The COLLECTED SHORT STORIES of KHUSHWANT SINGH

The COLLECTED SHORT STORIES of KHUSHWANT SINGH

RAVI DAYAL Publisher
Delhi

Published by
RAVI DAYAL Publisher
51 E Sujan Singh Park
New Delhi 10003

Distributed by
ORIENT LONGMAN LTD.
Bangalore Bombay Calcutta
Guwahati Hyderabad Madras Lucknow
New Delhi Patna

First published 1989
Second impression 1990
Third impression 1990

ISBN 0 86311 063 0

Composed by Spantech Publisher Pvt. Ltd., Delhi
Printed by Rekha Printers Pvt. Ltd., New Delhi 110020

For Naina
my one and only grandchild
in the hope that she will write
more and better stories than
her grandpa

Acknowledgements

The stories numbered 2, 6 and 10 in the Contents of this volume first appeared in *Canadian Forum*; those numbered 3, 5 and 14 first appeared in *Harpers*, *Saturday Night* and the *Statesman* respectively. 'The Bottom-Pincher' was first published in *London Magazine*, *Stories 8* (1973) and the introductory essay, 'On the Short Story', is a shortened version of an article by Khushwant Singh which appeared in *The Kenyon Review* (Vol. xxi, no. 126, issue 4, 1969). Stories 1–14 first appeared in volume form in *The Mark of Vishnu and Other Stories* (Saturn Press, London, 1950); 15–19, in *The Voice of God and Other Stories* (Jaico, Bombay, 1957); 22–31 in *A Bride for the Sahib and Other Stories* (Hind Pocket Books, Delhi, 1967); and 20 in *Black Jasmine* (Jaico, 1972). When first published, story number 18 appeared in a shorter version and under the title 'Little Man, You've Had a Busy Day'.

Contents

On the Short Story

Who says the short story is dead? In India it has only recently had its rebirth, and literary pundits who make horoscopes have forecast a long and prosperous life for it.

In India, as in most other developing countries, where paper, printing, and mass literacy are a phenomenon of recent years, the two literary forms that were cultivated most were poetry and folk drama—both memorized and thus passed on from generation to generation. To a lesser extent so also was the fable (*lateefa*)—short, calculated to convey a lesson using a minimum of words, and almost universally ending with a punch line which rounded off the tale. The novel was practically unknown until the British introduced it into the country.

With the turn of the century, things began to change. Poetry began to lose ground. Although poetic symposia (*kavi sammelan*) remained as popular as ever, not as many people cultivated the habit of reading poetry in print. Drama suffered because of the absence of theatres and professional actors: only religious themes based on old classics continued to be performed as before in the open, very much in the style of passion plays in Europe. Although Indians began to write novels, they were ill-at-ease with them. The only literary form which had its roots in tradition, and could avail itself of the vast opportunities opened up by printing and the rapidly increasing demand for literature, was the short story. For some years its only serious rival was poetry. In the last decade, the issue was decided in favour of the short story for one simple reason—short stories could always be translated, poetry could not.

Even to this day, some of our best short stories are written by little-known authors and published in obscure magazines which do not pay anything to their contributors. And it takes a long time before the story in question gets to be talked about in literary circles and translated into other languages. But there is little doubt that in all of India's major fourteen languages the standard of short-story writing is uniformly high and their popularity unrivalled. Let me illustrate with some examples. In the last 100 years two events that exercised the imagination of all Indians were the impact of British rule and the division of their country into India and Pakistan. An enormous amount of writing—novels, poems, plays, and short stories—has been produced, with the British Raj and the tragic partition of India as their main themes. And, in both, the short story has been more successful than the novel, poetry, or drama.

Prem Chand wrote many novels on the theme of the Raj and the decadence of India. In none of them did he sum up the psychological impact as well as he did in a dozen pages of an utterly contrived short story titled 'The Resignation.' It tells about a meek Hindu Babu (most educated Indians were Babu-clerks) working in a British firm run by a beefy, bullying Englishman who made it a point to be discourteous to his Indian employees—who in their turn took the Sahib's rudeness as a part of their job. The Babu's wife, however, looked upon her husband as a hero. Every evening when the Babu came home she asked him what had happened in the office. And every day he told her of the Sahib's behaviour. 'I hope you put him in his place,' she would say. 'Of course, he dare not speak like that to me. I will give him a piece of my mind if he does.' So over the years the Babu came to lead a double life: a snivelling, toadying sycophant in the office; a brave, upright, and outspoken man at home. (True of most Indians during most of British rule in India.) The climax came one afternoon when the Sahib had imbibed too much liquor and vented his spleen on the Babu. When the Babu came home and was narrating the incident to his wife, the conflict became too much for him. While the wife was laying out his dinner and being 'proud of him' for having stood up to the Englishman, the Babu determined to enact what in fact he was only boasting of having done. He left his dinner uneaten and rushed out of his home with his umbrella (a Babu symbol). He went back to his office, found the Sahib still inebriated (with power as well as with alcohol). The Babu slapped his letter of resignation on the table, smacked the Sahib on the head with the umbrella, and triumphantly marched back to his home to enjoy the meal so lovingly laid out by his adoring wife.

The story, an entire fabrication exaggerated in the portrayal of all three characters, captured the 'turning worm' spirit of the mass of Indians more than E.M. Forster's *A Passage to India* or any other novel known to me.

The partition of India, accompanied by savage rioting that took a toll of more than 500,000 lives and uprooted ten million people from their homes, has been the theme of innumerable novels (including the author's own *Train to Pakistan*, Balachandra Rajan's *The Dark Dancer*, and Mulgaonkar's *A Bend on the Ganges*). Here again it is a patently absurd and contrived short story which portrayed the senseless tragedy with greater effect than any of the novels or reams of sob stuff in verse.

Saadat Hassan Munto, a Punjabi Muslim, made his name as a novelist, short-story writer, and leader of the extreme left-wing litterateurs. He had a natural bent for the erotic. Many of his stories were banned for obscenity and at least once he was jailed (for his portrayal of a Eurasian lady officer in the army as a woman of easy virtue). Munto was also an ardent nationalist and refused to accept the theory that the Hindus and Muslims were two different nations. Munto pretended to ignore the fact of partition and chose to live in Bombay rather than return to his home town, Lahore, which became the capital of West Pakistan. The communal massacres and the tension between India and Pakistan became too much for him. His mind was seriously disturbed and he was taken back to Lahore, where he died soon after in a mental asylum.

'Toba Tek Singh' (translated by me as 'Exchange of Lunatics' in the collection of short stories *Land of the Five Rivers*) is in some ways Munto's summing up of his own life and that of his homeland. The scene is the lunatic asylum of Lahore. Time—some months after the partition, when movements of refugees, exchanges of lands, properties, etc., have been completed; only lunatics of either side remain to be exchanged. High-level government deliberations result in a detailed scheme to transfer lunatics to the border on a particular day, the coldest of the year. In the lunatic asylum at Lahore, for several months the main topic of conversation has been the establishment of Pakistan. A Muslim lunatic believes he is Mr Jinnah, and makes speeches (often quoting the founding father) supporting Pakistan. A Sikh lunatic believes he is the Sikh leader, Tara Singh, and makes sabre-rattling speeches opposing Pakistan (often quoting Tara Singh's actual words). And still another lunatic, usually ensconced aloft a tree, believes he is God, who will ultimately determine the course of events. When asked for guidance, 'god' usually replies, 'We have not yet made up our mind.' There is the 'hero' of the story, Bishen Singh, who has been in the asylum a great many years and whose sole concern with the partition is on which side his village, Toba Tek Singh, where his daughter lives, is going to be. He consults the 'leaders' concerned and seeks the guidance of 'god,' and getting no satisfaction from them relapses into the gibberish which he has been chanting like a litany ever since being admitted to the asylum. Comes the fateful day when Hindu and Sikh lunatics take tearful leave of their Muslim friends and are driven to the border. All along the route Bishen Singh goes on asking everyone, 'Which side is Toba Tek Singh?' No one has heard of this obscure hamlet. The group waits for long hours in bitter cold at the check-post on the border, with Bishen Singh pestering everyone about Toba Tek Singh. Ultimately, almost frozen to death, he crosses over to India and on asking an Indian policeman the location of his village is told that Toba Tek Singh has gone to Pakistan. Bishen Singh tries to run back, and meets his death in the no-man's-land between the two countries.

In this mad and macabre setting, Munto has told the tragicomedy of a people rent asunder by the insane fires of hatred.

The reason why the short story is in desuetude in the Western world, while it thrives in India, is that as a literary form it demands adherence to a set of rules. Indian writers subscribe to these rules; modern European and American writers do not. These rules, though not as rigidly prescribed as the seventeen syllables of the haiku, should nevertheless be clear enough to anyone who wishes to express his thoughts in a short story:

1, a short story must in fact be short. It cannot be a short novel, any more than a novel can be a long short story. Just as a large painting needs a larger canvas and is better done in oils than in water colours, and just as a miniature is better done on ivory or parchment and in stone colours with its lines drawn with the precision of a hair brush, so it is in writing. A novel is on a large canvas, a story is like a miniature painting. Personally, I would fix 3500 words as the outside limit for a short story.

2, a short story must be built around one incident or a series of incidents illustrating one theme or portraying one character or the equation between that one character and others.

3, a short story can be as fantastic and its characters and situations as fanciful as the writer cares to make them—provided they have the ring of truth and a 'message' to convey.

4, a short story must have a distinct beginning, middle, and end.

5, a short story must have, like a scorpion's sting in its tail, a curlicue which sums up the story.

These rules are, of course, personal and arbitrary. I believe that the world's great short-story writers have subscribed and perhaps unconsciously still do subscribe to them. Reread George Orwell's 'Shooting an Elephant,' or anything by Somerset Maugham, who, despite lack of style, and the absence of anything significant to say, is for me the greatest spinner of short stories of all times.

Posthumous

I am in bed with fever. It is not serious. In fact, it is not serious at all, as I have been left alone to look after myself. I wonder what would happen if the temperature suddenly shot up. Perhaps I would die. That would be really hard on my friends. I have so many and am so popular. I wonder what the papers would have to say about it. They couldn't just ignore me. Perhaps the *Tribune* would mention it on its front page with a small photograph. The headline would read 'Sardar Khushwant Singh Dead'—and then in somewhat smaller print:

We regret to announce the sudden death of Sardar Khushwant Singh at 6 p.m. last evening. He leaves behind a young widow, two infant children and a large number of friends and admirers to mourn his loss. It will be recalled that the Sardar came to settle in Lahore some five years ago from his home town, Delhi. Within these years he rose to a position of eminence in the Bar and in politics. His loss will be mourned generally throughout the Province.

Amongst those who called at the late Sardar's residence were the P.A. to the Prime Minister, the P.A. to the Chief Justice, several Ministers and Judges of the High Court.

In a statement to the press, the Hon'ble the Chief Justice said: 'I feel that the Punjab is poorer by the passing away of this man. The cruel hand of death has cut short the promise of a brilliant career'.

At the bottom of the page would be an announcement:

The funeral will take place at 10 a.m. today.

I feel very sorry for myself and for all my friends. With difficulty I check the tears which want to express sorrow at my own death. But I also feel elated and want people to mourn me. So I decide to die—just for the fun of it as it were. In the evening, giving enough time for the press to hear of my death, I give up the ghost. Having emerged from my corpse, I come down and sit on the cool marble steps at the entrance to wallow in posthumous glory.

In the morning I get the paper before my wife. There is no chance of a squabble over the newspaper as I am downstairs already, and in any case my wife is busy pottering around my corpse. The *Tribune* lets me down. At the bottom of page 3, column 1, I find myself inserted in little brackets of obituary notices of retired civil servants—and that is all. I feel annoyed. It must be that blighter Shafi, Special Representative. He never liked me. But I couldn't imagine he would be so mean as to deny me a little importance when I was dead. However, he couldn't keep the wave of sorrow which would run over the Province from trickling into his paper. My friends would see to that.

Near the High Court the paper is delivered fairly early. In the house of my lawyer friend Qadir it is deposited well before dawn. It isn't that the Qadirs are early risers. As a matter of fact, hardly anyone stirs in the house before 9 a.m. But Qadir is a great one for principles and he insists that the paper must be available early in the morning even if it is not looked at.

As usual, the Qadirs were in bed at 9 a.m. He had worked very late at night. She believed in sleep anyhow. The paper was brought in on a tray along with a tumbler of hot water with a dash of lime juice. Qadir sipped the hot water between intervals of cigarette smoking. He had to do this to make his bowels work. He only glanced at the headlines in bed. The real reading was done when the cigarette and lime had had their effect. The knowledge of how fate had treated me had to await the lavatory.

In due course Qadir ambled into the bathroom with the paper in one hand and a cigarette perched on his lower lip. Comfortably seated, he began to scan it thoroughly and his eye fell on news of lesser import. When he got to page 3, column 1, he stopped smoking for a moment, a very brief moment. Should he get up and shout to his wife? No, he decided, that would be an unnecessary demonstration. Qadir was a rationalist. He had become more of one since he married a woman who was a bundle of emotions and explosions. The poor fellow was dead and nothing could be done about it. He knew that his wife would burst out crying when he told her. That was all the more reason that he should be matter-of-fact about it—just as if he was going to tell her of a case he had lost.

Qadir knew his wife well. He told her with an air of casualness, and she burst out crying. Her ten-year-old daughter came running into the room. She eyed her mother for a little while and then joined her in the wailing. Qadir decided to be severe.

'What are you making all this noise for?' he said sternly. 'Do you think it will bring him back to life?'

His wife knew that it was no use arguing with him. He always won the arguments.

'I think we should go to their house at once. His wife must be feeling wretched,' she said.

Qadir shrugged his shoulders.

'I am afraid I can't manage it. Much as I would like to condole with his wife—or rather widow—my duty to my clients comes first. I have to be at the tribunal in half an hour.'

Qadir was at the tribunal all day and his family stopped at home.

Not far from the city's big park lives another friend, Khosla. He and his family, consisting of a wife, three sons and a daughter, reside in this upper-class residential area. He is a judge and very high up in the bureaucracy.

Khosla is an early riser. He has to rise early because that is the only time he has to himself. During the day he has to work in the Courts. In the evenings he plays tennis—and then he has to spend some time with the children and fussing with his wife. He has a large number of visitors, as he is very popular and enjoys popularity. But Khosla is ambitious. As a lad he had fancied himself as a clever boy. In his early youth his hair had begun to fall off and had uncovered a large bald forehead. Khosla had looked upon it as nature's confirmation of his opinion about himself. Perhaps he was a genius. The more he gazed upon his large head in the mirror, the more he became convinced that fate had marked for him an extraordinary career. So he worked harder. He won scholarships and rounded off his academic career by topping the list in the Civil Service examination. He had justified the confidence he had in himself by winning laurels in the stiffest competitive examination in the country. For some years he lived the life of a contented bureaucrat. In fact, he assured himself that he was what people called 'a success in life.'

After some years this contentment had vanished. Every time he brushed the little tuft at the back of his head and ran his hands across his vast forehead he became conscious of unrealized expectations. There were hundreds of senior civil servants like him. All were considered successes in life. The Civil Service was obviously not enough. He would work—he would write—he knew he could write. There it was written in the size of his head. So Khosla took to writing. In order to write well he took to reading. He amassed a large library and regularly spent some hours in it before going to work.

This morning Khosla happened to be in a mood to write. He

made himself a cup of tea and settled in a comfortable armchair by the electric radiator. He stuck the pencil in his mouth and meditated. He couldn't think of what to write. He decided to write his diary. He had spent the previous day listening to an important case. It was likely to go on for some days. The court room had been packed and everyone had been looking at him—that seemed a good enough subject. So he started to write.

Khosla was disturbed by the knock of the bearer bringing in the paper. He opened the news-sheet to read the truths of mundane existence.

Khosla was more interested in social affairs, births, marriages and deaths, than events of national or international import. He turned to page 3, column 1. His eye caught the announcement and he straightened up.

He just tapped his notebook with his pencil, and after a wake-up cough informed his wife of the news. She just yawned and opened her large dreamy eyes wide.

'I suppose you will close the High Court today?' she said.

'I am afraid the High Court doesn't close at just any excuse. I'll have to go. If I have any time I'll drop in on the way—or we can call on Sunday.'

The Khoslas did not come. Nor did many others for whose sorrow at my demise I had already felt sorrowful.

At 10 o'clock a little crowd had collected in front of the open space beneath my flat. It consisted mainly of people I did not expect to see. There were some lawyers in their court dress, and a number of sightseers who wanted to find out what was happening. Two friends of mine also turned up, but they stood apart from the crowd. One was a tall, slim man who looked like an artist. With one hand he kept his cigarette in place, the other he constantly employed in pushing his long hair off his forehead. He was a writer. He did not believe in attending funerals. But one had to hang around for a little while as a sort of social obligation. It was distasteful to him. There was something infectious about a corpse—so he smoked incessantly and made a cigarette smoke-screen between himself and the rest of the world.

The other friend was a Communist, a short, slight man with wavy hair and a hawkish expression. His frame and expression belied the volcano which they camouflaged. His approach to every-thing was coldly Marxist and sentiment found no place in it. Deaths were unimportant events. It was the cause that mattered. He consulted the writer in a polite whisper.

'How far are you going?'

'I plan dropping off at the coffee house,' answered the other. 'Are you going the whole way?'

'No ruddy fear,' said the Communist emphatically. 'Actually I had to be at a meeting at ten, and I was planning to be free of this by 9.30—but you know our people haven't the foggiest idea about time. I'll get along to the Party office now and then meet you at the coffee house at 11.30. Incidentally if you get the opportunity, just ask the hearse driver if he is a member of the Tongawalla Union. Cheers.'

A little later a hearse, drawn by a bony brown horse arrived and pulled up in front of my doorstep. The horse and his master were completely oblivious of the solemnity of the occasion. The driver sat placidly chewing his betelnut and eyeing the assembly. He was wondering whether this was the type likely to produce a tip. The beast straightaway started to piddle and the crowd scattered to avoid the spray which rebounded off the brick floor.

The crowd did not have to wait very long. My corpse was brought down all tied up in white linen and placed inside the hearse. A few flowers were ceremoniously placed on me. The procession was ready to start.

Before we moved another friend turned up on his bicycle. He was somewhat dark and flabby. He carried several books on the carrier and had the appearance of a scholarly serious-minded professor. As soon as he saw the loaded hearse, he dismounted. He had great respect for the dead and was particular to express it. He put his bicycle in the hall, chained it, and joined the crowd. When my wife came down to bid her last farewell he was visibly moved. From his pocket he produced a little book and thoughtfully turned over its pages. Then he slipped through the people towards my wife. With tears in his eyes he handed the book to her.

'I've brought you a copy of the *Gita*. It will give you great comfort.'

Overcome with emotion, he hurriedly slipped back to wipe the tears which had crept into his eyes.

'This,' he said to himself with a sigh, 'is the end of human existence. This is the truth.'

He was fond of thinking in platitudes—but to him all platitudes were profound and had the freshness and vigour of original thought.

'Like bubbles,' he said to himself, 'human life is as momentary as a bubble.'

But one didn't just die and disappear. Matter could not immaterialize—it could only change its form. The *Gita* put it so beautifully—

'Like a man casts off old garments to put on new ones . . . so does the soul, etc., etc.'

The professor was lost in contemplation. He wondered what new garments his dead friend had donned.

His thoughts were disturbed by a movement between his legs. A little pup came round the professor's legs licking his trousers and looking up at him. The professor was a kind man. He involuntarily bent down and patted the little dog, allowing him to lick his hands.

The professor's mind wandered—he felt uneasy. He looked at the corpse and then at the fluffy little dog at his feet, who after all was part of God's creation.

'Like a man casts off old garments to put on new ones . . . so does the soul . . .'

No, no, he said to himself. He shouldn't allow such uncharitable thoughts to cross his mind. But he couldn't check his mind. It wasn't impossible. The *Gita* said so, too. And he bent down again and patted the pup with more tenderness and fellow feeling.

The procession was on the move. I was in front, uncomfortably laid within the glass hearse, with half a dozen people walking behind. It went down towards the river.

By the time it had passed the main street, I found myself in solitude. Some of the lawyers had left at the High Court. My author friend had branched off to the coffee house, still smoking. At the local college, the professor gave me a last longing, lingering look and sped up the slope to his classroom. The remaining six or seven disappeared into the District Courts.

I began to feel a little small. Lesser men than myself had had larger crowds. Even a dead pauper carried on a municipal wheelbarrow got two sweepers to cart him off. I had only one human being, the driver, and even he seemed to be oblivious of the enormity of the soul whose decayed mansion he was transporting on its last voyage. As for the horse, he was positively rude.

The route to the cremation ground is marked with an infinite variety of offensive smells. The climax is reached when one has to branch off the main road towards the crematorium along a narrow path which runs beside the city's one and only sewer. It is a stream of dull, black fluid with bubbles bursting on its surface all the time.

Fortunately for me, I was given some time to ruminate over my miscalculated posthumous importance. The driver pulled up under a large peepul tree near where the road turns off to the cremation ground. Under this peepul tree is a tonga stand and a water trough for horses to drink out of. The horse made for the water and the driver clambered off his perch to ask the tonga-drivers for a light for his cigarette.

The tonga-drivers gathered round the hearse and peered in from all sides.

'Must be someone rich,' said one. 'But there is no one with him,' queried another. 'I suppose this is another English custom—no one to go with funerals.'

By now I was thoroughly fed up. There were three ways open to me. One was to take the route to the cremation ground and, like the others that went there, give myself up to scorching flames, perhaps to be born again into a better world, but probably to be extinguished into nothingness. There was another road which forked off to the right towards the city. There lived harlots and other people of ill-repute. They drank and gambled and fornicated. Theirs was a world of sensation and they crammed their lives with all the varieties which the senses were capable of registering. The third one was to take the way back. It was difficult to make up one's mind. In situations like these the toss of a coin frequently helps. So I decided to toss the coin; heads and I hazard the world beyond; tails and I go to join the throng of sensation seekers in the city; if it is neither heads nor tails and the coin stands on its edge, I retrace my steps to a humdrum existence bereft of the spirit of adventure and denuded of the lust for living.

Karma

Sir Mohan Lal looked at himself in the mirror of a first class waiting room at the railway station. The mirror was obviously made in India. The red oxide at its back had come off at several places and long lines of translucent glass cut across its surface. Sir Mohan smiled at the mirror with an air of pity and patronage.

'You are so very much like everything else in this country, inefficient, dirty, indifferent,' he murmured.

The mirror smiled back at Sir Mohan.

'You are a bit of all right, old chap,' it said. 'Distinguished, efficient—even handsome. That neatly-trimmed moustache—the suit from Saville Row with the carnation in the buttonhole—the aroma of eau de Cologne, talcum powder and scented soap all about you! Yes, old fellow, you are a bit of all right.'

Sir Mohan threw out his chest, smoothed his Balliol tie for the umpteenth time and waved a goodbye to the mirror.

He glanced at his watch. There was still time for a quick one.

'Koi Hai!'

A bearer in white livery appeared through a wire gauze door.

'Ek Chota,' ordered Sir Mohan, and sank into a large cane chair to drink and ruminate.

Outside the waiting room Sir Mohan Lal's luggage lay piled along the wall. On a small grey steel trunk Lachmi, Lady Mohan Lal, sat chewing a betel leaf and fanning herself with a newspaper. She was short and fat and in her middle forties. She wore a dirty white sari with a red border. On one side of her nose glistened a diamond nose-ring, and she had several gold bangles on her arms. She had been talking to the bearer until Sir Mohan had summoned him inside. As soon as he had gone, she hailed a passing railway coolie.

'Where does the zenana stop?'

'Right at the end of the platform.'

The coolie flattened his turban to make a cushion, hoisted the steel trunk on his head, and moved down the platform. Lady Lal picked up her brass tiffin carrier and ambled along behind him. On the way she stopped by a hawker's stall to replenish her silver betel leaf case, and then joined the coolie. She sat down on her steel trunk (which the coolie had put down) and started talking to him.

'Are the trains very crowded on these lines?'

'These days all trains are crowded, but you'll find room in the zenana.'

'Then I might as well get over the bother of eating.'

Lady Lal opened the brass carrier and took out a bundle of cramped chapatties and some mango pickle. While she ate, the coolie sat opposite her on his haunches, drawing lines in the gravel with his finger.

'Are you travelling alone, sister?'

'No, I am with my master, brother. He is in the waiting room. He travels first class. He is a vizier and a barrister, and meets so many officers and Englishmen in the trains—and I am only a native woman. I can't understand English and don't know their ways, so I keep to my zenana inter-class.'

Lachmi chatted away merrily. She was fond of a little gossip and had no one to talk to at home. Her husband never had any time to spare for her. She lived in the upper storey of the house and he on the ground floor. He did not like her poor illiterate relatives hanging about his bungalow, so they never came. He came up to her once in a while at night and stayed for a few minutes. He just ordered her about in anglicized Hindustani, and she obeyed passively. These nocturnal visits had, however, borne no fruit.

The signal came down and the clanging of the bell announced the approaching train. Lady Lal hurriedly finished off her meal. She got up, still licking the stone of the pickled mango. She emitted a long, loud belch as she went to the public tap to rinse her mouth and wash her hands. After washing she dried her mouth and hands with the loose end of her sari, and walked back to her steel trunk, belching and thanking the gods for the favour of a filling meal.

The train steamed in. Lachmi found herself facing an almost empty inter-class zenana compartment next to the guard's van, at the tail end of the train. The rest of the train was packed. She heaved her squat, bulky frame through the door and found a seat by the window. She produced a two-anna bit from a knot in her sari and dismissed the coolie. She then opened her betel case and made herself two betel leaves charged with a red and white paste, minced betelnuts and cardamoms. These she thrust into her mouth till her cheeks bulged on both sides. Then she rested her chin on her hands and sat gazing idly at the jostling crowd on the platform.

The arrival of the train did not disturb Sir Mohan Lal's sang-froid. He continued to sip his Scotch and ordered the bearer to tell him when he had moved the luggage to a first class compartment. Excitement, bustle, and hurry were exhibitions of bad breeding, and Sir Mohan was eminently well-bred. He wanted everything 'tickety-boo' and orderly. In his five years abroad, Sir Mohan had acquired the manners and attitudes of the upper classes. He rarely spoke Hindustani. When he did, it was like an Englishman's—only the very necessary words and properly anglicized. But he fancied his English, finished and refined at no less a place than the University of Oxford. He was fond of conversation, and like a cultured Englishman he could talk on almost any subject—books, politics, people. How frequently had he heard English people say that he spoke like an Englishman!

Sir Mohan wondered if he would be travelling alone. It was a Cantonment and some English officers might be on the train. His heart warmed at the prospect of an impressive conversation. He never showed any sign of eagerness to talk to the English as most Indians did. Nor was he loud, aggressive and opinionated like them. He went about his business with an expressionless matter-of-factness. He would retire to his corner by the window and get out a copy of *The Times*. He would fold it in a way in which the name of the paper was visible to others while he did the crossword puzzle. *The Times* always attracted attention. Someone would like to borrow it when he put it aside with a gesture signifying 'I've finished with it.' Perhaps someone would recognize his Balliol tie which he always wore while travelling. That would open a vista leading to a fairyland of Oxford colleges, masters, dons, tutors, boat-races and rugger matches. If both *The Times* and the tie failed, Sir Mohan would 'Koi Hai' his bearer to get the Scotch out. Whisky never failed with Englishmen. Then followed Sir Mohan's handsome gold cigarette case filled with English cigarettes. English cigarettes in India? How on earth did he get them? Sure he didn't mind? And Sir Mohan's understanding smile—of course he didn't. But could he use the Englishman as a medium to commune with his dear old England? Those five years of grey bags and gowns, of sports blazers and mixed doubles, of dinners at the Inns of Court and nights with Piccadilly prostitutes. Five years of a crowded glorious life. Worth far more than the forty-five in India with his dirty, vulgar country-men, with sordid details of the road to success, of nocturnal visits to the upper storey and all-too-brief sexual acts with obese old Lachmi, smelling of sweat and raw onions.

Sir Mohan's thoughts were disturbed by the bearer announcing the installation of the Sahib's luggage in a first class coupe next to the engine. Sir Mohan walked to his coupe with a studied gait. He was dismayed. The compartment was empty. With a sigh he sat down in a corner and opened the copy of *The Times* he had read several times before.

Sir Mohan looked out of the window down the crowded platform. His face lit up as he saw two English soldiers trudging along, looking in all the compartments for room. They had their haversacks slung behind their backs and walked unsteadily. Sir Mohan decided to welcome them, even though they were entitled to travel only second class. He would speak to the guard.

One of the soldiers came up to the last compartment and stuck his face through the window. He surveyed the compartment and noticed the unoccupied berth.

''Ere, Bill,' he shouted, 'one 'ere.'

His companion came up, also looked in, and looked at Sir Mohan.

'Get the nigger out,' he muttered to his companion.

They opened the door, and turned to the half-smiling, half-protesting Sir Mohan.

'Reserved!' yelled Bill.

'*Janta*—Reserved. Army—*Fauj*,' exclaimed Jim, pointing to his khaki shirt.

'*Ek dum jao*—get out!'

'I say, I say, surely,' protested Sir Mohan in his Oxford accent.

The soldiers paused. It almost sounded like English, but they knew better than to trust their inebriated ears. The engine whistled and the guard waved his green flag.

They picked up Sir Mohan's suit-case and flung it on to the platform. Then followed his thermos flask, brief-case, bedding and *The Times*. Sir Mohan was livid with rage.

'Preposterous, preposterous,' he shouted, hoarse with anger. 'I'll have you arrested—guard, guard!'

Bill and Jim paused again. It did sound like English, but it was too much of the King's for them.

'Keep yer ruddy mouth shut!' And Jim struck Sir Mohan flat on the face.

The engine gave another short whistle and the train began to move. The soldiers caught Sir Mohan by the arms and flung him out of the train. He reeled backwards, tripped on his bedding, and landed on the suit-case.

'Toodle-oo!'

Sir Mohan's feet were glued to the earth and he lost his speech. He stared at the lighted windows of the train going past him in quickening tempo. The tail-end of the train appeared with a red light and the guard standing in the open doorway with the flags in his hands.

In the inter-class zenana compartment was Lachmi, fair and fat, on whose nose the diamond nose-ring glistened against the station lights. Her mouth was bloated with betel saliva which she had been storing up to spit as soon as the train had cleared the station. As the train sped past the lighted part of the platform, Lady Lal spat and sent a jet of red dribble flying across like a dart.

The Mark of Vishnu

'This is for the Kala Nag,' said Gunga Ram, pouring the milk into the saucer. 'Every night I leave it outside the hole near the wall and it's gone by the morning.'

'Perhaps it is the cat,' we youngsters suggested.

'Cat!' said Gunga Ram with contempt. 'No cat goes near that hole. Kala Nag lives there. As long as I give him milk, he will not bite anyone in this house. You can all go about with bare feet and play where you like.'

We were not having any patronage from Gunga Ram.

'You're a stupid old Brahmin,' I said. 'Don't you know snakes don't drink milk? At least one couldn't drink a saucerful every day. The teacher told us that a snake eats only once in several days. We saw a grass snake which had just swallowed a frog. It stuck like a blob in its throat and took several days to dissolve and go down its tail. We've got dozens of them in the lab. in methylated spirit. Why, last month the teacher bought one from a snake-charmer which could run both ways. It had another head with a pair of eyes at the tail. You should have seen the fun when it was put in the jar. There wasn't an empty one in the lab. So the teacher put it in one which had a Russels viper. He caught its two ends with a pair of forceps, dropped it in the jar, and quickly put the lid on. There was an absolute storm as it went round and round in the glass tearing the decayed viper into shreds.'

Gunga Ram shut his eyes in pious horror.

'You will pay for it one day. Yes, you will.'

It was no use arguing with Gunga Ram. He, like all good Hindus, believed in the Trinity of Brahma, Vishnu, and Siva, the creator, preserver, and destroyer. Of these he was most devoted to Vishnu. Every morning he smeared his forehead with a V mark in sandalwood paste to honour the deity. Although a Brahmin, he was illiterate and full of superstition. To him, all life was sacred, even if it was of a serpent or scorpion or centipede. Whenever he saw one he quickly shoved it away lest we kill it. He picked up wasps we battered with our badminton rackets and tended their damaged wings. Sometimes he got stung. It never seemed to shake his faith. More dangerous the animal, the more devoted Gunga Ram was to its existence. Hence the regard for snakes; above all, the cobra, who was the Kala Nag.

'We will kill your Kala Nag if we see him.'

'I won't let you. It's laid a hundred eggs and if you kill it all the eggs will become cobras and the house will be full of them. Then what will you do?'

'We'll catch them alive and send them to Bombay. They milk them there for anti-snake-bite serum. They pay two rupees for a live cobra. That makes two hundred rupees straightaway.'

'Your doctors must have udders. I never saw a snake have any. But don't you dare touch this one. It is a *phannyar*—it is hooded. I've seen it. It's three hands long. As for its hood!' Gunga Ram opened the palms of his hands and his head swayed from side to side. 'You should see it basking on the lawn in the sunlight.'

'That just proves what a liar you are. *The phannyar* is the male, so it couldn't have laid the hundred eggs. You must have laid the eggs yourself.'

The party burst into peals of laughter.

'Must be Gunga Ram's eggs. We'll soon have a hundred Gunga Rams.'

Gunga Ram was squashed. It was the lot of a servant to be constantly squashed. But having the children of the household make fun of him was too much even for Gunga Ram. They were constantly belittling him with their new-fangled ideas. They never read their scriptures. Nor even what the Mahatma said about non-violence. It was just shotguns to kill birds and the jars of methylated spirit to drown snakes. Gunga Ram would stick to his faith in the sanctity of life, he would feed and protect snakes because snakes were the most vile of God's creatures on earth. If you could love them, instead of killing them, you proved your point.

What the point was which Gunga Ram wanted to prove was not clear. He just proved it by leaving the saucerful of milk by the snake hole every night and finding it gone in the mornings.

One day we saw Kala Nag. The monsoons had burst with all their fury and it had rained in the night. The earth which had lain parched and dry under the withering heat of the summer sun was teeming with life. In little pools frogs croaked. The muddy ground was littered with crawling worms, centipedes, and velvety lady-birds. Grass had begun to show and the banana leaves glistened bright and glossy green. The rain had flooded Kala Nag's hole. He sat in an open patch on the lawn. His shiny black hood glistened in the sunlight. He was big—almost six feet in length, and rounded and fleshy, as my wrist.

'Looks like a King Cobra. Let's get him.'

Kala Nag did not have much of a chance. The ground was slippery and all the holes and gutters were full of water. Gunga Ram was not at home to help.

Armed with long bamboo sticks, we surrounded Kala Nag before he even scented danger. When he saw us his eyes turned a fiery red and he hissed and spat on all sides. Then like lightning Kala Nag made for the banana grove.

The ground was too muddy and he slithered. He had hardly gone five yards when a stick caught him in the middle and broke his back. A volley of blows reduced him to a squishy-squashy pulp of black and white jelly, spattered with blood and mud. His head was still undamaged.

'Don't damage the hood,' yelled one of us. 'We'll take Kala Nag to school.'

So we slid a bamboo stick under the cobra's belly and lifted him on the end of the pole. We put him in a large biscuit tin and tied it up with string. We hid the tin under a bed.

At night I hung around Gunga Ram waiting for him to get his saucer of milk. 'Aren't you going to take any milk for the Kala Nag tonight?'

'Yes,' answered Gunga Ram irritably. 'You go to bed.'

He did not want any more argument on the subject.

'He won't need the milk any more.'

Gunga Ram paused.

'Why?'

'Oh, nothing. There are so many frogs about. They must taste better than your milk. You never put any sugar in it anyway.'

The next morning Gunga Ram brought back the saucer with the milk still in it. He looked sullen and suspicious.

'I told you snakes like frogs better than milk.'

Whilst we changed and had breakfast Gunga Ram hung around us. The school bus came and we clambered into it with the tin. As the bus started we held out the tin to Gunga Ram.

'Here's your Kala Nag. Safe in this box. We are going to put him in spirit.'

We left him standing speechless, staring at the departing bus.

There was great excitement in the school. We were a set of four brothers, known for our toughness. We had proved it again.

'A King Cobra.'

'Six feet long.'

'*Phannyar.*'

The tin was presented to the science teacher.

It was on the teacher's table, and we waited for him to open it and admire our kill. The teacher pretended to be indifferent and set us some problems to work on. With studied matter-of-factness he fetched his forceps and a jar with a banded Krait lying curled in muddy methylated spirit. He began to hum and untie the cord around the box.

As soon as the cord was loosened the lid flew into the air, just missing the teacher's nose. There was Kala Nag. His eyes burnt like embers and his hood was taut and undamaged. With a loud hiss he went for the teacher's face. The teacher pushed himself back on the chair and toppled over. He fell on the floor and stared at the cobra, petrified with fear. The boys stood up on their desks and yelled hysterically.

Kala Nag surveyed the scene with his bloodshot eyes. His forked tongue darted in and out excitedly. He spat furiously and then made a bid for freedom. He fell out of the tin on to the floor with a loud plop. His back was broken in several places and he dragged himself painfully to the door. When he got to the threshold he drew himself up once again with his hood outspread to face another danger.

Outside the classroom stood Gunga Ram with a saucer and a jug of milk. As soon as he saw Kala Nag come up he went down on his knees. He poured the milk into the saucer and placed it near the threshold. With hands folded in prayer he bowed his head to the ground craving forgiveness. In desperate fury, the cobra hissed and spat and bit Gunga Ram all over the head—then with great effort dragged himself into a gutter and wriggled out of view.

Gunga Ram collapsed with his hands covering his face. He groaned in agony. The poison blinded him instantly. Within a few minutes he turned pale and blue and froth appeared in his mouth. On his forehead were little drops of blood. These the teacher wiped with his handkerchief. Underneath was the V mark where the Kala Nag had dug his fangs.

The Butterfly

'Meet my friend Charles,' said I, introducing him to the doctor.

'The name is Romesh Chandra', said Charles, shaking the doctor's hand. 'Pleased to meet you.'

This was usual. He was introduced as Charles by his friends and he corrected them with 'The name is Romesh Chandra.' But it hadn't always been that way. As a matter of fact, when I first met Charles I could not even suspect that he could be a Romesh Chandra. He came to the University from a mission school in Simla, with a batch of Anglo-Indians. The 'Me-shun Squad' we called them, and they did not mind the description. The squad consisted of Smiths, Stanleys and Johnsons. Even the Indians in their lot had English names. Hence Charles was Charles—more intimately known as Old Charlie.

Charles' appearance and dress was a complete challenge to any suggestion of his being a Romesh Chandra. He wore a sola topee at a jaunty angle with the strap tightly passing under his chin. On one side of his hat he had stuck a grey feather. It was very much like a pigeon's. Charles informed us that it belonged to a bird called an ostrich which was rare, not to be found in India. Charles' jackets had leather patches at their elbows just as the English. The crease of his grey bags was as a razor's edge. As for Charles' speech, we who came from native institutions thought that perhaps the King's English derived its royal prefix from the way King Charles spoke. Some words Charles used we had never heard. What impressed us more was that even the Oxford dictionary did not know of them. There was the invariable 'Yus mun' or 'No mun' or 'Say mun' before each sentence. There were 'chips' for rupees and 'flicks' for cinemas and the college principal was 'Old Prinny'.

When Charles came to the University he had to live in the hostel with us Indians. Anglo-Indians had a hostel of their own, and in spite of what Charles was and despite what he did he could not get admission into that select residence. But Charles was true to his loyalties. He rarely talked to us and only ate at our mess when he ran out of cash and could not eat lamb chops with mint sauce in English restaurants. He spent the day with his Anglo-Indian friends. At college they kept together and spent the intervals between classes in reminiscences of their school days or their exploits in the local Anglo-Indian colony. We hung round greedily, lapping up bits of their coversation.

'Say, mun, whatchya think of Phylis?'

'Phyllis? Gosh, mun. Some girl!'

'And Gladys! Phew. Cinders, mun, cinders!' And so on.

We always wanted to get Charles to tell us about the Anglo-Indian colony when he came back late in the evenings. He looked as if he had a lot to tell but we were not the sort who could understand. When we asked him if he had had any fun Charles replied with a studied silence and a smile.

One evening he was communicative. He asked us if we had ever slept with a white woman. We confessed we had not. We hadn't even with a black or a brown one. But what was a white woman like? Good? Charles did not answer. He just rolled his eyes up and showed us the whites. We begged of him to let us into the details. He gave them to us with all the genius of an amorous artist and we left for our room envying Charles and feeling uncomfortable.

Then, without any apparent reason, Charles began to change. He began to mix more with us than with his Anglo-Indian friends and we felt flattered. He dropped hints about his Indian origin. For 'back home in Brighton' we often caught him saying 'back home in Bheyra.' He even told us confidentially that his real name was Romesh Chandra.

One evening Charles gave us inside information of white women in low, subdued tones. He said they were much overrated—and added with a whisper in our ears that there was nothing to them except their white skin and the Indians were much better. We said we had always suspected that to be so and since Charles must know what was what about a white woman we were glad to have our suspicions confirmed. In any case we decided that Charles was very patriotic in his preference for Indian women.

Some time later we discovered the reasons for Charles' patriotism. He had been getting on famously with Betty Brown until her Anglo-Indian beau, Jacob, got a job in the Police as a sergeant. Charles was dropped. He didn't have a khaki uniform, nor a Sam Brown belt, nor the silver letters 'P.P.' for Punjab Police on his shoulders.

He didn't have a motorcycle with a pillion seat. In any case, all said and done, Charles was a nigger.

Charles had decided to take this let-down to heart, but his heart discovered a prop before it could break. Out of the barren wastes of sandy Shahpur came a girl cousin to join the University. She was only sixteen but already faintly perceptible signs of young woman-hood had appeared on her bosom. Her embarrassment at being stared at caused her to look down most of the time, giving her a coy, bashful appearance. She wore a sari, of coarse white handspun cloth, and even on the coldest days in January she went about in sandals. Charles missed a heart-beat the first time she greeted him with folded hands and a scarcely audible 'Namaste.' She was like the goddess Saraswati in a picture which Charles' mother owned. Charles had been in love with that picture since his infancy. The goddess stood in celestial white on a large pink lotus with the snow-clad mountains behind her. In the corners in the foreground, a couple of elephants raised their trunks in salutation. Charles decided this cousin was Saraswati. From the tiny red spot on her forehead down to the tips of her pink toes it was the Hindu goddess come to life—stepping out of the Vedas, descending from the heights of snow-bound Kailash, floating down the Ganges on a gorgeous lotus, and somehow, face to face with Charles.

Charles went native with a bang. He was constantly with us (when not with his cousin) and referred to his Anglo-Indian friends as buggers or bastards. He swore that they were both, since he knew all that there was to know about them. We agreed that he must be right and marvelled at the variety of his sexual experiences. Charles' dress also suffered a change. At first the feather in his hat disappeared and then the hat itself. His grey bags and leather-lined coat had a dramatic exit. On a cold December evening he happened to be out walking with one of us along the canal bank. He was out of cash and had been angling for a safe bet to get some. Ultimately he announced that he would jump into the canal with his clothes on if we gave him five rupees. Charles won the bet and returned to the hostel wet and shivering with cold, but triumphantly flourishing a five-rupee note. His one pair of trousers now hung six inches above his ankles. This misfortune was Charles' excuse to wear Indian dress. Handspun cloth was cheap and his cousin wore it all the time. So the feather-sola-hatted-grey-bagged Anglo-Indian changed into a khaddar-clad Indian.

Romesh took his new role seriously. To emphasize the change, the title 'Sriyut' appeared before his name and we were told that all really Indian Indians used the prefix to show that they were Indians. We who were merely Misters felt a little foreign by contrast. Romesh made us feel unpatriotic in many other small ways. He always carried books written in Hindi or Urdu. He discussed Kalidas and Ghalib and Munshi Prem Chand, and considered them infinitely better than any foreign writer. We said nothing as we knew nothing. But we had our suspicions about Romesh's newly-acquired erudition.

Romesh's greatest act of patriotism was only known to a select few. We often saw him produce a tattered parchment from his leather case and study it closely. Whenever we got near him, he hurriedly put it back in the case as if its contents were a great secret. In fact, they were, and Romesh had been working on it for several months. To a select number of his persistent inquirers he broke the great news that he carried with him a list of Englishmen he was going to shoot. He produced the parchment and laid it before our admiring eyes. We examined it closely. It had several important officers of the Police and the Indian Civil Service on it, ending with J. Jacob, Inspector Punjab Police. At our suggestion, the list of con-demned men was enlarged. Romesh quietly folded the parchment and put it back in his pocket. From the expression on his face we felt sorry for the relatives of the doomed officials.

For several days we woke up earlier than usual to see the news-paper announcing the assassinations. But apparently Romesh had given his victims a few days of grace in which to mend their ways. When we asked him, he told us that everything was ready—he only needed a few assistants. We naturally had prior engagements and regretted our inability to assist him. Romesh was rude to us and called us cowards. We didn't retaliate because there was some truth in what he said. But some of us suspected that Romesh was pulling our leg and decided to pull his in turn.

We told Romesh that we already had a secret terrorist organization and if he wanted to join we would welcome him. Romesh turned pale, but after what he had called us he had little choice. One night we blindfolded him and drove him out of the town to an attic which we had hired. Here we uncovered his eyes and he saw an assembly of hooded men. Romesh was sworn to secrecy and before a large picture of Lenin he took a solemn oath to serve the proletarian cause with his blood—and if he failed there was the ominous warning written in large letters above Lenin's bald head—'Death to Traitors!' Romesh had just begun to feel heroic after the oath when a whistle was heard and a hooded man rushed in to announce that someone had betrayed us. We pulled out our revolvers and levelled them at Romesh and demanded a quick explanation. He stuttered and stammered and shook like an aspen leaf. Then someone laughed. Romesh went home much humbled.

The story of Romesh's terrorist venture spread and people began to laugh at him. Even his cousin found it amusing. That hurt Romesh very much. He hadn't expected it from her. It was like Saraswati throwing away her dignity and poise and cocking the snook. But his Saraswati was to let him down again. She left the University and married a pot-bellied bureaucrat.

Romesh was dejected and in his depression he began to moult once more. He rarely talked to anyone and spent many hours reading Karl Marx, Engels and Lenin. Communism brought relief to Romesh's tortured soul. To his inward fears it brought succour and confidence. To his already belligerent personality it lent more punch and pugnacity. After many months of spiritual tonic manufactured by the Left Book Club, Romesh emerged from his self-imposed seclusion a new man. The Hindi-reading chrysalis burst its shell and blossomed into a Marxist butterfly. Sriyut Romesh Chandra was dead. Comrade Romesh Chandra—or Comrade Charlie—was born.

As in the past, Charles took his new role seriously. He joined the Communist Party. He organized the tonga-wallahs and sweepers into powerful unions. At his command the sweepers went on strike till the city stank of filth. At his command the tongas stopped plying and people stayed at home and prayed that Charles would change his mind.

We who knew Charles refused to take him seriously, and waited.

Charles had ordered a strike of the tonga-wallahs. There was always an excuse for that. The Corporation had refused to increase their fares. The policemen always demanded too much bribe. The magistrates dealt out too much summary injustice and inequitable fines. So the tonga-wallahs struck and the city was deprived of its only means of transport. Charles was triumphant and celebrated the successful strike by standing us beer. Next day the authorities decided to act. The tonga-wallah union was declared illegal and the tonga drivers were ordered back on the roads on pain of confiscation of licences.

We knew that this meant trouble and Charles and trouble didn't go together. In the morning a tonga went round carrying a large red flag announcing a meeting of tonga drivers in the evening. Charles was not in the tonga nor was he mentioned among the speakers. In the afternoon there was an announcement by beat of the drum that the authorities had declared the meeting unlawful. We understood why Charles was not in the list of speakers. He was sure to be out of town on urgent business, or in bed with a belly ache. We decided to go and see the fun.

At the square near the railway station there was a vast crowd. Separated from this seething mass were two groups in the middle. One was of some two hundred tonga drivers squatting on the ground. In their centre was a man with a red flag. About thirty yards from the tonga-wallahs were four rows of fifty policemen each, armed with rifles. In front of these serried rows several Anglo-Indian sergeants strolled up and down impatiently. Jacob was amongst them. He slapped his jack-boots with a leather-covered stick. Charles had escaped him.

A tall, dark man rose from the midst of the circle of tonga drivers and stood beside the red flag. He started to speak. There was silence and ears were strained to listen to his words.

'Comrades!' he shouted, 'the hour of trial has come. We must face it. We are labourers and justice is on our side.'

He was interrupted by one of the Anglo-Indian sergeants, who walked into the circle and produced a yellow piece of paper demanding the dispersal of the meeting within five minutes. He caught the speaker roughly by the scruff of the neck and pushed him towards a couple of constables who handcuffed him and led him to a jail van.

The drivers were now leaderless. We heard loud arguments of loss of daily earnings, of women and children starving if they went to jail, and of their leaders deserting them. Some slunk out of the circle amid cries of shame from the others and disappeared into the crowd. Then more followed and it seemed that within the prescribed five minutes the meeting would disperse.

Then all of a sudden, out of nowhere Charles appeared. We saw his small, slim figure walking across the gap separating the crowd from the tonga drivers. He nervously pressed his tousled hair with both his hands. A little cheer went up from the tonga drivers as

Charles got in their midst and grabbed the red flag.

'Comrades!' he shouted, and looked round the assembly. With both hands uplifted, he started to sing the 'Internationale,' which his terrifed comrades took up with mock bravery.

The police commissioner knew his job. A little more show of force and he would get them rattled and be done with them. He shouted the command to fix bayonets. Two hundred steel bayonets glistened against the setting sun and were fixed onto the rifles. The singing died down and more tonga-wallahs fled back into the crowd. Charles was there, still holding the flag, with half-a-dozen comrades clinging to his trousers. Once again his voice rang out: 'Comrades!' and he lifted his two arms and the little band started singing the 'Red Flag.'

'Shun!'

'Standing load!'

'Aim!'

Two hundred bayonetted rifles were drawn shoulder high with their ugly nozzles pointing at Charles and his companions. Our blood ran cold and sweat stood on our foreheads. They couldn't shoot people for assembling at a meeting. But apparently they meant to. The commissioner's baton was raised aloft. He dropped it with a jerk.

'Fire!'

The rifles were pointed to the sky and a terrific volley rent the silence. Only the flag was hit and several holes appeared in the red cloth. But the noise was terrific and the crowds fled in terror. Charles' companions deserted him. Two of them tried to drag him back with them but he brushed them aside.

Now Charles stood alone in the vast square. A small figure with a large flag. The rifles were still pointed at him and the smoke from their nozzles slowly drifted towards him. There was absolute silence. For some minutes Charles stood and placidly surveyed the scene. Facing him were the policemen, the symbol of all that he hated and despised. His countrymen had deserted him. He slowly raised the red flag and his solitary voice broke the petrified silence with 'Hindi hum chalees crore' ('We four hundred million Indians')! Then he slowly marched towards the armed policemen singing lustily.

Out of the police ranks stepped Jacob and stood in Charles' way with his arms stretched to stop him. Charles came up to him till his face almost touched Jacob's.

'Shut up!' yelled the sergeant, hitting a hard back-hander across Charles' face. But Charles didn't stop singing.

'O.K., you bastard, you asked for it!'

Jacob lashed out with his baton and hit Charles till he drew blood. Our butterfly had been bludgeoned.

The police did not bother to take Charles. He was left in the square terribly beaten and unconscious. We picked him up and took him home to be nursed. We got a nice-looking European nurse to take care of him. He remained unconscious most of the night and we were much bothered.

In the early hours of the morning he came to, and we gathered round him expecting to see him in agony. But Charles was all smiles and triumph. He was in poetic rapture.

'Comrades!' he shouted, 'comrades, to the barricades!'

'Barricades of hearts and souls.'

'Hurl your song like a bomb,' he went on with gusto.

'Now, now, Mister,' said the pretty nurse severely, 'don't excite yourself.'

Charles hadn't noticed her. He did now, and smiled.

'The name is Romesh Chandra. Charles for short. Pleased to meet you.'

The Interview

There was a knock on the door. Before I could say 'Come in,' the receptionist tip-toed in, shutting the door behind her. 'A Mr Towers to see you,' she whispered.

'Has he an appointment?'

'No. He won't say what he wants either. He just said he wanted to see you. Shall I say you are busy?'

The door opened again—without a knock—and in walked a hulking man in shirt sleeves. He was followed by a blonde in her fading forties and a little girl.

'Hello there! I see you are going to have your morning coffee and I thought I'd join you. Towers is the name, Stan Towers. And this is my wife Margery and little Pam. Say hello, Pam.'

Pam said hello and collapsed into the leather chair sucking a lollipop. I shook hands with Margery, who produced a weary smile. She sat down on the arm of Pam's chair and stared at the wallpaper, looking utterly bored.

'Cream and sugar for me and the wife,' said Mr Towers, dismissing the receptionist. 'Pam'll stick to her lollipop, won't you, Pam?'

Pam sat up, pulled out a dribbling lollipop to say a slow motion 'Yeah,' and collapsed into the chair again.

Towers sat down on my desk and pulled out his packet of cigarettes. He pulled one half an inch out of the pack and held it out to me. I shook my head. 'No thanks, I . . .'

Towers lit it for himself and calmly surveyed the room, charging it with smoke and expectancy.

'We were passing through and didn't know what to do. We've seen the sights and Marge doesn't care for them anyhow. So I says to Marge I'll tell you what we'll do. We'll go and see the American Ambassador and the Indian High Commissioner. But you don't know them, she says to me and I said that's how we'll get to know them. And so we did. We saw both of them. I said then, let's see the Public Relations Officer. That's his job. So here we are. You don't mind, do you? Of course you don't.'

Of course. Of course.

I looked at Marge. A smile faded in and it faded out. She didn't seem to mind anything.

'We come from Chicago—you know Chicago?'

'I'm afraid I have never been to Chicago.'

'Not Shikago. Shik ahgo, Shik ahgo.'

'Shikahgo.'

'That's right, Shikahgo. I am a numismatist. Do you know numismatism? Of course you do. Silly of me to ask a Public Relations man.'

I smiled nervously. Of course. Of course.

'If I may say so, I am one of the world's nine leading numismatists. My articles have appeared in the best numismatical journals, including your own annual number of the Calcutta *Numismatical Journal*. Do you know the Calcutta Numismatical Society?'

'Oh yes. It's very well known.'

'I thought you would. Germany had many famous numismatists. One doesn't know what's happened to them now.'

'Maybe the Russians have taken them over, like they took over Krupp's works,' said I, throwing a feeler.

'Krupp's was only armaments, you know,' he added a little uneasily. 'They must be dead. That just leaves Professor Charbonneau of France and your own Dr Banerjee. Doesn't it, Marge?'

Marge smiled back to life and smiled out of it. Numismatics. Numismatics. The word went round and round eluding recognition. Not Krupp's. Not Ballistics. Numismatics. Banerjee. Banerjee.

'You know Banerjee? Silly of me to ask. You must have heard of him.'

There was no way out. 'No, I haven't had the opportunity of meeting him personally. But of course one hears about him all the time.'

'I thought you would know about him. You must meet him when you get back. Tell him I asked you to. We've been carrying on a very interesting controversy in *The Numismatist* about the age of a treasure unearthed near Tutankhamen's tomb.'

'I haven't had the pleasure of reading that. But I have seen Dr Banerjee's book on the excavations at Mohenjodaro. It was Dr Banerjee, wasn't it?' I queried dubiously.

'I don't know about this one. Didn't know he was an archaeologist as well.'

The door opened. The girl brought in coffee and biscuits. I felt like a boxer saved by the bell on the count of nine.

'Oh, Miss Forbes, will you give this chit to Miss Merriman?' I scribbled a small note and slipped it in her hand. While she handed round the coffee I quickly opened a conversation with Marge.

'And what do you think of India, Mrs Towers?'

'Oh, fine.'

'Wouldn't you like to go there?'

'Yeah, very much.'

'Oh yes, you would like it very much. So different the people and the country. I am sure you would like it.'

'Sure.'

I turned to Pam. She had finished sucking her lollipop and was placidly picking her nose. 'Wouldn't you like to go to India Pam?'

Pam blushed with guilt. Her parents glowered at her. Marge gave her a handkerchief.

Towers returned to the assault.

'I am very interested about this book of Banerjee's you talk about. Did you say it was about Mohenjodaro?'

'Maybe I am mixing him up with someone else.'

'No, no. I am sure you are not. There were things in Mohenjodaro which would be of enormous interest to a numismatist. Banerjee must have written about these.'

Numismatics. Numismatics.

'Oh yes, he must have. It was such a long time ago that I saw the book. I don't really remember what he was mainly interested in.'

Numismatics. Numismatics.

The door opened once more. Miss Merriman came in holding an open book. Her glasses were balanced on the tip of her nose. She just smiled at the Towers and mumbled.

'Numismatics. Numismatics. Here we are—from the Latin word numisma; pertaining or relating to . . .'

'Miss Merriman, you haven't met Mr Towers. He is one of the world's greatest numismatics. Mr Towers, this is Miss Merriman, my secretary. She is very interested in numismatics.'

With triumphant relief I relieved Miss Merriman of the dictionary and the tell-tale chit.

'Oh, are you now?' beamed Mr Towers, gripping the hand of his new victim and shaking it vigorously. 'It is a pleasure to meet someone interested in numismatics. As I was saying, people do not realize the contribution that numismatics has made in reconstructing ancient history.'

'Don't they?' queried the baffled Miss Merriman.

'No, indeed they do not,' emphasized Mr Towers, warming to the subject. 'Numismatics is the one science which has helped to fix the chronology of all historical excavations. We would have known nothing about the Indo-Greek, Indo-Scythian, or even the Indo-Parthian periods but for numismaticians. Why, Dr Banerjee has even been able to trace the entire genealogy of the Kings of Kathiawar and the Western Kshatrapas.'

'Yes, indeed,' commented Miss Merriman dubiously.

'I was telling you about Mohenjodaro,' I burst in quickly, pretending to read out of the dictionary. 'Mohenjodaro has yielded valuable material to the numismatician.'

'Aha,' exclaimed Mr Towers, 'I said so, didn't I? Let's see—is that Banerjee's book?'

Before I could do anything, Mr Towers had the dictionary out of my hand.

The Portrait of A Lady

My grandmother, like everybody's grandmother, was an old woman. She had been old and wrinkled for the twenty years that I had known her. People said that she had once been young and pretty and had even had a husband, but that was hard to believe. My grandfather's portrait hung above the mantelpiece in the drawing-room. He wore a big turban and loose-fitting clothes. His long white beard covered the best part of his chest and he looked at least a hundred years old. He did not look the sort of person who would have a wife or children. He looked as if he could only have lots and lots of grandchildren. As for my grandmother being young and pretty, the thought was almost revolting. She often told us of the games she used to play as a child. That seemed quite absurd and undignified on her part and we treated it like the fables of the Prophets she used to tell us.

She had always been short and fat and slightly bent. Her face was a crisscross of wrinkles running from everywhere to everywhere. No, we were certain she had always been as we had known her. Old, so terribly old that she could not have grown older, and had stayed at the same age for twenty years. She could never have been pretty; but she was always beautiful. She hobbled about the house in spotless white with one hand resting on her waist to balance her stoop and the other telling the beads of her rosary. Her silver locks were scattered untidily over her pale, puckered face, and her lips constantly moved in inaudible prayer. Yes, she was beautiful. She was like the winter landscape in the mountains, an expanse of pure white serenity breathing peace and contentment.

My grandmother and I were good friends. My parents left me with her when they went to live in the city and we were constantly together. She used to wake me up in the morning and get me ready for school. She said her morning prayer in a monotonous sing-song while she bathed and dressed me in the hope that I would listen and get to know it by heart. I listened because I loved her voice but never bothered to learn it. Then she would fetch my wooden slate which she had already washed and plastered with yellow chalk, a tiny earthen ink pot and a reed pen, tie them all in a bundle and hand it to me. After a breakfast of a thick, stale chapatti with a little butter and sugar spread on it, we went to school. She carried several stale chapatties with her for the village dogs.

My grandmother always went to school with me because the school was attached to the temple. The priest taught us the alphabet and the morning prayer. While the children sat in rows on either side of the verandah singing the alphabet or the prayer in a chorus, my grandmother sat inside reading the scriptures. When we had both finished, we would walk back together. This time the village dogs would meet us at the temple door. They followed us to our home growling and fighting each other for the chapatties we threw to them.

When my parents were comfortably settled in the city, they sent for us. That was a turning-point in our friendship. Although we shared the same room, my grandmother no longer came to school with me. I used to go to an English school in a motor bus. There were no dogs in the streets and she took to feeding sparrows in the courtyard of our city house.

As the years rolled by we saw less of each other. For some time she continued to wake me up and get me ready for school. When I came back she would ask me what the teacher had taught me. I would tell her English words and little things of western science and learning, the law of gravity, Archimedes' principle, the world being round, etc. This made her unhappy. She could not help me with my lessons. She did not believe in the things they taught at the English school and was distressed that there was no teaching about God and the scriptures. One day I announced that we were being given music lessons. She was very disturbed. To her music had lewd associations. It was the monopoly of harlots and beggars and not meant for gentle folk. She rarely talked to me after that.

When I went up to University, I was given a room of my own. The common link of friendship was snapped. My grandmother accepted her seclusion with resignation. She rarely left her spinning wheel to talk to anyone. From sunrise to sunset she sat by her wheel spinning and reciting prayers. Only in the afternoon she relaxed for a while to feed the sparrows. While she sat in the verandah breaking the bread into little bits, hundreds of little birds collected round her creating a veritable bedlam of chirrupings. Some came and perched on her legs, others on her shoulders. Some even sat on her head. She smiled but never shoo'd them away. It used to be the happiest half-hour of the day for her.

When I decided to go abroad for further studies, I was sure my grandmother would be upset. I would be away for five years, and at her age one could never tell. But my grandmother could. She was not even sentimental. She came to leave me at the railway station but did not talk or show any emotion. Her lips moved in prayer, her mind was lost in prayer. Her fingers were busy telling the beads of her rosary. Silently she kissed my forehead, and when I left I cherished the moist imprint as perhaps the last sign of physical contact between us.

But that was not so. After five years I came back home and was met by her at the station. She did not look a day older. She still had no time for words, and while she clasped me in her arms I could hear her reciting her prayer. Even on the first day of my arrival, her happiest moments were with her sparrows whom she fed longer and with frivolous rebukes.

In the evening a change came over her. She did not pray. She collected the women of the neighbourhood, got an old drum and started to sing. For several hours she thumped the sagging skins of the dilapidated drum and sang of the home-coming of warriors. We had to persuade her to stop to avoid overstraining. That was the first time since I had known her that she did not pray.

The next morning she was taken ill. It was a mild fever and the doctor told us that it would go. But my grandmother thought differently. She told us that her end was near. She said that, since only a few hours before the close of the last chapter of her life she had omitted to pray, she was not going to waste any more time talking to us.

We protested. But she ignored our protests. She lay peacefully in bed praying and telling her beads. Even before we could suspect, her lips stopped moving and the rosary fell from her lifeless fingers. A peaceful pallor spread on her face and we knew that she was dead.

We lifted her off the bed and, as is customary, laid her on the ground and covered her with a red shroud. After a few hours of mourning we left her alone to make arrangements for her funeral.

In the evening we went to her room with a crude stretcher to take her to be cremated. The sun was setting and had lit her room and verandah with a blaze of golden light. We stopped half-way in the courtyard. All over the verandah and in her room right up to where she lay dead and stiff wrapped in the red shroud, thousands of sparrows sat scattered on the floor. There was no chirping. We felt sorry for the birds and my mother fetched some bread for them. She broke it into little crumbs, the way my grandmother used to, and threw it to them. The sparrows took no notice of the bread. When we carried my grandmother's corpse off, they flew away quietly. Next morning the sweeper swept the bread crumbs into the dust bin.

The Voice of God

Bhamba Kalan and Bhamba Khurd are two little villages with hardly half a mile between them. As a matter of fact, the littering of mud huts, the tomb of Syed Bulhey Shah and the Mission School almost link Bhamba Kalan and Bhamba Khurd together; hence they are generally referred to as just Bhamba.

The village is mainly inhabited by Sikh peasants, who own all the land around it. The Moslems till the lands of their Sikh masters or ply the lesser trades as potters and weavers. There are some Christians who live in a cluster of huts on the outskirts of the habitations who do the menial work. Then there are the Hindu shopkeepers who sell provisions—oil, soap, salt, spices, cloth, scissors, mirrors, and Japanese toys.

Nothing that is important ever happens in Bhamba. Once a year there is a gathering at the tomb of Syed Bulhey Shah when people from the neighbouring villages—Moslems, Hindus and Sikhs alike—come to the fair. Their womenfolk make offerings at the tomb and buy charms to induce their barren wombs to yield. Once a year the Sikhs go to the fair at Amritsar with their long swords carried on their shoulders. Besides these, the only excitement is provided by periodical visits of the police. Someone would break someone else's head in a drunken brawl; someone would abduct somebody's wife or daughter; someone would be indiscreet in distilling illicit liquor. Sometimes no one would do anything and the police would simply come to drink the illicit liquor and eat the eggs and chickens. From the homes of the inhospitable the police would recover arms, liquor or opium, and they would be sent to jail or learn to be hospitable.

Besides these diversions, life in Bhamba has little change. In the morning, while men work in the fields and boys graze cattle, women work at home grinding corn, cooking or spinning, After midday they all relax. The flour mill starts working. It has a diesel oil engine with an exhaust pipe rising above the village roofs. On top of the exhaust pipe the miller has fixed an earthen pot which turns the engine's puffing into shrill blasts. Its monotonous notes are heard

for miles around Bhamba. It is the background music to afternoon
siestas and lazy gossip.

One spring afternoon the residents of Bhamba were basking in
the sunshine in little groups doing nothing. The men sat on their
haunches, staring blankly at the mud walls, listening to the music
of the mill. The women sat on their string cots gossiping and rubbing
clarifed butter into each other's scalps. There was a bumper crop in
the offing, and the vast stretch of yellow and green mustard gave
the countryside an appearance of peace and prosperity.

All at once the village was astir. Children went running about
the alleys shouting excitedly. A motor car ploughed its way through
the dusty track towards Bhamba raising clouds of dust behind it. It
was a smart brown station wagon with five or six people in it. The
car drove up hooting furiously. Children ran behind it or stood on
its rear bumper. Village dogs were all around, barking and snapping
at the mudguards. The car came to a halt in the village square, and
the clouds of dust raised by it rolled up and enveloped it.

When the dust drifted away five men stepped out with handkerchiefs to their noses. In front was the English Deputy Commissioner,
Mr Forsythe—a short stout man in khaki with a sola topee tightly
strapped under his chin. He was escorted by two policemen and his
chauffeur. With him was Sardar Sahib Ganda Singh, Honorary
Magistrate, a big landowner who lived in and owned the neighbouring village, Ganda Singh Wala.

The zaildar and three lambardars of Bhamba stepped out from
the crowd of villagers and greeted the Englishman with salams and
a chorus of welcome. The Sahib had never been to Bhamba before.
What auspicious occasion had brought the defender of the poor,
the king of kings, the merciful, to these parts?

The Deputy Commissioner smiled affably and made for the house
of the zaildar. Mr Forsythe sank into a low cane chair while his
companion, Ganda Singh, sat next to him on a green one made of
steel. The villagers closed round the circle of chairs, still a babel of
welcomes.

Forsythe took off his sola topee, uncovering a pink bald head.
He mopped his forehead with his handkerchief and with a gesture
indicated to the crowd that he wished to speak. There was silence.
Forsythe continued to mop his forehead to let the silence sink into
the crowd and increase their expectancy. Then he introduced
Ganda Singh in eloquent terms.

Ganda Singh did not need an introduction. Everyone in the district knew him. He had helped the Government and had been granted lands, titles and an Honorary Magistracy. He was a well-known patron of thugs. His men robbed with impunity and shared the proceeds with the police. His liquor stills worked in broad daylight, and even excise staff were entertained to many varieties of liquor fermented in dung heaps. Ganda Singh's hospitality was lavish. There was food and drink in plenty. For men who mattered, he even provided dusky village maidens—naive and provocatively unwilling.

Ganda Singh was the most hated man in the district, and he knew it. Wherever he went, he was accompanied by two armed men. A black leather cartridge belt charged with bullets ran across his chest from the shoulder to the hips, ending in a pouch containing a loaded revolver. Everyone in Bhamba had seen him before. His starched turban had one end proudly plumaged above his head and the other hanging behind the nape of his neck. His eyes were darkened with antimony and his glossy black beard, neatly trimmed and oiled, gave him a lecherous look. He was tall and corpulent. He wore a white shirt which hung just above his knees and a pair of baggy punjabi trousers whose blue silk cord was displayed under the hem of the shirt. On his feet he wore a pair of black pumps which squeaked as he walked.

Forsythe paid tributes to Ganda Singh as the pride of the district. He was glad to learn, he said, that the Sardar was proposing to contest the forthcoming elections to the Punjab Legislative Assembly. He had been nominated by the leaders of the Sikh community and had the full approval of the Government.

There were whispers and subdued talk but Forsythe did not attach any importance to them. He dismissed the crowd and then proceeded to talk revenue business with the zaildar and the lambardars.

While Forsythe was busy with one lambardar, Ganda Singh canvassed the others a few yards away with his arms round their shoulders. He told them that the Sahib was very 'merciful to him' and he could get him to do anything the lambardars wanted. One wanted a licence for a gun. Another's name had been sent up to the Deputy Commissioner to be made an assessor in the Court of Sessions. The third one's nephew had been run in under the Excise Act and his case was pending. Could the Deputy Commissioner drop a hint to the Magistrate that the accused was his own man?

Ganda Singh made a note of all these in his diary and got the lambardar's promise of 100 per cent poll in his favour. It was a matter of prestige for the Sikh peasantry, he added. More than that, he was of the same sub-caste as they were. As for his rival, the Nationalist candidate, he was not even an agriculturist! He was a lawyer from the city. The Kisan candidate was one of them, but then he had no religion. Besides that, the Government strongly disapproved of him and had frequently put him in jail for reasons of security.

Forsythe and Ganda Singh's party left in the evening. Their visit was like a stone dropped in Bhamba's placid pool whose ripples would take several days to subside. Peace had gone from Bhamba for some time to come.

Next day the residents of Bhamba were again basking in the sunshine listening to the whistling of the grinding machine and talking about Forsythe, when they were disturbed by the shouts of the children and the barking of the dogs. This time the intruder was a large cream-coloured lorry with a loudspeaker fixed on its roof. Along the mudguards on either side were fixed stout flag poles on which large-sized flags of the Nationalist party fluttered.

The lorry came to a halt in the village square. Before the dust drifted away and the occupants of the lorry could be made out, the loudspeaker blared out. After a little coughing a voice announced:

'Residents of Bhamba, do you know that elections to the Pubjab Assembly are imminent? Do you know your duty in these elections? Vote for Sardar Kartar Singh, Advocate, who is a nominee of the Nationalists!'

There was a pause. Then the voice at the microphone shouted the name of Kartar Singh and a dozen voices yelled back: 'Zindabad!' This was repeated several times in such explosions that dogs put their tails between their legs and slunk away.

Then Kartar Singh stepped out from the front seat. From the rear emerged a dozen young men dressed in Gandhi caps, shirts and dhoties of coarse handspun cloth. They carried bundles of posters.

Kartar Singh had never been to Bhamba before but several villagers knew him. They had engaged him in criminal cases for exorbitant fees. Even these villagers found it difficult to recognize him. They had seen him in European dress with black coat, tie and striped trousers. Now he was dressed in a long shirt, pyjamas and sandals.

Kartar Singh and one of his companions, a fat, dark man dressed like him, made for the zaildar's house, while the other men went about pasting posters in the village. The zaildar's door was shut and he could not be found. The villagers swore that he was with them when the lorry came and had left to make arrangements for the visitors. But the zaildar's little boy came out of his house and informed them that his father had just gone out to answer the call of nature. The villagers smiled and the crowd returned to the lorry. Kartar Singh and his companion clambered on to the roof and the microphone was handed over to them.

Kartar Singh introduced his companion, Seth Sukhtankar. The Seth was a well-known Nationalist leader who had been elected to the Punjab Assembly unopposed. He was also a millionaire, owning a chain of cloth mills. He had made his fortune during the movement to boycott foreign cloth. In the five years of the war the Seth's wealth had gone into astronomical figures. He had no sympathy with the Government, so he bought and sold in the black market with a clear conscience. While people starved and went naked, the Seth bought stacks of wheat and hoarded it. He sold this at fabulous prices. He was passionately anti-British. He wanted all Indians to unite. The main point of his speech was that if 400 million Indians united and spat in a tank, there would be enough spit to drown the entire English population in India. But somehow the facilities for such a mass suicide had never been provided. The Seth was also passionately anti-Socialist. Socialists were traitors. They had caused strikes in his mills at a time when he could have ousted all foreign goods from the market by dumping his own cheaper products. He decried them as foreign agents.

After Sukthankar, Kartar Singh himself spoke. He knew all about Ganda Singh. No one, he said, should vote for a man who trimmed his beard and drank liquor. He also warned the villagers against the insidious propaganda of the Kisans, who had no religion or morals, and who, besides wanting to share everyone's property, would share everyone's wives.

Seth Sukhtankar's party went as it had come, leaving clouds of dust with the loudspeaker blaring 'Zindabad!' to Kartar Singh's name.

Every day strangers came to Bhamba and made speeches. The private life of Ganda Singh was no longer private. But what of that? retorted Ganda Singh's men. He was a Sikh agriculturist and what agriculturist did not drink? Kartar Singh was only a city lawyer backed by Hindu moneylenders. Didn't Seth Sukhtankar offer money to the lambardars if they proclaimed their intention to vote Nationalist? Where did all the money for lorries, posters and voters come from? Kartar Singh was not too prosperous for a lawyer.

In spite of the slanders against each other, both the candidates agreed that the Kisan should be kept out. But no Kisan had yet come to Bhamba and the villagers awaited with anxiety the arrival of the representative of the godless, immoral traitors.

Then one spring afternoon when, as on any other spring afternoon, the villagers basked in the sunshine doing nothing, the Kisan came. He was not greeted by the village children or the dogs because no one heard him come. He rode up on a mare as white as his turban and the long beard that covered the best part of his chest.

It was Baba Ram Singh. Everyone in Bhamba had heard of him. He had been arrested several times in peasant movements and had spent the best part of his life in jail. All his property had been confiscated and he was homeless—yet all the homes of the countryside were open to him People touched his feet wherever he went and mothers brought their children to be blessed by him. He was popularly known as Babaji, because of his age and piety.

The villagers gathered round Ram Singh, kissing his stirrups and his dusty shoes. What had brought Babaji to Bhamba? He told them that he was contesting the elections to the Legislative Assembly. There was a murmur of applause. Then one villager asked him— surely the Nationalists could not put up two candidates? Kartar Singh, the lawyer, had told them that he was the Nationalist nominee. The Baba's answer chilled his audience to silence.

'Kisan!'

Kisan? But he was a god-fearing man who had spent his life serving the peasants. Traitor? But the Government had put him in jail for nearly twenty years and robbed him of his property. Immoral? Why, he was like the Guru himself. He did not drink nor trim his beard.

Baba Ram Singh did not stay very long. He wanted their votes because he would fight for their liberation from foreigners as well as exploiting landlords. He would fight the police bullies and the corrupt administration. He did not even mention the names of his rival candidates.

No Kisan ever came to Bhamba again. Nor did the Baba himself repeat his visit. He went alone from village to village and in his own peaceful way he blew away the might of Forsythe's Government and the corrupting cash of Sukhtankar like fluffs of thistledown before a gust of wind.

One day before the polling was to take place, he was arrested on a charge of making a seditious speech.

II

Bhamba like all neighbouring villages went to the polls. Smelly, dirty Sikh peasants tumbled out of Seth Sukhtankar's lorries drunk with Ganda Singh's liquor. But they knew who to vote for. Thousands went in and, being illiterate, named their candidate—and walked back home. The Seth's lorries did not take them back nor did Ganda Singh give them more liquor for sustenance.

The counting was done ten days later in Forsythe's office. A large crowd gathered outside yelling the names of Ganda Singh and Kartar Singh. Baba Ram Singh was not even mentioned. At 11 a.m. the stubby figure of Forsythe appeared on the steps of the office. He was wreathed in smiles as he read out the result:

1. Sardar Ganda Singh, Honorary Magistrate   10,560
2. Sardar Kartar Singh, Advocate   8,340
3. Baba Ram Singh   760

The last mentioned forfeited his deposit.

The people had spoken. The voice of the people is the voice of God.

A Punjab Pastorale

Peter Hansen was a young American from Illinois. His father was a Swede who had settled in the United States and made good as a stockbroker. Peter was given the best an American youth could desire in the way of schooling and university education, and in due course joined his father's firm. It did not take him long to discover that he was not meant for business. His spirit of adventure felt cramped in horizons clogged with sky-scrapers. He yearned for the wide open spaces and wanted to serve humanity. He gave up stockbroking and took to Christianity, left Illinois and came to India. His Mission ordered him to preach the gospel of Christ among the Sikh peasantry in the Punjab. This brought Peter Hansen to Amritsar.

Hansen plunged into the humanitarian business with American thoroughness. He drew up maps of the countryside and stuck little flags to mark the villages he would visit. He made lists in an indexed register of villagers he had to contact, together with details of their private lives. He bought an old American army motorcycle, and within a few weeks of his arrival Padre Hansen and his phut-phut became a familiar sight in the district.

Hansen was a missionary, but with a difference. He did not go about peddling religion. It was reform he was after—social reform, economic reform, educational reform, moral reform. His method, too, was different. He did not believe in preaching or proselytizing but in reform by example and personal contact.

'Once you get to know them,' he used to say, 'you can make them do anything.'

Hansen and I were destined to meet. I, too, had a heart for humanity, only I did nothing about it except talk. But Hansen did not know that. I was not religious, and had taken to Marxism. Even that did not bother Hansen, he was a bit of a Socialist himself. He happened to attend a meeting I was addressing.

'The country is ripe for revolution,' I was saying. 'It needs proper leadership to get it going. High falutin' talk of dialectical materialism and Marxist economics does not register on the rural mind. We must preach Socialism through example and personal contact. We must denounce police oppression, corruption and injustice in the law courts. Above all, we must get to know the people. Once you get to know them—you can make them do anything.'

Hansen and I shook hands and a partnership to further the cause of progress was made.

One hot May morning we decided to give our enterprise a trial. Hansen rigged himself out in his touring clothes—a white jockey cap, a tight-fitting vest, a pair of very short shorts, and sandals on his feet. I donned my socialist garments of the coarsest handspun khaddar, mounted Hansen's motorcycle pillion, and we shot out of Amritsar.

Some fifteen miles east of the city, there was a big canal which ran at right angles to the road. We crossed the bridge and turned off the metal road on to a cart-track. The track showed visible signs of wear and tear. Bullock-cart wheels had left deep ruts which ran criss-cross like intersecting tram lines. Hansen did not seem to notice them. He sped on with a grim resolve, his belly hugging the petrol tank. I held stoically on to his vest. I could find no protruding gadgets on which to rest my feet, and they dangled helpless above the hot exhaust pipes. I did not dare to protest. There were greater things in the offing, and I could not go down just because the going was rough. But I did go down. While Hansen's eyes were glued to the distant horizon as if straining to get a glimpse of the domes of Shangrila, we flew over a ditch at some 40 miles per hour. I was tossed in the air, and by the time I came down Hansen and his motor-cycle were several yards ahead on their philanthropic errand. I landed in the middle of a very dusty track. It didn't hurt much, but it was somewhat undignified. My turban had flown off and my long hair spread clumsily over my face. Hansen pulled up and looked concerned for a moment. Then he flashed his teeth at me like a cheap toothpaste advertisement, and burst out laughing.

'You look too darned funny for words,' he roared. 'Just as well it happened here. This is where we break off. Soorajpur is just across those fields, behind the keekar trees.' Hansen ran his motorcycle down the canal bank to a large peepul tree, still laughing. I collected my scattered belongings and joined him. I opened his water bottle, poured the water down my parched throat and splashed it on my dusty face. Then I stretched myself in the welcome shade of the peepul, and was at peace with my surroundings.

Soorajpur was just visible through the thick cluster of keekar trees. All around it stretched a vast expanse of wheat fields. The corn was ripe and ready for harvesting. A soft breeze blew across the golden cornfields like ripples over a lake. Under the trees the cattle and the cowherds lay in deep slumber. It was a scene typical of pastoral Punjab on a summer afternoon.

It was too peaceful to think of revolution. My enthusiasm was somewhat on the wane. I was willing to leave Soorajpur to its slovenly backwardness.

But Hansen's ardour had not cooled. Just as I had shut my eyes in peaceful contemplation, he started to talk.

'The last time I was here there was a crisis going on. The Sikhs would not let the Christians into their temple because the Christians were sweepers and skinned dead buffaloes.'

'Oh?' I inquired politely, 'what happened?'•

'I told the Christians to go and tell the Sikhs that they would give up skinning dead buffaloes if they were allowed in the temple. Just then a buffalo died right near the most popular village well and no one would touch it. The place was full of crows and vultures and the stink was terrible. I got round Moola Singh—you must meet the old man—and told him to persuade the Sikhs to think over the matter. He told his fellow Sikhs to remove the carcass themselves or let the Christians into the temple. Sure as ever, they came round. Now the Christians are paid twenty rupees for skinning a dead buffalo. They sell the hide for another thirty or forty rupees, and they walk in and out of the Sikh temple as they please. It was all really because of Moola Singh. Personal contact does so much. I've always said once you get to know these village folk you can make them do anything. And Moola Singh is a grand old fellow. Come along, we had better be moving.'

And so we started off again. This time Hansen was on the motor-cycle, and I was pushing it across ploughed fields and dry water courses. Hansen was apparently very popular. Everyone who saw him came around to greet him. He knew the names of all of them. In the traditional fashion, he shook them by both hands and put his hands across his heart. No one took any notice of me, nor volunteered to help me push the motorcycle.

I pushed hand-shaking Hansen and his motorcycle up a narrow alley to the centre of the village. We parked the machine by a well amidst a crowd of urchins and proceeded to Moola Singh's house,

which was a few yards away. Moola Singh was to be my first contact
and I was to deliver him all my Socialism. At night I was to address
a meeting at the temple with Moola Singh to back me up. Hansen
would visit the houses of the Christians who lived on the outskirts
of the village.

We caught Moola Singh unawares. Hansen's inquiries about
him had evinced no answer from the crowd walking along with us
towards his courtyard. When we got to his house, we saw his two
wives sitting under the shadow of a wall. One was rubbing clarified
butter into the head of the other. They too were reticent about
Moola Singh. Suddenly becoming aware of this mysterious silence,
Hansen turned to the crowd and asked the reason for it. Then all of
a sudden appeared Moola Singh on his threshold. He was a large
hulking man over six feet in height. His hair hung over his shoulders
and mingled with his beard. He was about sixty, but a youthful,
roguish smile played about his face.

He stretched his arms wide and gathered Hansen in a friendly
embrace. Through the mass of hair and beard I heard Hansen calling
out my name. Moola Singh held out one hand to me, still holding
the American by the other. He clasped him again and the two
swayed in a close, amorous embrace. Moola Singh was stinking of
drink. Saliva dribbled from his mouth on to his shaggy beard. It ran
down like threads of silver on Hansen's hazel-brown hair. Hansen
winced as the liquid ran through his hair on to his scalp. With a little
jerk he extricated himself from Moola Singh's grasp and pushed
him back gently.

Hansen was too well bred to lose his temper. He smiled his toothpaste advertisement smile and poked Moola Singh in the ribs.

'Bahut Sharab! Bahut Sharab!' he rebuked in Hindustani.

Moola Singh grinned. He caught both his ears with his hands
and stuck out his yellow tongue in a gesture of repentance.

'Never again, Sahib. This is the last time—*toba toba*. You come
to my house and I am stupidly drunk. If you forgive me this time
and promise to come again, I will not touch drink any more.'

Hansen forgave him and promised to come again. We left Moola
Singh's house a little depressed. I began to think that our ardour for
reform was somewhat adolescent. Hansen was wiping the dribble
off his hair with his handkerchief and cursing the Sikhs. The Christian
folk, he insisted, were so much nicer. They didn't drink. They didn't
grow long hair and beards which stank of sweat and stale clarified

butter. Since he had got to know them, they were living a clean Christian life—free of pagan superstition which beset the life of the hirsute Sikh. He dismissed the crowd with a firm wave of the hand and we walked down to the mission school.

We entered the Christian habitation with more optimism. Mr Yoosuf Masih, the teacher, welcomed us and put a garland of marigolds around Hansen's neck. Sweeper women and children gathered about him in a chorus of salams. Hansen patted the children and shook hands with their mothers. So much cleaner than the Sikhs, he said with a triumphant smile. He insisted on my going inside their huts and seeing for myself. The first hut had a large picture of the black, red-tongued, multi-armed goddess Kali hanging in the centre of a wall. Others also had pictures. In fact, we saw the entire Hindu pantheon: Shiva on his tiger skin with serpents twining around his neck; Ganesha riding the mouse, his lady love seated on his elephantine thigh; Saraswati standing in spotless white on a large lotus. Hansen saw them too. I smiled at him but he looked away. He shook hands with Mr Yoosuf Masih rather abruptly, promising to see him later in the evening. We then made our way back towards the village well to our motorcycle.

We walked a long way without speaking. Hansen was somewhat depressed. I was just bored and tired. As we approached the well, Hansen spoke.

'Queer country this! You do not know where to start. When you've begun, you are not sure if you are going about it the right way. When you look back to see how far you've got, you find that you've got nowhere. It's like a stream losing itself in the desert sand. It dries up so quickly that you cannot even find its traces.' I made no comment.

The sun went down and the shades of twilight gathered Soorajpur in their fold. The moon was in the first quarter and shed a soft, silky light in the narrow alleys. Hansen started talking again. If only Christian converts would free themselves from the clutches of superstition. If only Sikhs would give up dissipating and use their fine manhood towards something constructive. If ... if ... if ... The burden of the world's woes seemed to have descended on him and he looked miserable and woebegone.

Suddenly Hansen stopped talking. He sat up straight as if electrified. From Moola Singh's courtyard emerged a girl, barely sixteen, with two pitchers balanced on her stately head. She came towards the well where we were sitting. She wore a man's striped shirt. It had no buttons in the front and made a V formation running from her neck down to the middle of her flat belly. On either side, the V was mis-shaped by her youthful breasts. Hansen's eyes were fixed on her. His mouth was wide open. The girl drew several buckets of water from the well and we watched. The depression lifted, and the streets of slovenly Soorajpur were charged with romance and mellowed moonlight. The girl went, with the two pitchers balanced on her head. Her slim figure disappeared into Moola Singh's courtyard.

Hansen came back to earth. 'Oh my, oh my, that was sum'pn. She is old Moola Singh's daughter. Hardly believe it, would you? She is like a flower in the desert, and desert flowers always smell sweeter. They have to make up for the desert. I could almost write a poem about her.'

We sat by the well for a long time, feeling strangely happy. Hansen was trying hard to give his emotions a poetical form. 'I've got it,' he exclaimed, snapping his fingers and looking up at the sky—

    'She walks in beauty like the night,

    . . . . '

Kusum

Kusum Kumari was a good girl with a capital G. To Kusum being good was no effort at all. In fact, she could not help being good. Although she was only eighteen she looked twenty-eight, and her manner was that of a middle-aged woman, in her forties. She was short and somewhat fat. Her dark, oval face was spotted with darker small pox marks. On her stubby nose was a pair of gold-rimmed glasses whose thick lenses magnified her eyes to bovine proportions. The hair on her head was short and sparse. This she oiled till it looked as if it was glued to her scalp. It was tightly plaited at the back, stretching up her forehead and arching her eyebrows. As for Kusum's figure, it was, euphemistically put, filled up. One could not tell her bust or belly or behind distinctly. They were all contained in one squatty frame which Kusum draped in a simple white sari.

But Kusum made up for all that by being good and clever. She worked hard and had a string of first classes to her credit. Her glasses and her figure bore testimony to the many hours spent over books. Kusum was no trouble to her parents. She got up early and cycled to her college. She came back from college. She had no engagements. She had no distractions and she did not distract anybody.

Kusum had no use for modern fashions, nor did she have any interest in boys. She shunned sex. She had no use for make-up and cosmetics. She believed that people should be content with the skins God gave them, even if they were pock-marked. She believed in virtue and kindness. She believed in work and propriety. She believed that a woman's place was in the kitchen. She believed that girls should never be seen with their heads uncovered. Kusum was popular with old men and women, but young men took no notice of her. So she came to believe in the values nature had unkindly forced upon her.

On Kusum's nineteenth birthday some college girls sent her a lipstick and some rouge as a present. Kusum took this as a personal insult. She hid the things in a corner of her drawer and coldly announced that she had thrown them out of the window. She turned the face of her mirror towards the wall and decided to squash the desire to see herself.

Kusum hardly ever laughed. After her nineteenth birthday, she seldom smiled. She became more earnest, grimly earnest. She knew it made her uglier, but she could not help it. In any case, since no man ever took notice of her, there was no point in trying to look attractive. And since she looked unattractive, no man took notice of her.

Kusum's university life came to an end in April when she took her degree examination. Other girls came out of the examination hall and went on a binge with their friends and relations. Nobody came to meet Kusum and she collected her bicycle with the usual matter-of-factnes. Other girls could look forward to matrimony. Kusum had nothing to look forward to—nothing but her sparsely furnished room with her mirror facing the wall and a few textbooks.

Kusum cycled home with her mind a complete void. She was alone on the road and could afford to lose herself in thinking of nothing. She took the turning home on the wrong side of the road, and before she could collect her thoughts she ran into a young hawker with a basket of oranges on his head. She fell on him and then rolled over on the road. Her glasses were smashed. The bicycle was on the pavement. The hawker was just a bit shaken—not hurt. His basket of oranges was all right too. He smiled pleasantly.

'Miss Sahib, you should keep to your side of the road.'

Kusum was angry and the hawker's tone made her angrier.

'Are you blind? Can't you see where you are going?' she shrieked hoarsely.

The hawker looked around. The road was deserted. His smile became roguish.

'No, Miss Sahib, I am not blind, but I am one-eyed.'

He shut one of his eyes in a long, lecherous wink and made the sound of a loud kiss.

Kusum's face coloured. She was furious. She picked up the bicycle and got on hurriedly. In a hoarse voice she swore at the hawker.

'Pig ... ass.'

The hawker was not offended. He seemed to be enjoying the situation.

'Ass?' he questioned, lustfully winking with the other eye. 'Have you seen one?'

He held his right arm at the elbow with his left and moved it vigorously to demonstrate. Kusum was flustered—she had never been accosted before. She rushed home—rushed to her room and buried her face in a pillow.

Kusum lay buried in her pillow and her thoughts for several hours. The wrath disappeared but the picture of the rascally hawker winking and making lewd suggestions stuck in her mind. Nobody had ever done that to her before. Did the hawker find her attractive?

The sun went down and the pale moonlight crept into the room and lit the bed she lay on. Kusum was thinking of the hawker—now with tenderness and regret. 'Maybe', she said to herself, 'maybe'. She got up and opened the drawer where her lipstick and rouge lay hidden. She patted her cheeks with the rouge. She turned the face of the mirror towards her and pouted her lips to put on the lipstick. She undid her hair and shook her head to loosen it. The hair fell in profusion about her shoulders. She picked a rose bud from a vase and stuck it in her hair. She stepped back and tilted her head sideways to admire herself.

'Mirror, mirror, on the wall,
Who is the fairest one of all?'

An attractive dark-eyed girl with a mass of tumbled black hair adorned by a rose bud smiled back at her—'I should say so!'

The Riot

The town lay etherized under the fresh spring twilight. The shops were closed and house-doors barred from the inside. Street lamps dimly lit the deserted roads. Only a few policemen walked about with steel helmets on their heads and rifles slung behind their backs. The sound of their hobnailed boots was all that broke the stillness of the town.

The twilight sank into darkness. A cresent moon lit the quiet streets. A soft breeze blew bits of newspaper from the pavements on to the road and back again. It was cool and smelled of the freshness of spring. Some dogs emerged from a dark lane and gathered round a lamp-post. A couple of policemen strolled past them smiling. One of them mumbled something vulgar. The other pretended to pick up a stone and hurl it at the dogs. The dogs ran down the street in the opposite direction and resumed their courtship at a safer distance.

Rani was a pariah bitch whose litter populated the lanes and by-lanes of the town. She was a thin, scraggy specimen, typical of the pariahs of the town. Her white coat was mangy, showing patches of raw flesh. Her dried-up udders hung loosely from her ribs. Her tail was always tucked between her hind legs as she slunk about in fear and abject servility.

Rani would have died of starvation with her first litter of eight had it not been for the generosity of the Hindu shopkeeper, Ram Jawaya, in the corner of whose courtyard she had unloaded her womb. The shopkeeper's family fed her and played with her pups till they were old enough to run about the streets and steal food for themselves. The shopkeeper's generosity had put Rani in the habit of sponging. Every year when spring came she would find an excuse to loiter around the stall of Ramzan, the Moslem greengrocer. Beneath the wooden platform on which groceries were displayed lived the big, burly Moti. Early autumn, she presented the shopkeeper's household with half-a-dozen or more of Moti's offspring.

Moti was a cross between a Newfoundland and a spaniel. His shaggy coat and sullen look were Ramzan's pride. Ramzan had lopped off Moti's tail and ears. He fed him till Moti grew big and strong and became the master of the town's canine population. Rani had many rivals. But year after year, with the advent of spring, Rani's fancy lightly turned to thoughts of Moti and she sauntered across to Ramzan's stall.

This time spring had come but the town was paralysed with fear of communal riots and curfews. In the daytime people hung about the street corners in groups of tens and twenties, talking in whispers. No shops opened and long before curfew hours the streets were deserted, with only pariah dogs and policemen about.

Tonight even Moti was missing. In fact, ever since the curfew Ramzan had kept him indoors tied to a cot. He was far more useful guarding Ramzan's house than loitering about the streets. Rani came to Ramzan's stall and sniffed around. Moti could not have been there for some days. She was disappointed. But spring came only once a year—and hardly ever did it come at a time when one could have the city to oneself with no curious children looking on—and no scandalized parents hurling stones at her. So Rani gave up Moti and ambled down the road toward Ram Jawaya's house. A train of suitors followed her.

Rani faced her many suitors in front of Ram Jawaya's doorstep. They snarled and snapped and fought with each other. Rani stood impassively, waiting for the decision. In a few minutes a lanky black dog, one of Rani's own progeny, won the honours. The others slunk away.

In Ramzan's house, Moti sat pensively eyeing his master from underneath his charpoy. For some days the spring air had made him restive. He heard the snarling in the street and smelled Rani in the air. But Ramzan would not let him go. He tugged at the rope— then gave it up and began to whine. Ramzan's heavy hand struck him. A little later he began to whine again. Ramzan had had several sleepless nights watching and was heavy with sleep. He began to snore. Moti whined louder and then sent up a pitiful howl to his unfaithful mistress. He tugged and strained at the leash and began to bark. Ramzan got up angrily from his charpoy to beat him. Moti made a dash toward the door dragging the lightened string cot behind him. He nosed open the door and rushed out. The charpoy stuck in the doorway and the rope tightened round his neck. He made a savage wrench, the rope gave way, and he leapt across the road. Ramzan ran back to his room, slipped a knife under his shirt, and went after Moti.

Outside Ram Jawaya's house, the illicit liaison of Rani and the black pariah was being consummated. Suddenly the burly form of Moti came into view. With an angry growl Moti leapt at Rani's lover. Other dogs joined the melee, tearing and snapping wildly.

Ram Jawaya had also spent several sleepless nights keeping watch and yelling back war cries to the Moslems. At last fatigue and sleep overcame his newly-acquired martial spirit. He slept soundly with a heap of stones under his charpoy and an imposing array of soda water bottles filled with acid close at hand. The noise outside woke him. The shopkeeper picked up a big stone and opened the door. With a loud oath he sent the missile flying at the dogs. Suddenly a human being emerged from the corner and the stone caught him squarely in the solar plexus.

The stone did not cause much damage to Ramzan but the suddenness of the assault took him aback. He yelled 'Murder!' and produced his knife from under his shirt. The shopkeeper and the grocer eyed each other for a brief moment and then ran back to their houses shouting. The petrified town came to life. There was more shouting. The drum at the Sikh temple beat a loud tattoo—the air was rent with war cries.

Men emerged from their houses making hasty inquiries. A Moslem or a Hindu, it was said, had been attacked. Someone had been kidnapped and was being butchered. A party of goondas were going to attack, but the dogs had started barking. They had actually assaulted a woman and killed her children. There must be resistance. There was. Groups of five joined others of ten. Tens joined twenties till a few hundred, armed with knives, spears, hatchets, and kerosene oil cans proceeded to Ram Jawaya's house. They were met with a fusilade of stones, soda water bottles, and acid. They hit back blindly. Tins of kerosene oil were emptied indiscriminately and lighted. Flames shot up in the sky enveloping Ram Jawaya's home and the entire neighbourhood, Hindu, Moslem and Sikh alike.

The police rushed to the scene and opened fire. Fire engines clanged their way in and sent jets of water flying into the sky. But fires had been started in other parts of the town and there were not enough fire engines to go round.

All night and all the next day the fires burnt—and houses fell and people were killed. Ram Jawaya's home was burnt and he barely escaped with his life. For several days smoke rose from the ruins. What had once been a busy town was a heap of charred masonry.

Some months later when peace was restored, Ram Jawaya came to inspect the site of his old home. It was all in shambles with the bricks lying in a mountainous pile. In the corner of what had once been his courtyard there was a little clearing. There lay Rani with her litter nuzzling into her dried udders. Beside her stood Moti guarding his bastard brood.

The Rape

Dalip Singh lay on his charpoy staring at the star-studded sky. It was hot and still. He was naked save for his loin cloth. Even so, beads of perspiration rolled off from all parts of his body. The heat rose from the mud walls which had been baking in the sun all day. He had sprinkled water on the roof of the house, but that only produced a clammy vapour smelling of earth and cow dung. He had drunk as much water as his stomach would hold, still his throat was parched. Then there were the mosquitoes and their monotonous droning. Some came too close to his ears and were caught and mashed between his palm and the fingers. One or two got into his ears and he rammed them against the greasy walls with his index finger. Some got entangled in his beard and were squashed to silence in their snares. Some managed to gorge themselves on his blood, leaving him to scratch and curse.

Across the narrow alley separating his house from his uncle's, Dalip Singh could see a row of charpoys on the roof. At one end slept his uncle, Banta Singh, with his arms and legs parted as if crucified. His belly rose and fell as he snored. He had had bhang in the afternoon and slept with utter abandon. At the other end of the row several women sat fanning themselves and talking softly.

Dalip Singh lay awake staring at the sky. For him there was no peace, no sleep. Yet, on the other roof slept his uncle, his father's brother and murderer. His womenfolk found time to sit and gossip into the late hours of the night while his own mother scrubbed the pots and pans with ash and gathered cow dung for fuel. Banta Singh had servants to look after his cattle and plough his land while he drank bhang and slept. His black-eyed daughter Bindo went about doing nothing but showing off her Japanese silks. But for Dalip Singh it was work and more work.

The keekar trees stirred. A soft, cool breeze blew across the roof-tops. It drove the mosquitoes away and dried the sweat. It made Dalip feel cool and placid, and he was heavy with sleep. On Banta Singh's roof the women stopped fanning themselves. Bindo stood up beside her charpoy, threw her head back and filled her lungs with the cool fresh air. Dalip watched her stroll up and down. She could see the people of the village sleeping on the roofs and in the courtyards. No one stirred. Bindo stopped and stood beside her charpoy. She picked up her shirt from the two corners which fell just above her knees and held it across her face with both hands, baring herself from the waist to her neck, letting the cool breeze envelop her flat belly and her youthful bust. Then someone said something in an angry whisper and Bindo let down her shirt. She dropped on her charpoy and was lost in the confused outlines of her pillow.

Dalip Singh was wide awake and his heart beat wildly. The loathsome figure of Banta Singh vanished from his mind. He shut his eyes and tried to recreate Bindo as he saw her in the starlight. He desired her and in his dreams he possessed her. Bindo was always willing—even begging. Dalip condescending, even indifferent. Banta Singh spited and humbled. Dalip Singh's eyes were shut but they opened into another world where Bindo lived and loved, naked, unashamed and beautiful.

Several hours later Dalip's mother came and shook him by the shoulder. It was time to go out ploughing while it was cool. The sky was black and the stars brighter. He picked up his shirt which lay folded under his pillow and put it on. He looked across to the adjoining roof. Bindo lay fast asleep.

Dalip Singh yoked his bullocks to the plough and let them lead him to the fields. He went through the dark, deserted lanes of the village to the starlit fields. He was tired, and the image of Bindo still confused his mind.

The eastern horizon turned grey. From the mango grove the koil's piercing cries issued in a series of loud outbursts. The crows began to caw softly in the keekar trees.

Dalip Singh was ploughing but his mind was not in it. He just held the plough and walked slowly behind. The furrows were neither straight nor deep. The morning light made him feel ashamed. He decided to pull himself together and shake off his day-dreaming. He dug the sharp point of his plough deep into the earth and thrust his goading stick violently into the hind parts of the bullocks. The beasts were jerked into movement, snorting and lashing their tails. The plough tore through the earth and large clods of earth fell on either side under Dalip's feet. Dalip felt master of his bullocks and the plough.He pressed the plough deeper with savage determination and watched its steel point concupiscently nosing its way through the rich brown earth.

The sun came up very bright and hot. Dalip gave up the ploughing and led his bullocks to a well under the peepul tree and unyoked them. He drew several buckets of water. He bathed himself and splashed water over his bullocks, and followed them home dripping all the way.

His mother was waiting for him. She brought him freshly baked bread and spinach, with a little butter on it. She also brought a large copper cup full of buttermilk. Dalip fell to the food eagerly, while his mother sat by him fanning away the flies. He finished the bread and spinach and washed it down with buttermilk. He laid himself on a charpoy and was soon fast asleep. His mother still sat by him fanning him tenderly.

Dalip slept right through the morning and afternoon. He got up in the evening and went round to his fields to clear the water courses. He walked along the water channel which separated his land from his uncle's. Banta Singh's fields were being irrigated by his tenants. Since he had killed his brother Banta Singh never came to his land in the evening.

Dalip Singh busied himself clearing the water channels in his fields. When he had finished doing that he came to the water course and washed himself. He sat down on the grassy bank with his feet in the running water and waited for his mother.

The sun went down across a vast stretch of flat land, and the evening star shone, close to a crescent moon. From the village he could hear the shouts of women at the well, of children at play—all mixed up with the barking of dogs and the bedlam of sparrows noisily settling down for the night. Batches of women came out into the fields and scattered behind the bushes to relieve themselves. They assembled again and washed in rows along the water course.

Dalip Singh's mother came with the wooden token from the canal timekeeper, showing that Dalip's turn to water his field had started. Then she went back to look after the cattle. Banta Singh's tenants had already left. Dalip Singh blocked the water exit to Banta Singh's land and cut it open to his fields. After doing this he stretched himself on the cool grassy bank and watched the water rippling over the ploughed earth, shimmering like quick-silver under the light of the new moon. He lay on his back looking at the sky and listening to the noises from the village. He could hear women talking somewhere in Banta Singh's fields. Then the world relapsed into a moonlit silence.

Dalip Singh's thoughts were disturbed by the sound of splashing water close to him. He turned round and saw a woman on the opposite bank sitting on her haunches washing herself. With one hand she splashed the water between her thighs, with the other she cleaned herself. She scraped a handful of mud from the ground, rubbed it on her hands and dipped them in the running water. She rinsed her mouth and threw handfuls of water over her face. Then she stood up leaving her baggy trousers lying at her feet. She picked up her shirt from the front and bent down to wipe her face with it.

It was Bindo. Dalip Singh was possessed with a maddening desire. He jumped across the water course and ran towards her. The girl had her face buried in her shirt. Before she could turn round, Dalip Singh's arms closed round her under the armpits and across her breasts. As she turned round he smothered her face with passionate kisses and stifled her frightened cry by gluing his mouth to hers. He bore her down on the soft grass. Bindo fought like a wildcat. She caught Dalip's beard in both her hands and savagely dug her nails into his cheeks. She bit his nose till it bled. But she was soon exhausted. She gave up the struggle and lay perfectly still. Her eyes were shut and tears trickled down on either side, washing the black antimony on to her ears. She looked beautiful in the pale moonlight. Dalip was full of remorse. He had never intended hurting her. He caressed her forehead with his large rough hands and let his fingers run through her hair. He bent down and tenderly rubbed his nose against hers. Bindo opened her large black eyes and stared at him blankly. There was no hate in them, nor any love. It was just a blank stare. Dalip Singh kissed her eyes and nose gently. Bindo just looked at him with a vacant expression, and more tears welled in her eyes.

Bindo's companions were shouting for her. She did not answer. One of them came nearer and shouted for help. Dalip Singh got up quickly and jumped aross the water course and was lost in the darkness.

II

The entire male population of the village of Singhpura turned up to hear the case of Crown v Dalip Singh. The court room, the verandah and the courtyard were packed with villagers. At one end of the verandah was Dalip Singh in handcuffs between two policemen.

His mother sat fanning him with her face covered in a shawl. She was weeping and blowing her nose. At the other end, Bindo, her mother and several other women were huddled together in a circle. Bindo also wept and blew her nose. Towering above this group were Banta Singh and his friends leaning on their bamboo poles, in constant and whispered consultation. Other villagers whiled away their time buying sweets from hawkers, or having their ears cleaned by itinerant 'ear specialists'. Some were gathered round vendors of aphrodisiacs nudging each other and laughing.

Banta Singh had hired a lawyer to help the government prosecutor. The lawyer collected the prosecution witnesses in a corner and made them go over their evidence. He warned them of the questions likely to be put to them by the defence counsel. He introduced the court orderly and the clerk to Banta Singh and made him tip them. He got a wad of notes from his client to pay the government prosecutor. The machinery of justice was fully oiled. Dalip Singh had no counsel nor defence witnesses.

The orderly opened the court room door and called the case in a sing-song manner. He let in Banta Singh and his friends. Dalip Singh was marched in by the policemen but the orderly kept his mother out. She had not paid him. When order was restored in the court room, the clerk proceeded with reading the charge.

Dalip Singh pleaded not guilty. Mr Kumar, the magistrate asked the prosecuting sub-inspector to produce Bindo. Bindo shuffled into the witness box with her face still covered in her shawl and blowing her nose. The inspector asked her about her father's enmity with Dalip Singh. He produced her clothes stained with blood and semen. That closed the case for the prosecution. The evidence of Bindo corroborated by the exhibits was clear and irrefutable.

The prisoner was asked if he had any questions to put. Dalip Singh folded his handcuffed hands.

'I am innocent, possessor of pearls.'

Mr Kumar was impatient.

'Have you heard the evidence? If you have no questions for the girl, I will pass orders.'

'Thou of the pearls, I have no lawyer. I have no friends in the village to give evidence for me. I am poor. Show mercy. I am innocent.'

The magistrate was angry. He turned to the clerk. 'Cross-examination—nil.'

'But,' spluttered Dalip Singh, 'before you send me to jail, emperor, ask her if she was not willing. I went to her because she wanted me. I am innocent.'

Mr Kumar turned to the clerk again.

'Cross-examination by accused—Did you go to the accused of your own free will? Answer...'

Mr Kumar addressed Bindo: 'Answer, did you go to the accused of your own free will?'

Bindo blew her nose and wept. The magistrate and the crowd waited in impatient irritating silence.

'Did you or did you not? Answer. I have other work to do.'

Through the many folds of the shawl muffling her face Bindo answered.

'Yes.'

The Memsahib of Mandla

John Dyson dismounted on the summit of the hill and surveyed the scene. The red brick rest house was situated in the centre of a small clearing in the jungle. On all sides where the hill sloped down was a high wall of trees with creepers climbing from the trunks and spreading out like cobwebs among the branches. The only opening was on the side from which the road led down to the valley. One could see a densely wooded valley stretching away for several miles.

The baggage had already arrived and lay piled in the verandah. Near the servants' quarters the coolies were sitting on their haunches smoking, by turns, a small clay hookah. The overseer sat on a steel chair talking to them.

The hookah party at the servants' quarters broke up, and the overseer walked over to meet Dyson.

'Lovely garden,' said Dyson, addressing the overseer. 'Who's been looking after it?'

'There is an old mali, sahib. He's been living here some fifty years—as long as the house has been here.'

A skinny old man pushed his way through the crowd and bowed to Dyson with folded hands. '*Gharreeb purrwar* (defender of the poor), I am the mali. I have been a mali ever since I was fifteen. Jean Memsahib brought me here and now I am sixty. Jean Memsahib died here. I too will die here.'

'Jean Memsahib? Would that be Cotton's wife?' asked Dyson, turning to the overseer.

'No, Sir, no one knows much about her. She was a social worker—or a teacher—or a missionary, or something. She built this bungalow and had a school for children. Then she died suddenly and no one seems to know anything about her. The Government took over the building and converted it into a forest officers' rest house.'

The conversation was interrupted by the shouts of coolies coming up with the palanquin chairs carrying Mrs Dyson and her daughter Jennifer.

'Old mission school' said Dyson, waving towards the house. 'Not a bad spot, is it?'

The family surveyed the scene in silence. The setting sun lit the house, the lawns, the flower beds, and the teak forest with its creepers in a haze of golden light. It was quiet and peaceful. The distant murmur of the stream in the valley emphasized the stillness of the evening.

The coolies and the overseer left for the village in the valley before sunset. The Dysons got busy settling in. The bearers went about lighting hurricane lanterns, laying the dinner table, and fixing mosquito nets on the beds. Mrs Dyson and Jennifer went round inspecting the rooms. Dyson stretched himself on a large cane armchair in the verandah, lit his pipe and ordered a Scotch. He watched the setting sun fire the monsoon clouds in a blaze of burnished gold, then a copper red, orange, pink, white, and finally a sulky grey. The tropical jungle was hushed into an eerie stillness as the twilight sank into night. The birds settled down, and within a few minutes it was quite dark. Now the jungle was alive with a different variety of noises, the croaking of frogs and the calls of jackals and hyenas. As Dyson sat sipping his Scotch and smoking, the fireflies came out on the lawn almost up to where he was sitting.

The bearer announced dinner. The dining table was lit with candles. From the mantelpiece a hurricane lantern spread a sickly yellow light on the grey plaster walls discoloured by age and monsoon rains.

There was very little talk at the dinner table. Only the bearer coming in or going out with plates and courses, and the tinkle of crockery and cutlery broke the oppressive silence. Jennifer was fidgety. She had been exploring the house when the bearer had interrupted her with summons to the dining room. Suddenly she put down her knife and fork with a loud clatter—

'Look, mummy, there's a picture on the wall.'

Mrs Dyson shuddered and turned back to look. The distemper on the wall was discoloured by long lines where rain water had trickled down from the ceiling to the floor. There were many patterns on the wall which changed shape with the flickering of the lamp.

'Jennifer,' said Mrs Dyson hoarsely, 'do stop frightening me and get on with your dinner.'

The rest of the meal was eaten in silence. Jennifer was sent to bed when the coffee was brought in.

Mrs Dyson looked back at the wall once more. There was nothing on it.

'John, I don't like this place.'

Dyson lit his pipe with deliberation, pressing down the tobacco with a match box.

'John, I don't like this place,' repeated Mrs Dyson.

'You are tired. You'd better get to bed.'

Mrs Dyson went to bed. Her husband joined her after a while, and in a few minutes he was asleep and snoring.

Mrs Dyson could not sleep. She propped her pillows against the poles of the mosquito net and stared at the garden. It was a moonless night but the sky was clear and the lawn was dimly star-lit. Beyond the lawn was the forest, like a high black wall. The frogs and the insects, an occasional screech of a bird, the laugh of a hyena and the howling of jackals, filled the jungle with noises. This brought cold sweat on Mrs Dyson's forehead.

Many hours later a pale moon came up over the crest of the jungle and lit the garden with a sickly glow. The dew covered the lawn with gossamer white.

Mrs Dyson decided to take a walk to shake off the feeling of eerieness. The grass was cool and wet under her bare feet. As she walked she looked at the green trail she left in the dewy whitewash on the grass. She shook her head as if throwing off a weight, and took several deep breaths. It was fresh and exhilarating. There was nothing eerie and nothing to be frightened of.

Mrs Dyson strolled up and down the moonlit lawn for several minutes. Feeling refreshed, she decided to go back to bed. Just as she approached the verandah she stopped suddenly. A few paces ahead of her the lawn showed footprints. A trail continued to be marked by invisible feet to the edge of the clearing and then disappeared in the jungle. Margaret Dyson felt feverish and weak in the knees and collapsed.

When she recovered, it was nearly morning. The whole countryside was alive with the singing of birds. Mrs Dyson dragged herself to bed utterly exhausted.

When the bearer brought in the tea, the sun was streaming across the verandah. Dyson had had his breakfast and was ready to go out. At the further end of the lawn the overseer and coolies were waiting for him.

Dyson was back shortly before sunset. He ordered his whisky and soda and stretched out his legs for the bearer to unlace his boots. With a couple of whiskies in him he became jovial.

'What are we having for dinner? Smells like curried chicken. I am hungry—can't beat the country air!'

The family had their dinner in silence, Dyson enjoying the food. A jackal walked up the lawn almost to the dining room door and set up a howl. Mrs Dyson's fork fell from her hands. Before her husband could speak, she stood up and said in a hoarse whisper: 'John, I don't like this place.'

'Your nerves are in a bad way. It was only a jackal. I'll shoot a few. They won't disturb you. There's no need to be jittery. Did you sleep well last night?'

'Yes, thank you.'

'I saw you walking on the lawn, Mummy,' butted in Jennifer.

'You eat your pudding and go to bed,' answered Mrs Dyson.

'But I saw you, Mummy—you were in your white dressing gown and you looked inside my net to see if I was asleep and I shut my eyes. I saw you.'

Mrs Dyson went pale.

'Don't talk nonsense, Jennifer, and go to bed. I haven't got a white dressing gown and you know it.' Mrs. Dyson got up from the table and her husband joined her.

'Did you have a disturbed night?'

'I couldn't sleep at all. But, John, I haven't got a white dressing gown and I did not look into Jennifer's bed.'

'Oh, this is all hooey. Come on, Jennifer, finish your pudding and off to bed. I'll get my gun and shoot one of these jackals. Would you like a jackal for a fur coat, Jennifer?' said Dyson, affecting a hearty manner.

'No, I don't like jackals.'

Dyson got his gun, loaded it, and stood it against the wall near his bed. He lit his pipe and kept up a continuous conversation till it was time to go to bed.

'If you hear any jackals,' he said to his wife, 'just wake me up.'

'Yes, dear.'

Within a few minutes Dyson was fast asleep.

Jennifer was also asleep. But Mrs Dyson lay in bed with her eyes wide open staring through the net at the lawn and the wall of trees that was the jungle.

Out of the misty haze emerged a figure of a woman in a long white dressing gown. Her hair was tied in two plaits which fell on her shoulders. Her features were not discernible but her eyes had an inhuman brightness. Mrs Dyson turned cold, petrified with fear. She tried to scream, but only a muffled moan escaped her. John Dyson continued to snore.

The phantom figure started moving towards the verandah, fixing Mrs Dyson with a stare. When it was half-way across the lawn, a jackal scampered across and stood facing it. The animal raised its head and sent up a long howl, and immediately others joined in the chorus.

Mrs Dyson found her voice and her moan changed into a frantic shriek.

John Dyson got up with a start and darted for his gun. Before he could collect his wits and take aim the jackals dashed away in different directions. Dyson emptied both his barrels at one of them which was well out of range.

'Missed the bastard' Dyson muttered to himself.

Next morning the Dysons' nerves were more frayed than ever.

'I am sorry, dear, I frightened you last night,' said Dyson, 'I must get those jackals tonight.'

'John, didn't you see anything else?'

'Else, what else?'

'A woman in white. She was walking straight at us when you fired the gun.'

'Nonsense. I am sorry I missed the jackal. You must pull yourself together.'

'But, John, you must believe me. The first night I saw her foot-prints on the lawn.'

Mrs Dyson paused, and then got up. 'Come and see.'

She led her husband to the lawn, still milky white and shimmering in the sunlight. There were the footprints. Dyson followed them till he came to a clearing. In the centre of the clearing was a grave— an old dilapidated grave without any stone or inscription. The moss had grown all over it and from the cracks in the plaster grew weeds and ferns.

Dyson was shaken but did not change his tone. 'This is too damned silly for words,' he said.

When the overseer arrived Dyson sent for him in his office and shut the door behind him.

'Sunder Lal, what do you know about this house?'

'Not much, sir,' faltered the overseer. 'Many stories are told in the villages around here and superstitious folk believe them. The house has remained unoccupied for many yars, and even after the Government acquired it Indian officers refused to stay here. But the mali has been here all this time and seems quite happy.'

'Send for the mali.'

Sunder Lal fetched the mali.

'The Sahib wants to know about the house. Tell Sahib all you know.'

'Defender of the poor,' said the old mali speaking in Hindustani, 'the house was built by Jean Memsahib who came from Mandla. She had a school for children. It was on government land, and after many years of litigation the Government won and acquired it.'

'What happened to Jean Memsahib?' asked Dyson.

'She died in this house, Sahib. After the Government acquired the house she closed her school. Then she fell ill. She used to walk about in the garden during the rainy season and got malaria. She died after many attacks. Only Riaz, her Muslim bearer, and I were present. We went down to Mandla to inform the Sahibs there, but no one seemed to know about her. We buried her in the forest. Riaz left and is in Mandla working as a bearer. I stayed on with the Government.'

'How many people lived in this house after her death?'

'No one has lived here, Sahib. Officers come and go. People have spread tales about her cursing the place. But I have lived here more than fifty years and no harm has come to me.'

Dyson dismissed the overseer and the mali and went to his wife.

'Just had word with the mali and the overseer' announced Dyson nonchalantly, 'lot of poppycock about no one being able to stay in this house. The mali's been here for fifty years. In any case, I am going to stay right here and settle this ghost once for all.'

That night Dyson again loaded his gun and removed the safety catch. After dinner he drank several cups of black coffee. He had a hurricane lamp put beside his bed, and he began to look at some old copies of *Blackwood's Magazine* he had found in an almirah. Comforted by the light and the knowledge of her husband being awake, Mrs Dyson fell fast asleep, as soon as she put her head on the pillow.

For some time Dyson smoked his pipe and read. Then he dimmed the lantern and just smoked.

The night was darker than the two previous ones. It was clouded over and a damp breeze indicated rain. Some time well after midnight there was lightning and thunder and it began to rain—in torrents, as it does in the tropics. The breeze carried a thin cooling spray across the verandah into the mosquito nets. Mrs Dyson and her daughter slept through the lightning and thunder. The cool spray made Dyson sleepy. He began to nod and then dozed off sitting against his pillow.

A jackal came up close to the verandah and sent up a howl. Dyson woke up with a jerk. Just then the lamp flickered and went out. Through the net Dyson saw the outlines of a human figure standing at the foot of his bed. A pair of bright eyes fixed him with a steady stare. There was a flash of lightning and he saw her—the woman in white with plaits falling about her shoulders. The thunder which followed the lightning shook him into activity. With a cry of fear he leapt out of bed and groped for his gun, not taking his eyes off the figure beside his bed. He caught the butt and wildly went for the trigger. There were two loud reports. Dyson fell with the full discharge of the gun in his face.

The Great Difference

Haji Hafiz Maulana Abdus Salam Sahib, Maulvi Fazil-i-Deoband, etc., etc., was, above all these titles, the Fakhr-i-Millat, the pride of the faithful. He was a short, plump man, with a closely trimmed beard which framed his sallow, oval face in glossy black. He wore glasses the thickness of whose lenses bore testimony to his prodigious erudition. He was dressed in a loose-fitting chogha, very much like a dressing gown. On his head he bore a massive silk turban. He carried a rosary of green jade in his left hand; in the other an ebony black walking stick with an ivory handle. He always perfumed his beard and put a swab of scented cotton in his left ear.

The Maulana was undoubtedly a man of learning. Besides being a Hafiz he knew all that was worth knowing about the Holy Prophet Mohammad (May peace be upon him!) and the religion of Islam (May it ever increase!) Besides his well-deserved reputation for learning, the Maulana had also one for righteous living. Himself scrupulous in the observation of prayer and the traditions of the Hadith, he exhorted others to follow in the right path and checked many a Moslem from going astray. He was a gifted orator and his speeches were echoed in the heart of many a faithful who heard him spellbound. The Maulana was obviously the best choice for a representative to the World Congress of Faiths meeting at Paris.

A vast concourse of Delhi Moslems came to see the Maulana board the boat-train for Bombay. He stood in the open doorway of his second class compartment acknowledging the various salams with his hands raised to the level of his shoulders. As the train began to move a stentorian voice rang out the challenge '*Nara-e-Taqbeer!*' A thousand voices thundered back '*Allah-ho-Akbar.*' The Maulana Sahib raised his hands higher and his head bowed lower in acknowledgment. The train pulled out of the station midst deafening reminders that God was Great.

The Maulana Sahib shut the door of the compartment, unloaded his neck of the mass of marigold garlands, and placed them on his berth. Then for the first time he noticed the presence of another passenger in the compartment. I raised my hand in salutation, but the Maulana was too full of emotion to acknowledge. He sat by the open window of the carriage and stared across the stretching country-side through which we were passing. He was going to carry the message of Islam, the only true message, to the peoples of the West. The thought filled his entire being, and there was no room for me in it.

About an hour later the boat-train steamed in at the Mathura Railway Station. The platform was crowded with people carrying marigold garlands. Apparently Mathura, too, was sending one of its sons abroad. A party of four or five men came up to our compartment and read the reservation slip by the door. They shouted to the crowd and the whole mass surged towards us. All eyes were on our compartment.

First the luggage came in relays. Steel trunks, bedding, then several canisters and petrol tins. The canisters were full of earth and the petrol tins with water. Small labels pasted on the petrol tins stated in Devnagari script 'Ganga jal' (Ganges water). Then followed the owner of the luggage, Swami Vasheshvra Nanda.

Shri Swami Shri 666 Shri Guru Vasheshvra Nandaji, Maha Shastri, Mahamahopadhyaya, etc., etc., was symbolic of all that the Hindu religion stood for. He was born in Brindaban, the haunt of the romantic Sri Krishna—where each mango grove and every inch of the beautiful grassy bank of the river Yamuna was hallowed by its amorous associations with the dark, handsome lord of the flute and his milkmaids. From his early childhood Vasheshvra Nanda was of a meditative bent of mind. He frequented temples and spent many hours learning Sanskrit and the Vedas by heart. When his father proposed his initiation into the ancestral business of a sweets vendor, he ran away from home and spent some years in pious meditation in the jungles. He ultimately found his way into a yoga ashram, where his learning was immediately recognized and he was given the highest degree and appointed a research scholar. It was there that Vasheshvra Nanda had learnt English and probed into the mysteries of Western philosophy. The result had been his thesis entitled 'Mysticism of the Atharva Veda,' which had won him a doctorate of a well-known university. From then onwards he was known as a Swami and his reputation for learning accumulated prestige as a snowball collects snow.

Swami Vasheshvra Nanda's chief source of popularity was the

discovery of facts which proved the superiority of the Hindu over other systems of learning. To thrilled audiences he announced that all the West possessed was actually borrowed from the Hindu Shastras. European scholars had stolen invaluable Sanskrit documents, translated them into their own languages, and utilized this purloined learning in producing—their philosophy, their medicine, their science, their railway trains, motor cars, aeroplanes. There was conclusive evidence that the ancient Hindus had known all about these things. Thus, he said, the aeroplane had its Hindu ancestor in the *Garuda*, shaped like a vulture, on which Vishnu flew. Ram Chandra and Sita flew home from Ceylon in their *Viman*. Raja Chitra Sen took his beautiful wife in his *Viman* over the Himalayas and when he spat the spit fell into the palm of Rishi Galav and started the battle of the Mahabharata. In the excavations in the ruins of Banaras, a rusted steel wire had been found. It was clear as daylight that the Hindus had known all about the telephone. In other temples where no such wires were discovered, the Swami raised the irrefutable assumption that the Hindus even knew about ether waves and wireless telegraphy.

Hindus all over India clamoured for recognition of the Swami. At last even the Government yielded. It was rumoured that the Vicereine had sent for the Swami and begged of him the rare herb which caused barren women to conceive. Nine months after the Swami's visit to the Viceregal apartments, the Vicereine had been delivered of a male child. In the next honours list, the Swamiji was given the high distinction of Mahamahopadhyaya. A few months later Swami Vasheshvra Nanda was given international recognition and invited to represent Hinduism at the World Congress of Faiths in Paris.

The Swamiji was a tall, stout man, dressed in a saffron shirt and dhoti. He was bald, save for a long pigtail of black hair which dangled from the nadir of his skull to the back of his neck, where it was tied in a knot. This broad forehead was pasted with sandalwood. On his feet he wore high wooden sandals held on by a brass knob caught between his big toe and its neighbour.

The Swami stood in the door of the railway carriage and his admirers came in relays to garland him and touch his feet. He blessed them with an uplifted hand. Then the engine whistled and the Swamiji stood in the doorway to bless the throng. A man in green uniform came up, saluted the holy man, touched his feet and went back to a band of six or seven small boy scouts with drums and bag-pipes. They were the Hindu Boy Scout Sewak Sangh. He shouted the boys to order—one, two, three. The drum beat a loud tattoo and the bagpipes whined God Save the King. The engine gave another small blast and the train began to move. The crowd broke into a final crescendo of applause—'*Shri Vasheshvra Nanda ki jai!*' So we moved out of Mathura, the Maulana Sahib on my right and the Swamiji on my left. In the middle berth I lay back once more to glance into the many magazines I had collected for the journey— *La Vie Parisienne, Lilliput, Men Only, Razzle* and others.

For an hour or two my illustrious companions were too engrossed in their thoughts to bother about each other or me. But when it was time for lunch the Maulana Sahib unpacked a bundle of leavened chappatties and a plateful of meat, and spread them out on his seat. He invited the Swamiji and me to join him. The Swamiji folded his hands and refused. The food looked inedible but to prove my broad-mindedness I went over and shared it. The Swamiji produced a packet of dry fruit and bananas and placed them neatly on a freshly washed banana leaf. He ate by himself without even a suggestion of sharing it. It was obvious that he did not approve of either of us.

In the evening the Swamiji and I were left alone in the carriage. The Maulana filled his copper jug with a nozzle shaped like the letter S and shut himself in the latrine. Swamiji opened the conversation.

'You are a Sikh, aren't you?'

I admitted that I was.

'Then why did you eat the food of that Moslem? It may have been beef! Doesn't your religion forbid you to eat beef?'

I admitted that it did, but that did not bother me. The Swamiji protested.

'Even if you have no religious belief, you should not eat with Moslems. They are outcastes and dirty people. Didn't you see the very jug he carried into the latrine he uses for drinking water? It is most unbecoming of you a Sikh, whose ancestors fought the Moslems, to eat with him!'

I was willing to argue but the Maulana's appearance cut me short. He looked pleased with his performance. He splashed the last remaining drops of water from his offensive metal jug on his face, stroked his beard with his wet hands, and let his hands dry in the breeze as enjoined by the Prophet. The Swamiji turned away and stuck his face out of the carriage for fresh air.

A few minutes later the Maulana Sahib and I were left alone. At a small wayside station the Swamiji, who was determined not to enter the latrine used by the Maulana, hurriedly filled his brass jug—a round vase-like vessel without a handle or a nozzle—twined the sacred thread behind his left ear, and disappeared behind a bush. A little later he re-entered the compartment, emptied one of his canisters and rinsed his hands with the earth. He went out again, filled a bucket with water, and sat down on the crowded platform to have a bath.

The Maulana Sahib's tone was one of pity and contempt.

'I wonder when God will teach these Hindus some sense!'

Then he fished for sympathy.

'Even your Guru Baba Nanak, great personality, failed to get them off idol worship, cow worship, Ganga worship, and hundreds of other unintelligent things. He tried to unite Hindus and Moslems, but the Hindu is incapable of reason. He only understands the sword.'

I did not tell the Maulana about the Sikh injunction against eating Moslem kosher meat, nor the last Guru's exhortation to his followers not to associate with Moslems. The Swamiji had entered the carriage, fresh and dripping, and we relapsed into silence. The train was on the move once again.

As the sun set behind the forests of central India, my companions prepared themselves for prayer. The Maulana Sahib sat on his berth facing west with his hands raised to his ears. The Swamiji sat cross-legged with his hands resting on his knees and his eyes shut fast. I lingered over the nudes in my *Vie Parisienne*.

At the next halt the Maulana turned his face hurriedly to his right and left and blessed all that were in those directions. The Swamiji still sat rigid with his eyes closed. God was a whole-time job for him. Human beings rarely mattered. I fled from the carriage before the Maulana could invite me for dinner and went to the restaurant car for cold beer with veal and ham pie.

II

The World Congress of Faiths opened in Paris. I was given a ticket as a guest of both the Maulana Sahib and the Swamiji, and persuaded by them to hear their addresses. On the very first day I had good reason to take an interest in these spiritual assemblies.

We entered the great hall together, I in the middle to keep peace. The delegates rose, the visitors rose, and the applause was terrific.

The Maulana salamed acknowledgments. The Swamiji folded his hands. I just grinned. There was more applause when we were introduced by our names, religion and nationality.

'Mons. le Swami Vasheshvra Nanda—Hindou—Hindou.'

'Mons. le Hafiz le Haji le Maulana Abdus Salam—Moslem—Hindou.'

'Mons. K. Singh—Sheikh-Hindou.' (I did not protest.)

While other delegates were being introduced, a girl walked up to us with her autograph album. She looked too much a creature of the flesh to be seen in realms spiritual. But there she was—fair and buxom with her fuzzy hazel hair scattered in profusion about her shoulders. Her breasts were protestingly straight-jacketed under a soft, silky pullover. Her steatopygous behind was an invitation to lustfulness forbidden by the laws of man. We signed our names.

Could she come round and discuss some of her spiritual problems with us? My companions looked at me for a translation. Of course she could! That was what we were religious for! Would 6.30 p.m. that evening suit us? Yes? Unfortunately the Swamiji was due to address the assembly at that time, and I was expected to listen. But, suggested the Maulana Sahib, why couldn't she discuss Islam with him? He was free and would be pleased to solve the young lady's doubts. That was fixed. 6.30 p.m., the Hotel de Terminus—room No. 69, Haji Abdul Salam—spiritual instruction about Islam. The Maulana knew no French. The lady could only speak French.

The Swamiji was hurt. An innocent maiden being led astray by a lecherous cow eater? He must do something. It was the job of a Sikh to rescue women in distress. In any case, the lady must know about Hinduism before she could decide finally. So another appointment was made for the following evening. That time the Maulana was to address the assembly and the Swamiji would be free. The Swamiji, too, did not know French.

I insisted that my religion also should get a chance. Mlle. Jeanne Dupont (that was her name) put our names down in order, and left us smiling. She did not know there were so many religions. She would soon get to know the difference.

'Au revoir Messieurs.'

So the Maulana preached Islam to Mlle. Dupont, while I heard the Swamiji propound the philosophy of the Vedas at the Congress. Then the Swamiji preached Vedanta to Mlle. Dupont, while I heard the Maulana expound the gospel of the Prophet. But in my heart were the cogitations of things to come. On the third day I left the assembly for my proselytizing mission. The concierge of the hotel met me. A young lady had called and left a note for me. I tore open the envelope. There were two lines apologizing for her inability to let me know a day in advance, and in any case—'je comprends bien la différence.'

When Sikh Meets Sikh

When a Sikh meets another Sikh they both say '*Sut Sree Akal,*' which means simply 'God is truth.' More frequently one starts loudly proclaiming '*Wah guru jee ka Khalsa,*' which means 'The Sikhs are the chosen of God,' and the other joins him in completing it even more loudly with '*Wah guru jee ke Fateh*'—'And victory be to our God.' The latter form of greeting is fast gaining in popularity at the expense of the former. The reason for this is obvious. Just saying God is truth is as pointless as the European habit of referring to the time of the day and prefixing it as good. The other form goes further. It expresses both a truth and a hope. That the Sikhs are the chosen of God is something no Sikh has any doubt about—the Guru himself called them the Khalsa or the elect. And what could be more fitting than wishing victory to one's god all the time!

Although the Sikhs themselves rightly believe that they are the elect, there are other races who consider themselves chosen, other nations which call themselves A.1, and sects which style themselves the salt of the earth. As a matter of fact, in India itself other communities belittle the Sikhs as an odd people and have lots of stories making fun of them. Sikhs ignore these jests and have a lordly sort of superiority which they express in their day-to-day vocabulary. Thus all clean-shaven people are *Kirars*, which literally means cowards, or *Sirghassas*, which means bald-because-of-beating-on-the-head. A Sikh refers to himself as equal to a hundred and twenty-five thousand, or simply as an army.

Sikhs are not just a crude fighting type. Despite the many Victoria and Military Crosses they have won on the field of battle, they are essentially a peace-loving people. They were virtually the first community to prove the efficacy of passive resistance as a political weapon (and, paradoxically, also the first to organize a planned insurrection against British rule). The one thing which really marks them out is their spirit of pioneering. Although they number little over four million, there is hardly a country in the world without a Sikh—except perhaps Saudi Arabia and, now, Pakistan. There are

Sikh sentries, policemen and taxi-drivers in all countries from Northern China to Turkey. There are Sikh farmers and artisans in Australia, South Africa, the United States, Canada, and the countries of South America. There are Sikh doctors, pedlars and fortune-tellers in every country of Europe.

There is nothing racial or hereditary about the professions the Sikhs choose. A farmer in the Punjab may become a moneylender in Bombay, a carpenter in East Africa, a picker of fruit in California, or a lumber-jack in Canada. If necessary, he can train a troupe of love-birds to pick out cards telling fortunes to matelots in Marseilles—or just look more oriental himself and read ladies' hands at fun fairs. If all that fails, he can exploit his fine physique and cash in on feats of endurance. This brings me to the story of my meeting with Narinjan Singh—a farmer in the Punjab, a domestic servant in Shanghai, a fruit picker in San Francisco, an accountant in Vancouver, and an all-in wrestler in Toronto. I met him in Toronto.

For several days I had read his name in the papers and on hoard-ings. He was apparently quite a figure in the Canadian wrestling world and was due to fight someone called Mazurki, a Pole who also acted in the films. Narinjan Singh was known as Nanjo the Villain, Mazurki as Iron Mike. It seemed to be an important fight. In any case, Nanjo promised to be an interesting character. So I went to the auditorium.

The Maple Leaf Garden Auditorium was packed with nearly twenty thousand Canadian men, women and children. When I turned up to buy my ticket a couple of burly Mounted Policemen came up to me and said in a friendly way: 'You be careful.' They escorted me to my seat and one of them stood by in the gangway.

After the preliminary bouts the microphone blared forth: 'Atten-tion please, attention please. We now come to the last fight, between Nanjo Singh of India and Iron Mike Mazurki of Hollywood, Cali-fornia. Time—twenty minutes. Umpire—Steve Borman.'

A tremendous applause went up as the tall, lanky Pole walked down the gangway. He bowed to his admirers and entered the ring, followed by scores of autograph hunters. A minute later came the Indian, in a yellow turban and green dressing gown. The crowd hissed and booed. Unconcerned with the reception, he clambered into his corner, took off his turban and knelt in prayer—Moslem fashion towards Mecca. Then he unrobed. He was a short, squat man with brown bulging muscles, and a broad hairy chest. The umpire spoke to them in the centre of the ring. Then the fight started.

Nanjo was certainly the 'top cad' in the Canadian wrestling world. He was also an excellent actor. A Sikh, he turned to Mecca as the Canadians thought he should. He rudely pushed away autograph hunters and hit a couple of youngsters who made faces at him. In the ring he dug his fingers in his adversary's eyes, pulled his hair and bit him. In fact, he broke all the rules of wrestling and everyone saw him break them barring the umpire (who was not supposed to notice).

'This is all phoney, you know,' my neighbour informed me. 'Actually, Nanjo is as meek as a lamb. Nice guy once you get to know him.'

They all knew it was phoney, but it did not prevent them getting hysterical. When Nanjo twisted Mazurki's arms they shared the Pole's agony with sympathetic 'No! No's!' When Mazurki had Nanjo squirming under him they yelled: 'Kill the nigger.' So it went on for full fifteen minutes.

'Five minutes to go' announced the loudspeaker.

My neighbour braced himself and nudged me.

'Now the phoney bit ends and the fight begins.'

In a trice the Indian flung the lanky Pole, who had been sitting on his chest for the last five minutes, sprawling on the canvas. With a murderous yell he pounced upon Mazurki, caught the man's head between his thighs and twisted his arms behind his back. This was his famous 'cobra hold'. It squashed the head and strangled the victim at the same time. There was a petrified silence in the arena.

A raucous voice rang out: '*Mar dey Saley ko.*' Enthusiastically I joined my solitary countryman with a loud '*Mar dey.*' There was a shower of empty cigarette cases, paper balls and silver paper on my head and twenty thousand voices roared: 'Shut up.'

My neighbour was nervous. 'You better look out—people get a little worked up, you know.' The Mounty came close to me and warned me: 'Better keep quiet, mister, if you want to go home.'

The crowd rose from their seats and clustered round the ring. A woman ran up and put the lighted end of her cigarette on the Indians' ankle. But Nanjo wouldn't let go his victim. The police rushed in to get the spectators back in their seats and formed a cordon round the wrestlers. For some time Mazurki struggled and groaned, then he gave up. The referee stopped the fight and held aloft Nanjo's hand as the victor. The crowd booed and hissed and made towards him.

Half-a-dozen stalwart Mounties surrounded the wrestler and hustled him into his dressing room.

A quarter of an hour later, when the crowd had dispersed and it looked safe enough for a bearded and turbaned Indian to venture forth, I made for Nanjo's dressing room to collect some facts of his life. In the over-heated, stuffy room there were more than a dozen hulking masses of fat and flesh—Toronto's leading heavyweights. They were the best of friends. Nanjo and Mazurki were pounding each other's bellies with friendly blows and being obscenely intimate—'You son-ov-a-gun,' 'You son-ov-a-bitch,' and so on.

Nanjo saw me and a broad smile lit his face. 'Holy mackerel—see who's here—feller from my own country.'

I introduced myself and shook several sweaty hands. Nanjo's vocabulary of English words came to an end with 'Jeezez it's good to see you.' Then he broke into pure rustic Punjabi.

'I could floor the lot of them, but my manager won't let me. I have to lose. I have to act as a bad man and am often disqualified for fouling. What can I do?' Then with a characteristically Indian gesture he slapped his stomach. 'All for the belly. But when I have made enough I will show you what I can do. I'll floor the incestuous sister-sleepers. The whole bloody lot of them. Then I will go back to Hoshiarpur and till the land. I want to show my village to my wife.' He looked round the crowded room and shouted for his wife. A buxom blonde with a broad grin that bared several gold teeth emerged from the ring of wrestlers and greeted me with a loud 'How dyedo' and vigorous chewing of gum.

'She's a Sikh now. Her name is Mahinder Kaur. I've taught her some Punjabi. Baby tell the gentleman what I taught you.'

The blonde spat out her chewing gum.

'*Wah guru jee ka Khalsa.*

'*Wah guru jee kee Fateh.*'

Death Comes to Daulat Ram

There were things that happened the day Daulat Ram died which seemed more and more uncanny to his son when he sat back and recalled them in his mind.

It was on the morning of the 21st of July when Ranga got the first warning. He was sitting in a restaurant having his mid-morning cup of coffee. He was in the habit of going to the restaurant every day. It was a nice clean place tastefully done up with teak-wood panelling and gold lines on the margins. The carpet and upholstery were of a dark grey colour which set off the icy blue-white of the chandelier crystals like diamonds set in ebony. And the place was air-cooled. On a hot summer day, it was the coolest, quietest place in town.

It was not as hot as it can be in July. It had rained a little in the morning. The sky was still flecked with bulbous clouds. The humidity had dislocated the air-cooling plant. People came in, sat for a while, looked up at the ceiling for fans which were not there, cancelled their orders and went out. Only the regulars who came from neighbouring offices stayed on. Ranga was a regular.

The Goan three-piece band began to play. Ranga did not know what they played except that it was not the usual sort of light music. It was something which made him put down his cup and look up. He felt it had some sort of significance; at least he thought later that he had then felt that it had some *sort* of significance. As soon as the band finished the piece, the telephone hidden behind the bar began to ring. Ranga could not hear what the barman said but he could see from the way the barman lowered his head and put a finger in his right ear that he was asking the party at the other end to repeat what they had said. He took down something on a piece of paper, read it out to the caller and put down the receiver. The barman looked round the room trying to locate someone who looked like being the owner of the name on the slip of paper. His eyes went round like the searching beam of a lighthouse and stopped on Ranga. Ranga winced under his stare. The barman knew he was right and walked up to Ranga's table. 'You are wanted on the phone, Sir.'

Ranga did not pause to think why the barman had chosen to come to him first nor why without wanting to find out whether or not he was Ranga, had told him that he was wanted. When he came to think of it, he recalled having stood up before the barman had really got to his table. He also recalled that for some reason he had then felt that this was going to be bad news. It was not the first time that he had been rung up in the restaurant. Many of his friends knew of his habit of having coffee at 11 a.m. and of his preference for the restaurant. He always left the office with the announcement 'I am just going down for a cup of coffee. Send for me if it is something urgent.' Ranga knew it was not a friend nor the office. In fact he did not even ask who it was at the other end who said 'Come home at once, your father has been taken ill'.

It was said quite casually by a voice he subsequently believed to be an old man's. Ranga drove home straightaway. It was not the first time that Daulat Ram had been taken ill suddenly. He had trouble with his gall-bladder. Slight indiscretion in food developed into acute stomachache. It had to be eased with shots of morphia and medicine for the stomach. It never lasted long. He had to spend a couple of weeks in bed. He did that with good grace collecting his family around him and telling them how the source of all disease was the food one ate and how he was going to live happily ever after on temperance and boiled food eaten punctually and at home. 'Man does not die, he kills himself,' he would say with the conviction of a penitent. The chastened mood would last a few days after he was allowed out of bed. He would sip orange juice out of a cut-glass tumbler meant for whisky. He would insist on his guests having their Scotch to prove his will-power. 'Do have one,' he would say persuasively and add with a smile of beatific righteousness, 'I have given up drinking. After forty years of hard going, it is not easy but I don't miss it at all. In fact, I feel much better.'

The next stage would be to accept an invitation out. Then have a small whisky—'just one small whisky, the doctor had said one could do no harm'. One became two and two became three. Then he did not have to be asked out to have his whisky. He would order the servant in as casual a tone as if he was asking him to get his glasses from the study. If his wife went out of the room, he would gulp that down, and get another. He would drink this leisurely pretending it was the first. And a small second one before dinner could do no harm! If his wife as much as raised her eyebrow, he wanted to know why she nagged him. So the three or four whiskys, some sipped at leisure and some gulped in haste, were followed by a late dinner where 'the fried fish at so and so's was so much nicer than this boiled stuff. Why can't our cook make it like that?' or 'One must eat meat, eggs and, of course, greens and carrots. Proteins are necessary.' He had read a great deal about food and knew all the vitamins from A to Z. He ate them till the alphabet jostled the stones in his gallbladder. Then the inevitable attack with its agonizing belly-ache and loud groaning to drown his wife's 'You will not listen to me.' This was followed by the routine of nurses, doctors, morphia injections, telegrams to relations, whispered 'if it comes to the worst', the recovery and the chastened 'Man does not die, he kills himself'.

The first two or three times Ranga had received the news of these attacks with morbid foreboding. There was talk in the home of 'Let's see now, how old is father?' and 'Oh well that is not so old after all.' Then he had become somewhat callous. The first thing he would say was 'there he goes again.' But this time, as I have already said, Ranga somehow knew it was different. It was in the weather. The sun was fighting fiercely with big black clouds which kept blotting it out. There was no breeze and the trees in the garden hung their heads desolately. Even the house—it was odd, but there it was, even the house looked widowed. Perhaps it was the walls. The Ixora creeper which had covered the sides with its lush green leaves and bright orange flowers had fallen at places baring large bald patches of anaemic brick and stone.

There was an uneasy stillness about the whole thing. There was no one about the house. This was unusual. Normally the lawns were littered with children and grandchildren of various ages with their respective maid servants and hordes of children from the servants' quarters who were allowed to play with them. The chaprasi was not at his post beside the telephone in the entrance hall; the telephone had been taken off the hook. There were no cars on the drive-way to indicate the presence of callers; the chaprasi had obviously taken the opportunity to have a quiet smoke with his wife.

The chaprasi had overlooked the possibility of beggars trespassing into the house. He usually relied on the Alsatian dog, Moti, to keep them away. Moti was very dress-conscious. Anyone who was not dressed in European clothes was seen out with a rent or two in his dhoti. But that morning the only person about the house was a beggar. He sat right in the centre of the drive-way in front of the entrance. He had his head tucked between the knees with his arms round the legs. Moti stood a few yards away scrutinizing the figure, tilting his head first to the right, then to the left with a puzzled look in his eyes. He did not go up to greet Ranga as he stepped out of the car.

Neither the noise of the car driving in nor the banging of the door nor crunch of footsteps on the gravel disturbed the beggar.

'What do you want?' asked Ranga in a commanding tone. He had strong views on begging.

The man slowly raised his head. He was old, well in his eighties. A long white beard cascaded luxuriantly down his coarse grey shirt up to his navel. Silver locks escaped from all sides of his loosely wrapped turban. Even his bushy eye-brows had gone snowy-white. He fixed Ranga with a melancholy stare.

Ranga felt a little ashamed of himself. 'What do you want Babaji?' he repeated politely.

The old man just shook his head without taking his eyes off Ranga. Ranga felt as if he had been fixed in a picture frame. The man was obviously a beggar. The town was full of them after the partition of the Punjab. He must be one of the millions of refugees without a home. He might have lost his relations in a massacre and was too old to begin life again. That was not all. Ranga got a feeling that he had seen the man before.

'Where are you from, Babaji?'

The old man just shut his eyes. Tears rolled down his cheeks and were lost in his beard. Moti went up to the old man, sniffed at him and backed away whining. 'Have you no relation? No sons or daughters to look after you?'

The man shook his head again. Moti went up to him nervously and sneaked back to his master. Ranga felt it was silly to waste time talking.

'Go to the kitchen,' he said pointing to the servants' entrance. 'I'll tell the cook to give you food.'

Ranga walked away. He felt a peculiar heaviness in his foot-steps—almost as if the old man was pulling him back. Where had Ranga seen this man before? He looked back. The old man had put his head between his knees and apparently gone to sleep. He tripped over Moti and nearly lost his balance.

Daulat Ram's condition was no worse than when he was in the throes of an attack. He was groaning with his hands pressing his belly. He was surrounded by relations. A nurse was rubbing spirit on his arm. The doctor was pressing air bubbles out of his syringe. He jabbed in the needle and pushed in the morphia. Within a couple of minutes the opiate spread in his body and he fell asleep. The doctor packed his case, issued instructions to the nurse and left. The relations tiptoed out of the room. Ranga dragged the reluctant Moti by the collar.

It was outside the bedroom that Ranga realized that his.brother and sister were also there. Both lived far from Delhi and could not have been told of their father's condition. The brother said he had been summoned from an emergency conference. The sister had simply turned up for the week-end shopping in the capital. This was ominous. It had been a family tradition to die surrounded by friends and relations. No one in Ranga's family had died alone or suddenly. There was an uncanny something which brought people together—sometimes by letters and telegrams; sometimes it was just intuition which drove them to the bed of a departing relative.

There was no reason to invest this coincidence with morbid signi- ficance. The nurse had herself come out and announced that the patient was sleeping peacefully, no one was to go in and disturb him; Moti ought to be chained up, he had been coming in, putting his forefeet on the bed and looking at Daulat Ram. When lunch was served Ranga suddenly thought of the old beggar outside. He was talking to his brother across the table. He looked up and his grandfather's (Daulat Ram's father's) portrait caught his eye. 'Caught his eye,' was not an exaggeration. Although the picture had been there for almost twenty years it was the first time Ranga recognized the face beneath the massive turban with bushy eye-brows and the long silk-white beard. It was uncanny—it seemed as if the picture had also seen Ranga for the first time. Ranga turned pale. He gaped stupidly at the portrait of the benign old man in a match of 'who- blinks-first loses.' Soup dripped from the spoon suspended in mid-air.

'What's the matter?' asked his brother. 'You look as if you had seen a ghost.'

Ranga dropped the spoon in the plate with a splash. 'The beggar,' he muttered incoherently, 'The beggar.'

'What beggar?' asked his brother puzzled.

'I will be back in a moment,' answered Ranga, getting up from his seat. He rushed out of the house. The old man was not there.

Ranga came back to the dining room looking paler than before. 'He's gone. Where is Moti?

'What are you talking about? Who is gone?'

'Where is Moti?' repeated Ranga. 'I hope he has not gone into the bedroom.'

'No Sir,' answered the nurse wiping her mouth with a serviette. 'I closed the door. I will go and look.'

Everyone got up from the table to follow the nurse. The door of the bedroom was half-open. Ranga tiptoed in behind the nurse. Daulat Ram seemed fast asleep. Beside him on the bed was Moti; looking up with guilty, soulful eyes he began to whine. Ranga noticed that Daulat Ram was not breathing. He ran out of the room sobbing. 'The beggar. He's gone. He's gone.'

The Insurance Agent

'Hullo, Hullo, Hullo'—said he flinging out his arms. He clasped me in a bear-hug and emphasized his affection by squeezing me to his bosom several times.

'Hullo' I replied feebly, extricating myself from the hold. It was embarrassing; I could not even place him.

'Well old chap' said he slapping me on the back till my false teeth were shaken out of place. 'How's life? How is the wife, and the children? How's everyone?'

'Thank you. Thank you' I replied humbly, putting my false teeth back in place. 'Everyone is well. Thank you.'

Had he mistaken me for someone? I was a bachelor and a respectable bachelor at that. I had no children.

'That's fine—that's fine' he continued. But he was not looking at me anymore. He was surveying the crowd in the party and absent-mindedly murmuring 'fine, fine.'

A friend who had spotted me came up. Before we could greet each other, the stranger had opened his arms wide again with a triumphant 'Ah', followed by 'Hullo, Hullo, Hullo' and clasped my friend to his bosom. He slapped my friend on the back and asked about the health of his wife and children. My friend sheepishly replied they were well. He too was a bachelor and to the best of my knowledge had sired no offspring.

'Who is this chap?' I asked my friend when the man had gone further up the room.

'Never seen him before,' he replied. 'I thought he was an old friend of yours from the way he was talking to you.'

'What about the way he greeted you?' I retorted. 'Let us ask the host.'

We threaded our way through the crowd and found our host. 'Who is this friend of yours?' asked my friend.

The man in question had just released someone from his embrace and was advancing towards another with arms wide open, shouting 'Hullo, Hullo, Hullo.'

'I like that' answered our host. 'He came in with you, I thought you had brought him.'

'Certainly not' protested my friend. 'Never set my eyes on the chap. He must be with someone else.'

'Perhaps . . .' said the host apologetically. 'It does not matter. He seems to know so many people. My friends' friends are always welcome in my home—particularly if they are the friendly type.'

'Friendly type' was an understatement. This man was on positively amorous terms with everyone. He had just finished embracing the last remaining unembraced member of the party and was proceeding towards us near the door.

'Well old chap' he exclaimed, holding the host by his shoulders. 'Wonderful party. Absolutely wonderful. Thank you for asking me—Must fly now. I've got to go to another two. I know they won't be half as interesting as this one, but I must tear myself away. Good-bye.' He waved both his arms, and shouted 'good-bye all' to the crowd and vanished.

'Who was the man?' That was the question everyone was asking everyone else in the party. It seemed no one knew him. If no one knew him, how did he come to the party? No one knew the answer to that either. Malicious people said the man was a gate-crasher. But that, as I have already said, is what people with malice said.

He was a newcomer to our city, but from that day onwards we began to see him everywhere—at public receptions, private parties, political meetings, religious meetings, social gatherings. At weddings, christenings and funerals. He was always the centre of attraction.

His effusive 'Hullo, Hullo, Hullo' boomed over the babel of talk.

Mr Swami—for that the newspapers told us practically every morning was the name of the gentleman, was obviously a great favourite of the press. There was no function where he was not present (and he was present at most functions), where he did not figure prominently in the photographs—receiving guests, whether or not he was one of the hosts, garlanding people, even if there was no occasion to do so, or, just talking to a V.I.P. when the cameraman was about. In fact there was some kind of telepathic contact between Mr Swami and the press photographers. As soon as Mr Swami curled his drooping moustache to a rakish angle towards his eyes you could swear that a cameraman had entered the room. Next Mr Swami adjusted his tie. When he lost interest in the conversation he was having, you knew that a secret message had flashed an S.O.S. in his brain: 'operation photograph'. Mr Swami left you in the middle of your sentence and advanced towards some place with his arms generously extended to embrace someone. He got to his mark as the camera bulb flashed and shutter clicked. He was never out of focus. He was always helpful to the cameraman if the latter was so ignorant as not to know Mr Swami. 'Do send me a copy of the photograph. The name is Swami, S W A M I; that's right, Swami. Here, here is my card.'

Malicious people said Mr Swami loved publicity and paid press cameramen for the photographs that appeared in the papers. But that as I have already said was what malicious people said. Mr Swami was always protesting that he did not like publicity and made fun of others who did. There certainly was no reason why Mr Swami should have to pay any photographer. He knew everyone that mattered; from Mr Swami's dialogue it appeared that everyone who mattered knew Mr Swami—knew him well, consulted him on all important matters and set store on Mr Swami's advice.

'As I was telling Winston the last time I was in England' was a familiar opening sentence of Mr Swami's pronouncement on international affairs.

'Who is Winston?' somebody would ask timidly.

'Don't you know Winston? Winston Churchill of course. Old friend of mine. Known him for years. I said to him "Look Winnie, if you mean to win the war you must do so and so."'

The so and so was Mr Swami's advice to Mr Churchill. Mr Churchill had apparently appreciated Mr Swami's advice and had suggested his speaking to other leaders. Mr Swami's views on the international situation were punctuated with Winstons, Joes, Ferdinands, Eamons, Ikes, and many others. He was equally familiar with national figures in the political and industrial field. In fact, Mr Swami dropped Christian names of the mighty with the cool nonchalance of a man ejecting betel-spit.

Malicious people said Mr Swami was a snob. But that, as I have already said, was what people with malice said.

Mr Swami was always willing to talk to humbler folk like ourselves and even consult us about his own personal affairs. 'Look' he would say putting his arms round our shoulders, 'Can I have a word with you—alone?' In conspiratorial whispers he would ask, 'What sort of place is France? You've lived there long enough—you should know!'

'France' we would say 'is a nice place. A very nice place' we would say—was Mr Swami planning to spend a holiday there?

Mr Swami would smile 'Holiday? I have no time for a holiday. Work! But look, keep it under your hat. I haven't made up my mind yet.'

Mr Swami had consulted others about the United States, England, Scandinavian countries, Italy, Switzerland, and they were all told to keep it under their hats till Mr Swami had made up his mind. We did not know what Mr Swami was having to make up his mind about. Had he been offered the post of Ambassador? He never said so himself—but the look in his eye—the look of indecision, concern, responsibility, all combined to leave no doubt that Mr Swami was, in fact, having to choose between being an ambassador or a governor of some state. If we asked Mr Swami later whether he had made up his mind, he would just smile wearily and say 'I wish I could have said yes—but they won't spare me from the office. There is so much to do and so few people to do it.'

Malicious people said Mr Swami was putting it on and his work was of no importance. Now, that certainly was not correct. We did not know what work Mr Swami did except that it was vastly important. Mr Swami had frequently dropped hints that he dealt with life itself. Whatever that meant, it was obviously very lucrative. Even though short of frame, Mr Swami had a dear little paunch you could not ignore. Only prosperous people have paunches of that sort. Mr Swami's was always covered with expensive waistcoats and a gold chain that ran across in two waves meeting conically above his navel. He was well dressed sometimes in European and Indian costumes—just as the occasion required: his hair smartly set and moustache stiffened with wax, an aura of perfume enveloped his person. His shoes were polished bright and had the squeak only new ones have. Besides the dress and appearance there were other signs of prosperity. He belonged to all the clubs and societies in the town. And although he protested that he had no time for clubs—he was seen in three or four every evening. That was not all. Those of us who knew him saw his prosperity with our eyes. Even when he bought a pan for one anna, or a box of matches for two annas he presented a hundred rupee note. 'Never carry small change' was his motto. 'Too bulky. Just hundred rupee notes.' He would let us see that his wallet was crammed with wads of green paper. If that isn't prosperity, I am a pauper!

We discovered the nature of Mr Swami's occupation after he had been in the town for some time. He had by then visited everyone in their homes, inquired about the health of everyone's wives and children. He occasionally dropped in on people's offices—just dropped in while passing. No one could resent Mr Swami's visits because he never had an axe to grind and showed so much interest in ones' health. He could talk on practically every subject under the sun. He was also a bit of a philosopher. The way he talked about the world being an illusion, the uncertainty of life and the inevitability of death made you feel sad for yourself. 'The one absolute certainty about life is death' Mr Swami used to say prophetically—and then add with a penetrating look: 'It's not so bad for the ones who die—but for those that are left behind.' Straightaway from being sad about your own impending demise, you become sad for those that you were going to leave behind.

Malicious people said this was only sales talk. But that as I have already said is what only people with malice said. How could it be sales talk without their knowing what Mr Swami had to sell? Besides, what Mr Swami said was profoundly true. He only made profound truths appear profounder and have a personal bearing. Let me explain what I mean.

One morning the papers informed us that the wife of the retired president of our city Corporation had died. Now the president had been retired so long that people had forgotten of his existence. He was over eighty years old, not rich and, then, of no social distinction. He was really not a snob. Cup of tea and malicious people did not expect Mr Swami to be wasting his time at his wife's funeral. But they were wrong. Mr Swami was very much there. He had been deeply moved by the passing of the lady, and was in acute distress. He embraced us all—not with an 'Ah, Hullo, Hullo, Hullo' but wailing 'Ho, Ho, Ho' and crying bitterly. We too were deeply moved and believed that he must be a close relation of the deceased. Actually Mr Swami had never met either the retired president or his wife. But then Swami was a sensitive type who wanted to share other peoples' sorrows. When the old president came out, Mr Swami clasped him to his bosom and wept loud and long. He really needed more consoling than the man who had lost his wife. On regaining his composure he was soon busy comforting members of the bereaved family. He talked philosophically of the transitory nature of life and how everyone had to die one day.

'God has been kind to you sir' he said with a deep sigh addressing the ex-president—'He has taken your dear wife—may her soul rest in heaven—but spared you to look after your children and grand-children. See what a catastrophe it would have been if you had gone first and the burden of providing for the family had fallen on your wife!'

The old man agreed that God was just and merciful. But he too would go soon and God would no doubt look after his family.

'Yes of course, of course,' said Mr Swami, 'God is great and provides for his creatures, but it is also man's duty to provide against the future. God gave him brains to do that.'

The old man agreed with Mr Swami about God's munificence and man's duty. The dialogue between them went on at this philoso-phic level till we reached the cremation ground. There was again much crying and consoling. Now Mr Swami was being a great help to the ex-president in his sorrow—so the people left the two alone. Mr Swami produced a piece of folded paper from his pocket and read from it to the ex-president. We thought it had some sacred text from the way the two bent over each line. Apparently the old man subscribed to all the sentiments expressed in the sacred text, because we saw him scribble on the paper at several places. The old man's conversion was obviously of satisfaction to Mr Swami because he began to smile. He patted the old man on the back and left before the funeral was over. He said he had to go to another one.

Malicious people said that Mr Swami was an insurance agent and had sold the old man a life insurance policy. But that, as I have already said, is what malicious people said.

The Fawn

I shaded the dial of my watch. The glow-worm green of the radium showed a quarter to six.

'What is the time?' asked my companion.

'Getting on to six.'

'The sun will be up soon, I wish that shikari would hurry back. Let's have some coffee while we are waiting.'

I got the thermos-flask out of the car and poured out the coffee in two celluloid tumblers. We warmed our hands round the tumblers and breathed the hot humid coffee vapour.

The moon was in its last quarter. The countryside was bathed in a soft silvery whiteness. A fine mist lay on the ground. Above the dark line of trees a faint glow of light had begun to appear. We could just see the outlines of the village. It was an ungainly heap of mud huts and built on high ground. The minarets of a mosque showed above the rest.

For some time we sat enveloped in silence, sipping our coffee. My friend began to talk:

'Isn't it peaceful? So different from the life we usually lead. I look forward to these week-ends to get out of the rut of life at home. I have been doing so for nearly twenty years—ever since I became my own master. At least once in seven days I run away from life and be myself.'

After a pause he added, 'Anyone would in my shoes.'

He was obviously wanting me to ask him to carry on. 'Why particularly you?'

'I don't know. I've had a raw deal in life.' He paused for encouragement. He did not need much.

'We all have our ups and downs,' I suggested.

'All people don't have their mothers die when they are six years old; they don't have step-mothers producing hordes of step-brothers and step-sisters. And that is not all. My father died and I have had to look after them. Instead of drowning the lot as I would have liked to, I have to love them and care for them. Don't you see, one has to squash real hate under a weight of make-believe affection? Now and then one wants to get away from it all.'

He lit a cigarette and stretched himself on the grass. Having got it off his chest he felt he ought to ask me the same question.

'You don't have to escape from anything, do you?'

'Nothing in particular. I like the peace and quiet. After the hectic life in the city regulated by one's wrist watch it is refreshing to get out somewhere where time seems to come to a stop. The human system needs a break from the tyranny of the clock.'

'I suppose it does. Although it's really never bothered me. It has become so much a part of my life. I don't need the alarm clock to wake me up or tell me it's time to get to office. The office clocks could be set right at 1 o'clock when I step out for lunch. It is all really one's imagination. If you don't think about something, you won't notice it. Just lock up all the clocks in the house and give up wearing your watch and see the difference it will make. You will do all the things in time without being agitated.'

'That's just making a clockwork of your system. I would rather have it this way. An outing in the country with a gun gives me the break I want. I do not mind if I kill nothing. In fact I find killing somewhat wicked.'

Over the line of trees in the east the dawn began to break. The village began to come to life. From the mosque we heard the sound of the splashing of water. A little later the muezzin's sonorous cry broke the morning stillness, repeating in a monotonous sing-song 'Allah-o-Akbar'—'God is Great.'

Our shikari returned to report there were no birds on the lake. A party had been there the day before and shot a large number. Herds of deer were said to be in the neighbourhood. We got the guns out of the car and loaded them with buck-shot. My friend got out a razor blade from the car locker and stuck it in the folds of his sola hat. We followed our guide round the village on to the open fields.

The sun came up bright and hot on a vast expanse of undulating countryside. Patches of cultivation were jigsawed with rock and pampas grass. There were no trees or cover of any sort. My friend looked uneasy.

'This is no place for shooting,' he grumbled, 'the animal could see us from a mile.'

He was right. Every time we came up on high ground we saw herds of deer scatter away. For me time had come to a stop. I walked on fascinated by the sight of the deer leaping over the corn and scrub. The fluffy plumes of pampas waved us on as they bent to the soft morning breeze. My friend's uneasiness gave way to agitation. He slapped the butt of his gun irritably.

We continued our trek with the sun now directly over our heads. My friend looked hot and bothered and mopped his face and bald head with his handkerchief. It seemed that this was going to be just a long walk with our guns on our shoulders. That was what I wanted. Even my companion seemed to be reconciling himself to the idea of going back without a bag. We trudged on listening to the monotonous patter of our feet and the more monotonous calling of barbets.

All of a sudden there was movement in some bushes on our right. Before we could bring our guns to our shoulders a doe cleared our path in one big leap. Then in long springy strides she passed out of range. She stopped on top of a mound to look back. My friend pressed me down with a heavy hand. We crouched in the tall grass.

'Wait,' he said in a whisper, 'she must have a fawn nearby, otherwise she would not stop like that. We will get them both.'

He was right again. A fawn came awkwardly ambling on to the path. It didn't see us. My friend took a quick aim and fired. The shot hit the ground some feet away from the animal sending up a cloud of dust. The fawn turned round with a look of surprise. It sprang into the air and came down on the same spot. It frisked round in a circle twice. It stopped and held up its head to display its tiny antlers. The mother bayed in warning. The fawn ran up to her and then back towards us. It stopped a few yards away, sprang into the air three or four times and wagged its little stubby tail. The doe bayed again. The fawn turned round to look at its mother. My friend took careful aim and fired a second time. The bullet pierced the soft silk-white skin of the fawn's belly and brought out its entrails. It leapt up once more and fell on the dusty ground kicking its legs in the air.

My friend dropped his gun and rushed to his prey. The fawn was almost shot in two but it was still vigorously shaking its head and legs. He put his heavy boot on one of its antlers. Tears rolled down the fawn's large handsome eyes as it looked up. My friend took out the razor blade from his sola hat and slit the animal's throat, swearing at it all the time. A stream of warm purple blood gurgled out of the fawn's jugular veins. A quiver ran all over its body and it lay still. A white film came over its dark lustrous eyes.

My friend looked at his hands smeared with blood. 'Filthy mess' he exclaimed, 'bloody filthy mess.' He tore up a few blades of grass to wipe them. 'I wish I did not have to do this ceremonial cutting of the throat,' he continued, 'but you know what an orthodox Muslim household is! No one would touch anything I shot unless I had also pronounced a pious "Bismilah" and sent the beast's soul flying to paradise.'

'I did not hear you say "Bismilah"' I said quietly.

He laughed. 'I promise to say it when I get the mother. We will get her all right. You just wait and watch.'

'Let us have some lunch first,' I said, looking at my watch, 'it is after two.'

He laughed again. 'Wrist watch says 2 p.m. It is time to be hungry. I thought you were escaping from all that. All right, let us get over the lunch. We must not lose the mother.'

We sat under a tree drinking beer and eating sandwiches. My friend lit a cigar and pretended to relax. But all the time his eyes scanned the horizon. The doe was about, baying sometimes to our right, sometimes to our left. She never came close enough to be shot. Involuntarily, I looked at my watch and then dropped my hand quietly. My friend noticed that.

'Wrist watch says it is time to go home?' he asked with a smile.

'We ought to be moving if we want to be in time for dinner,' I answered.

'Have it your own way,' he said heaving himself up. 'But you cannot get away from that wrist watch. Why don't you leave it at home when you come? You should leave all your bothers at home. Look at me' he added holding out his hands. They were dirty with patches of crimson on his fingers.

We started back to the village with the shikari carrying the dead fawn across his shoulders. Whenever we stopped to rest we saw the doe somewhere about following us. By sunset we got back to our car near the village. My friend ordered the shikari to put the fawn in the luggage bunk at the back of the car and leave it open. We sat down some paces away from the car to sip our scotch and soda.

The sun went down and the shades of evening closed about us. The village noises settled down to rest. My companion was feeling pleased with himself.

'I feel happy at the end of a day like this,' he said. 'Good exercise.

Good sport. No backbiting, no bickering, no hatred, no unkindness. It is a clean life. One goes back to the world with more charity and understanding...'

I lay on my back gazing at the dark blue sky. The stars had begun to come out. I could not get the picture of the man slitting the throat of the fawn out of my mind. I was not listening, but when he stopped talking, I sat up. In the dusk I saw the car silhouetted against the twilight. Its bunk lay open like the jaws of some monster. The head of the dead fawn dangled from the rear fender. Behind the car was the mother sniffing at the corpse. There was a loud report. The doe collapsed near the mudguard of the car. I heard my friend swear triumphantly and rush towards his prey with his razor blade. 'In the name of God—Bismilah' he yelled and got on with his gory task.

The countryside relapsed into silence once more. The sonorous call of the muezzin broke the stillness of the gloom, 'Allah-o-Akbar.'

I looked at my watch again. It was time to go home.

Man, How the Government of India Run!

'**M**an, how you think the Government of India is run? How?'

Sunder Singh hurled this question across the stenographers' room to his two colleagues sitting opposite him. Ghosh Babu from Bengal spat the betel off his chin with the hem of his dhoti and made the monosyllabic comment:

'True.'

'Hey you, Mr Madrasi!' continued Sunder Singh turning aggressively to Sambamurthy. (Sunder Singh's knowledge of his country was conventionally Punjabi. Anyone south of Bombay was a Madrasi.) 'What you say?'

Sambamurthy also refused to be hustled into answering such vital questions in a hurry. He blew the dust in the keyboard of his typewriter and then looked at the excitable Sikh with his large, expressionless eyes.

'What you say?' repeated Sunder Singh impatiently. Sambamurthy shook his head from side to side and added one more word to his Bengali colleague's observation:

'Quite true.'

'Of course, quite true, man!' roared Sunder Singh, standing up and gesticulating. 'I say what do they know about work, these secretaries, additional secretaries, joint secretaries, deputy secretaries, under secretaries and God knows how many other kinds of factories?' He laughed at his own little joke and went on, 'All they do is attend meetings, drink cups of tea, dictate a few memos·and then go home to their memsahibs pretending they are tired because they have been so busy. Ha! busy! we know how busy! Don't we?'

They agreed they did. And you couldn't dismiss their opinions lightly because they did work in the Government of India and knew the way its intricate mechanism operated. What appeared to be an entangled cobweb of red-tape to the outside world was playing cat's-cradle to these three. They knew the rules and regulations of bureaucracy by heart; understood the importance of notings, minutes and memoranda; were familiar with the wayward conduct of files which travelled to and fro interminably from official to official like warp and woof weaving the fabric of administration. Their analysis was simple and based on experience. If typists and stenographers did not put sense and order into the minutes of meetings which had little of either, decisions taken by the big-wigs would remain completely unintelligible. If they did not put up the necessary papers for signature to officers, matters would come to a standstill.

And which senior officer knew the rules of procedure as well as they and who could make a file vanish mysteriously and as mysteriously make it re-appear? Was it a great wonder then that, although Messrs Sunder Singh, Sambamurthy and Ghosh were only three of the 30,000 who poured in and out of the enormous beehives which are the secretariats of the Government of India, they felt that the administration rested squarely on their shoulders? They knew that great decisions were not made by a concert of minds but by one or two persons and passed on to others, and that the moving force behind most institutions came from a small core of people and they were seldom the ones on top.

Having arrived at an amicable agreement about their importance, Sunder Singh rang the bell. A chaprasi opened the door and looked inquiringly at all three.

'Tea or coffee?' asked Sunder Singh generously; then answered the question himself. 'Two teas, and one coffee for Mr Madrasi. Quick. Any biscuit, shiskit? No? O.K. Two teas, one coffee. Quick.' He emphasized the urgency by clicking his thumb and finger to the sound 'phuta phut, phuta phut.'

'Today is the first time I came late,' repeated Sunder Singh, for the third time going over the incident which had occasioned the earlier outburst. 'That fellow says to me "Sunder Singh, you are late. How do you think the Government of India can run if everyone comes late to office?" I wanted to say "You don't talk Mister, you never come to office before 11 a.m. Today for the first time you are punctual and I for reasons beyond control am five minutes late and you give me a lecture to drink!" But you know how I am. I said this little fellow, this yesterday's child, why should I speak rashly to him: it will only spoil my mouth. I just said: "Sorry, Sir, you want me to take a letter?" "No" he said, "I have no time now, I will send for you later. But I don't like people being late".' 'Ha,' exploded

Sunder Singh and then mimicked his boss's voice. 'I don't like people being late. What say you Ghosh Babu?'

'There is no justice in this world,' exclaimed Mr Ghosh philoso-phically.

'Absolutely no justice,' added Sambamurthy.

The tea and coffee arrived. The three gentlemen left their res-pective tables and typewriters and put their chairs in the centre of the room; a fourth was put in their midst for the tray. Sunder Singh poured out the tea and coffee and the three relaxed for a half-hour interlude from work.

'In Europe,' said Ghosh Babu who read a great deal, 'they all stop work at eleven to have tea or coffee or cocoa, or some stronger beverage; they call it elevenses.'

'Very wise,' said Sambamurthy. '*All work and no play makes Jack a dull boy* is a famous English saying.' Sambamurthy was full of English quotations and clichés.

'But,' protested Sunder Singh. 'This is not play. Man, you get everything wrong. This is rest from work. Ghosh Babu, how long time they get for elevenses?'

'About half-an-hour,' replied Ghosh with authority. 'You see, they have no chaprasis, bearers, cooks or other servants. They make their own tea or coffee or go to hotels or restaurants.'

'Work stops completely?' asked Sunder Singh.

'Completely.'

'Wonderful.'

'We get no time off for elevenses,' complained Sambamurthy. 'We should bring it up before the Clerks' Association.'

'Yes, we should ask for half-an-hour break. Let us see,' said Sunder Singh looking at the clock. 'It is now 10.45. From 10.45 a.m. to 11.15 a.m.'

'That will be a popular demand,' replied Sambamurthy appro-vingly. 'I shall propose it.'

The decision brought a glow on their faces. They sat back and sipped their beverages noisily. When the coffee and teapots were empty Sunder Singh rang for the chaprasi. As he reappeared through the door the three brought out their wallets with a chorus of protests.

'No, no, no, my turn today.'

'No, mine. You paid yesterday.'

As usual, the more energetic Sikh won. He forced the wallets back into his colleagues' pockets, thrust the money and the tray into the chaprasi's hands and pushed him out of the office. They picked up their chairs and went back to their seats in front of the typewriters.

The time was 11.15 a.m.—the end of the unofficial 'elevenses.'

'Well, what is the news?' asked Sambamurthy, again blowing through the keyboard of his typewriter.

Sunder Singh rang the bell. The chaprasi reappeared.

'Oi, go and get the papers from the Ministry library. Say the Bara Sahib wants them all for half an hour.'

Five minutes later the chaprasi was back with a bundle of daily papers which he parcelled out province-wise.

The three plunged into the papers with eagerness. Ghosh Babu was politically inclined and read about things that were happening in the world. He also felt it his duty to educate his friends in international affairs and broaden their outlook. He picked out the important items and read them out loudly and then made suitable explanatory comment. To arouse their interest, he uttered exclamations like 'Arrey Baba' or 'Bap rey Bap!' Sambamurthy found news from his province of consuming interest and announced party intrigues and alignments with such prefatory noises as 'Aye, aye, aye.' Sunder Singh started with the back page and seldom got beyond the middle of the paper.

'Wah wah,' he exploded before Ghosh could tell him of the latest position in the East-West conflict or Sambamurthy of the feud between Brahmins and non-Brahmins. 'The Home Ministry won its volleyball match against Defence. They will be playing us at lunch-time today. I must ring up our team.'

Sunder Singh got busy with the telephone. All the members of the side had read the important news, but the comment on the match and forecasts on the fate which awaited the Home Ministry side took some time.

'We'll give them such a beating they will remember it all their lives,' exclaimed Sunder Singh exultantly each time he put the receiver down.

'You must come to the match,' he said addressing his colleagues. 'It is most important.'

Ghosh Babu put down the paper on his typewriter.

'If it is not too late. You never know when these Sahibs return from their tiffin.'

'Never before three o'clock, man! Don't you know how to appear busy? Always go late for lunch even if you have nothing to do so that your wife at least thinks you have been working very hard.'

Sambamurthy agreed. Although he was not the sporting kind, he felt an obligation to cheer up his Ministry—particularly his room-mate who was the great stand-by of the team.

They all returned to their papers. The time was a quarter to twelve.

Sunder Singh finished the sports page and turned to the next most important subject—the matrimonial advertisements. His eyes glowed as he went down the column. 'Ghosh Babu, this one is for you: "Wanted a match for an issueless virgin widow." If she is a virgin she has to be issueless. What he means by this?'

'If she is from the Punjab, you can never tell,' answered Sambamurthy grinning from ear to ear. 'We don't have such peculiar women in the south. This one sounds O.K.' Sambamurthy read out a detailed ad from the south. 'Mr Singh, if you were not married you could apply. Just send your horoscope. They won't know you have a beard and get frightened.'

'Why you people want horoscopes and not photos? What you see in horoscope?' demanded Sunder Singh.

'Beauty is only skin deep,' answered Sambamurthy coolly. 'Good fortune is much more useful.'

'And you people full of prejudice,' accused Sunder Singh. 'Castes and sub-castes. And also thinking of money all the time. Look at these from the Punjab! All say C & D no bar. You know what that means? Caste and dowry no bar.'

The three friends discussed the matrimonial conventions of their respective provinces and their own eligibility if given another chance—for they were all married and with children. This was a part of their daily routine in office—and perhaps the most absorbing part of it for they never missed it. The friendly banter continued till it was mid-day.

Sunder Singh took his coat off and hung it on a nail in the wall above his chair. He rolled in a couple of sheets of paper with the carbon sandwiched in between in the machine and typed a few lines starting with 'Dear Sir, reference your letter number...'and left it incomplete.

'I must have an early lunch if I want to play well. You bring your food to the volleyball ground.'

Ghosh and Sambamurthy nodded their heads.

He rang the bell.

'*Dekho*,' he said conspiratorially to the chaprasi. 'If the Sahib rings for me before 12.30 just tell him that I must have just gone somewhere—to the bathroom or for some work. Say my coat is there and things on the table. If it is after that, say we've just this minute gone for our lunch.'

The chaprasi smiled.

'Why you smile?' asked Sunder Singh, 'Don't we do this for you?'

Sunder Singh left his colleagues and went down to the canteen. He ordered himself a large meal of chapatties, several varieties of curries to be followed by ice-cream. He ate it leisurely and washed it all down with a hot cup of tea. Then joined the canteen manager in pan-chewing and office gossip.

'Tell me, Sardar Sahib, what is your great hobby these days?' asked the canteen manager who was a fellow Punjabi.

'Hobbies?' asked Sunder Singh indignantly. 'Where is the time for hobbies? From morning to night one is in this sister-sleeping office. By the time one returns home there is no energy left for anything. This is no life.'

'Somebody has to do the work, Sunder Singhji,' said the manager trying to make up. 'If you don't, who will?'

Sunder Singh acknowledged the gesture gracefully but did not want to leave the manager in any doubt about the amount of work he did: the manager was the focal point of a great deal of office gossip.

'Many people run private businesses to supplement their service salaries. I don't know how they find the time to do so! I don't get a moment to raise my head off the table. I could certainly do with a little additional income. What with a wife and children—but where is the time?'

'Besides, people like you and I cannot do such things,' said the manager, warming up. 'The government pays you a salary—whatever it is—to work in the office for it, not to run a private business. It is not honest. Is it?'

'No of course not. And where is the time or the energy after the brain-picking in the office.'

People started coming in for lunch and interrupting the conversation. Sunder Singh shook hands with the manager and left. It was 1.15 p.m. Another fifteen minutes for the game to start.

He sauntered out into the sun and made for the lawns alongside the secretariat. Clerks sat in little groups sharing the contents of their tiffin carriers; others were huddled round hawkers of sweet-meats, fruits and savouries. In the centre of the lawn a volleyball net was being put up between two high poles and a number of young men were limbering up for the match. Sunder Singh was greeted with loud 'hullos' and much back-slapping and handshaking. After all he was not only the most popular man in the Ministry but also the mainstay of his side; and this was the semi-final match. If they won, there would be a grand display at the finals with some Minister or high offical to do the prize distribution.

Sunder Singh took off his turban, rolled his long hair into a chignon and tied it with a handkerchief. He sat down on the grass amidst his team-mates to undo his shoes and discuss the tactics of the game.

The match started at 1.30 p.m. and was watched by hundreds of cheering, yelling, barracking clerks, stenographers, superintendents and others of the general category, amongst them Ghosh Babu and Sambamurthy. There was a sense of complete abandon. The little conscience at their having left their offices early had vanished with the beginning of the official lunch-hour break of 1–2 p.m. and the knowledge that bosses who left for their lunches late seldom returned before 3–4 p.m. after having their afternoon siestas.

The match was closely contested and came to an impasse at two games all. There was a short break and then the fifth and final came to decide the fate of the two most vital ministries of the Government of India. Sunder Singh who had played well in the four games excelled himself at the crucial moments of the match. He leapt like a tiger and put the punch of a cannon behind each ball he sent smashing down over the net to the other side. The defences of the Home Ministry crumbled and Sunder Singh's side carried the day amidst thunderous applause which shook the drowsy members of the secretariat and brought them to their windows. There was no doubt who the conquering hero was. Although he was drenched in sweat, his grateful colleagues embraced him; some even kissed him on his thick beard. He lay down exhausted but triumphant.

Iced aerated waters were served to both the teams; Sunder Singh's friends insisted on treating him to sweets at the stalls. He accepted because he did not want to hurt their feelings. Only the clock kept ticking in his mind and making him uncomfortable. At 3.45 he dragged himself away from his admirers and hurried back to his office. As he entered the long corridor he assumed a tired, busy look, like others in the place.

Ghosh Babu and Sambamurthy were already in their places. They greeted him with enthusiasm and showered praises on his great performance. They told him how the telephone hadn't stopped ringing since they came back, all asking for Sunder Singh and wanting to congratulate him. Sunder Singh was too modest a man to ring up himself so his friends informed the office of his return. Within a few minutes their room was full of other clerks and stenographers, all patting him on the back and shaking him by the hand. By the time they left, it was 4 p.m. Sunder Singh felt a little uneasy.

'Did the Sahib or anyone send for me or look in here?'

'No, no, it is all right. He is at another meeting. The chaprasi got another stenographer to take down the minutes.'

Sunder Singh felt much better.

'We must offer you tea for what you have done,' said Ghosh and Sambamurthy.

Once more the bell rang and the chaprasi was ordered to bring in two teas and a coffee. Anyhow it was after 4 p.m. and the one thing the English had taught and the Indians had learnt was the sanctity of afternoon tea. The seniormost officer would hesitate to disturb the juniormost clerk if he was at tea.

It was conventional to discuss postings, transfers, promotions and office intrigue with the evening tea. But Sunder Singh's mind was too full of his afternoon's sporting achievement to bother about trifling matters like the adverse report given to him by his last boss or the dog-in-the-manger attitude of the present one who, despite his acid remarks, had written 'cannot be spared' when Sunder Singh applied for a transfer to a job with better prospects. Success dissolves envy and breeds charity towards everyone. This afternoon's performance had been a crowning success which made Sunder Singh look kindly on his superiors. And then there were his colleagues' philosophical views on the tortuous path of success.

'Mr Singh,' said Sambamurthy sipping his coffee. 'As I have said before, the secret of success in government service is very simple.

You only have to get on with the man just above you and forget everyone else. It has nothing to do with work or ability or anything like that. Say "Yes Sir, Yes Sir" to everything he says; call at his house on festivals with garlands or sweets for his family; play with his children, if he has any, or flirt madly with his wife if he hasn't; do little jobs for his household like getting the electrician or carpenter when required—and you will get A+ for everything. Then nobody can touch you. Promotion after promotion. You may even become an Under Secretary.' An Under Secretary was the height of a stenographer's ambition.

'That, Mr Madrasi, I can never do,' said Sunder Singh proudly—forgetting that he had done all these with the knowledge and advice of his two colleagues. 'Never,' he repeated, smacking his chest with the open of his palm. 'You can ask me to do as much work as you like—day and night—but boot-licking, never! What you say, Ghosh Babu?'

Ghosh Babu agreed that the three of them could never debase themselves as others did to get on. If merit and hard work were the only criteria, they were willing to compete with anyone in the world. On this note of agreement, they shook hands and departed.

It was 5 p.m.—time for the office to close.

Sunder Singh was amongst the thousands of cyclists who wound their way along the broad roads running from the secretariat buildings to the distant townships where only clerks with their large families and measly wages could afford to live. They all looked tired after a hard day's work and Sunder Singh felt more tired than the others. He usually stopped *en route* to buy fruit or vegetables from hawkers who lined his route homewards—some on pavements—some with their wares strapped on the carriers of their bicycles. This evening he just pushed on listlessly till he got home.

The welcome at home had a regular pattern. His five-year-old son came rushing out to greet him and get a short ride on his father's bicycle. This evening Sunder Singh brushed him off a little irritated, and without a word of greeting to his wife he stretched himself on the charpoy in the centre of their little courtyard. His three-year-old daughter clambered up and wanted to jump on his belly as she did every evening, but Sunder Singh put her down and asked her to go away. The children slunk away a little frightened and went to their mother in the kitchen.

'Are you tired?' asked his wife at last. 'Did you have too much work to do today?'

'There is too much to do every day. Woman, how you think the Government of India run if we did no work?'

The Man With a Clear Conscience

I am a man with a clear conscience because I am a good man. I am one of the types of good men who understand evil and what causes men, and for that matter women and children as well—all of whom are born good, to become victims of evil circumstances and turn bad. I am not intolerant. I am not the sort of puritan who goes about passing judgments on people who have fallen on bad days and therefore strayed from the straight and narrow path of virtue. I have read many books on sociology and know that the causes of crime are too complicated to be easily labelled and punished. As a matter of fact I belong to the school of thought which believes that every criminal act is a censure against society and each time a man or woman is sent to the gallows or is put in prison, society admits its own failure. I do not judge. I know well that God's ways are infinite; we humans should try to comprehend them with humility and not with arrogance.

This description of myself may give some people the impression that I am an insufferable sort of prig with a smug smile of righteousness on my face. That is not so. Although I smile most of the time, it is not through any feeling of righteousness but because I believe that to smile is better than to scowl or have a face without any expression at all. And I am very sufferable because not only do I not pass judgments on evil-doers, I do not even pass them on those who readily do so. God's ways, as I have already said, are infinite; who am I to say this man or that is wrong in saying or doing what he does?

This in turn may give some people the impression that I am one of the arm-chair types who spend their time finding the pros and cons of everything without ever doing anything practical. That also is not correct. In my own humble way I do quite a lot. If I see people quarrelling in the street, I stop to settle their argument. I never let a tonga driver flog his horse when I am a passenger; and yet I never chide the driver for being harsh for who knows what hidden frustrations want to find expression in the act of whipping! Coming to theft, I have known my own servants pilfer. Sometimes it is little things like taking a swig out of my bottle of whisky and adding water to make up the volume; sometimes it is more like taking money out of my wallet in the assurance that I never know how much I carry and would not miss a rupee or two. But I am shrewd and have tackled the situation in my own way by offering the man whisky myself, or by increasing his pay or sending for his wife or child and giving them a rupee or two with such remarks as: 'Your husband (or father) cannot live within his pay, so you better take this.' My nights are never disturbed because I sleep the sleep of the just.

I have said all this to give you an idea of the sort of person I am, because without that you may not be able to appreciate the incident which I want to relate—an incident about a thief.

It happened not so long ago in Calcutta. If you do not know Calcutta, let me tell you a little about it because it is important to this story. It is a big city—one of the biggest in the world. It has four million people packed in a small space. It is over-crowded, filthy and full of beggars. It is also a very cruel city because the people who live here have become hardened against suffering. Here everyman's hand is against his neighbours because there is not enough money to be made and too many people wanting to make it; so besides beggars, prostitutes and pavement-dwellers which abound in any big but poor city, Calcutta is full of tricksters, pick-pockets and common thieves.

The incident took place on a hot summer afternoon when most people were having their siesta: the rich in their air-cooled rooms; the poor on shaded pavements or beneath trees. I disapprove of the habit of resting in the afternoon and was out exploring the city. I was walking along a footpath which ran between the tramlines and the metalled road. On one side were the fashionable shops of Chow-ringhee; on the other, the great maidan, the only open space in the teeming metropolis. The road and the maidan were deserted. It was as still in the glare of the middle of the day as it is after midnight. No motor-cars, no rickshaws, no pedestrians—nothing but the shimmer of heat on the metalled road and the flat monotony of parched grass with groups of people lying like corpses under the generous shades of banyan trees. Taxis were also parked under them on the lawn. The drivers slept on the seats with their legs sticking out of the windows.

All of a sudden there was a commotion under one of the trees.

Two burly Sikh taxi drivers began to beat a small Bengali dressed in a vest and khaki shorts. One of them caught his arms from the rear. The other grabbed his tuft of hair with his left hand and began hitting him with his right as hard as he could, drawing blood with each blow; and with each blow he came out with some foul abuse in which Sikh peasants specialize. 'This to rape your mother . . . this to rape your sister . . . this to rape your daughter . . . and this to this and this.'

Suddenly the city was awake. Windows opened and people looked into the glare with their eyes blinking. Men came running from all directions gesticulating and shouting—'Stop, stop. Don't kill the man.' I also ran to the scene. Some of the people there before me appealed to me to intervene. They did so because I am a Sikh and they believed I would have influence on fellow-Sikhs. I am neither big nor burly nor brave. But a good cause breeds courage even in a timid man; and all said and done I am not all that timid. I too am a Sikh. I walked up, broke through the ring of spectators and grasped the taxi-driver's hand raised to strike in mid-air.

'Stop beating this man. Do you want to kill him?' I roared angrily. With my other hand I freed the Bengali's tuft of hair from the other Sikh's grasp. The poor Bengali sank down on his knees, put his arms round my legs and buried his head between my knees. He began to cry loudly.

'Save me from these men,' he wailed. 'For God's sake, save me.'

The two Sikh taxi drivers closed on me from either side. They were both a foot taller than I and much more hairy and fierce to look at.

'And who are you?'

'I am nobody, but I am not going to let you do violence to this poor little man who is half your size. Aren't you ashamed of beating him?'

'Ashamed?' sneered one of them. 'Do you know who he is?'

'No! and I do not care. You are not going to hit him.'

'No?'

'No,' I shouted defiantly.

The Bengali sobbed: 'Save me from them. For God's sake, save me.'

'He is a thief,' said the first Sikh. 'He was taking off the valve-caps of the wheel of my cab; I caught him red-handed.' He produced two little valve-caps from his pocket, put them on the palm of his hand and showed them to the spectators; he sneered, sticking his palm under my nose.

'See.'

He caught the Bengali by his hair again and pulled his head back from between my knees. 'Weren't you stealing, you bastard? Didn't I catch you with your hand on the rear wheel? Tell him, otherwise I will rape your...'

'Save me from them. For God's sake, save me.' Terror was written in his eyes. There were cuts on his cheeks and blood flowed from the corners of his mouth.

'Did you steal these?' I asked him in my firm vicarish voice and once more made the Sikh release his head. He again put his face against my knees and began to whimper: 'No, I did not steal. Please save me from these men. For God's sake, save me.'

The other Sikh gave him a hard kick in the back. 'Liar,' he roared. 'He is the world's biggest liar. I saw him steal with my own eyes.'

They pulled him back, slapped him on the face and began searching his shirt and shorts' pockets. Out came bolts, nuts, screws, small bulbs and other little items which belong to motor-cars. They held them up for everyone to see.

'Does this put any sense in your head?'

The taunt was meant for me. But the Bengali once more sought shelter against my leg, whimpering in the same way.

'Why did you steal?' I asked him.

'I haven't had anything to eat for three days. I was hungry.'

'Liar!' shouted one of the Sikhs again. 'First he said he had not stolen; now he says he has not eaten for three days. Does he look like a man who has not eaten for three days? Just look at him.'

Once more the wretch was dragged back and shown to the spectators. He certainly did not look famished. But then three days do not reduce a man to a skeleton. And who could say what three days of hunger could make a man do!

'I will pay for whatever he has taken, if you forgive him,' I announced, a little pompously.

'We don't want your money,' snarled one of the taxi drivers. 'He is a thief and a liar. We are going to hand him over to the police. They will teach him what it means to steal.'

The spectators agreed. 'There is too much theft already and unless these chaps are severely punished, there will be no peace in this city.'

This was a challenge. The man was a thief. But what made him thieve we did not know. Perhaps he was one of the millions of refugees from Pakistan who swarmed the city looking for a livelihood. Perhaps he had a wife and children who would starve if this man was gaoled—which he undoubtedly would be.

'Listen brothers,' I appealed to the crowd. 'This man is a thief; this man is a liar. But he has had enough punishment. Why do you want to send him to prison? His family which is innocent will suffer.'

The thief confirmed my fears. 'Yes' he wailed at the top of his voice, 'my wife and three little children will starve. I have never done this sort of thing before; they will die of shame. Please forgive me; I will never steal again.'

'He is lying again,' said one of the spectators stepping out of the ring. 'I have seen him arrested for theft in this very maidan a few months ago. Weren't you caught thieving before?'

The man again clutched my knees and began to cry louder than before. He had no answer. Nor had I. He was a habitual thief and a liar. He probably had no family; and if he did have one, they must have got used to his going in and out of gaol. He was a menace to society and obviously the best thing to do was to put him away somewhere.

I did not let them beat him anymore. They tied his hands behind his back with their turbans and led him away to the police station. I heard him crying and wailing to me for help till he was round the corner. But I had done my duty. My conscience was clear. I tried to dismiss the incident from my mind.

Might he have a wife waiting for him somehere under some bridge where beggars live? No! he was a liar, one could not believe anything he said. I had done my duty. My conscience was clear.

I walked back to my hotel and ordered myself a large Scotch and soda. It looked wonderful with blocks of ice floating on top and the glass nicely frosted. Mayn't his children be crying for food? I ordered another. Of course he had no children! How could anyone believe anything said by a man like him! I had done my duty. My conscience was clear.

I took the second whisky and the third and the fourth and signed a chit for Rs 16. I had no appetite for dinner and went to my air-conditioned bed-room. Shouldn't I have asked him if he had a wife and children and where they lived? I might have saved them the anguish of waiting all night and perhaps given them the Rs 16 for food! Why should I let the talk of a thief and a liar bother me? I had done my duty. My conscience was clear. I was going to sleep the sleep of the just.

I changed into my night clothes. I picked up my trousers to put them under the pillow to be pressed. Then I noticed that the sides of the legs below the knees where the thief had hidden his face were spattered with blood.

Black Jasmine

'This is Martha—Martha Stack. Do you remember me? We were together in Paris thirty years ago.' The voice was creamy: unmistakably American Negro.

'Martha!' shouted Bannerjee enthusiastically into the mouthpiece. 'Of course I remember you! What on earth are you doing in Delhi? Why didn't you let me know you were coming?'

'Didn't know myself till the last minute before the plane left New York. But here I am in the Ashoka. Simply dying to see you again.'

'One moment Martha!' He put the palm of his hand on the mouthpiece, spoke to his wife, and resumed the dialogue. 'Come for dinner and meet the family.'

'Love to! Didn't know you had a family.'

'Wife and grown up children. Boy, twenty; girl, fifteen. Its been a long time you know! Thirty years! What about you?'

'No family no more. I've run through two husbands. Am by myself now', she laughed. 'Much nicer.'

'I'll call for you at seven. I hope you will be able to recognize me, I've gone somewhat grey and fat.'

'Don't worry honey, we all get old and fat', she replied. 'See you around seven. *Namastey*. Haven't forgotten that.'

Bannerjee put down the receiver. He tried to look bored. His wife put him out of countenance: 'Old girl friend?' she asked with a smile.

'No girl friend. A woman I met a the Sorbonne thiry years ago.'

'That's not what you told me first! Isn't she the one in your album? Must be quite a smasher.'

'Wasn't too bad to look at; but negroid. Thick lips, fuzzy hair and that sort of thing. We were the only coloured students in the class; so we were sort of thrown together.'

He realized his voice did not ring true. He avoided his wife's eyes. 'I'll have to fetch her from the Ashoka', he announced and went back to his study.

Odd, he said to himself, thirty years ago he had tried to impress

his friends with his association with Martha. He had her photograph
in his album. The picture of the attractive Negro girl in a large
straw hat worn at a coquettish angle, with the inscription, 'Love—
Martha' invariably aroused curiosity. 'And who is Martha?' his friends
thumbing through the album would ask. 'Ask no questions and
you'll hear no lies', he would answer with a smile. And now he had
to pretend that she had been little more than an acquaintance. That's
what marriage does to people; they have to lie about the most
innocent of relationships.

Innocent? Well, almost. His mind went back to the vacation term
lectures on *Literature Francais pour les Strangers* at the Sorbonne. They
were about thirty boys and girls in the class—mostly American
with a sprinkling of Dutch and Scandinavian. He and Martha were
the only coloured students in the group.

Martha attracted attention from the very first day. She sat away
from the others. She was taller than most of the men, coloured and
uncommonly attractive. On the second day some boys introduced
themselves to her and sat beside her. On the third she came up to
Bannerjee. 'Do you mind if I sit next to you? I am Martha Stack, I
am American', she said holding out her hand. 'My name is Bannerjee',
he replied half standing up, 'I am from India.'

Thereafter they had sat alongside in the class.

Bannerjee was usually an early arriver. He put his note-book on
the seat beside him to indicate that it was 'taken'. He waited for
Martha. Her receding forehead and fuzzy hair showed above the
stream of incoming students. She walked slowly, her hips swayed
rhythmically. She dropped gently into the seat beside Bannerjee.
'And how are we this morning? For God's sake don't get up each
time you see me.' The fragrance of Jasmine spread about her. Why
hadn't her parents named her 'Yasmeen'? Such a pretty name and
much more appropriate than Martha. During the lessons Bannerjee's
eyes would stray to his neighbour: her broad, powerful wrist adorned
with a bracelet of gold coins which jingled as she wrote, her dark,
brown arms and then her breasts—large for her bony frame but
taut as unripe mangoes. When she went out, Bannerjee watched
her slender form and swinging buttocks.

Bannerjee's admiration remained impersonal till the boys began
to tease him. 'You lucky blighter! You're the only one she seems to
notice.' But Bannerjee could not bring himself to make a pass at
her. She was too tall for him. Her dress was too loud; if he took **her**

out, people were bound to comment. In any case it was a bit silly to come all the way to Europe and bed a woman blacker than yourself!

Martha took the initiative. One morning as they were walking out of the class together she asked him casually, 'care to join me for a cup of coffee?' And after the coffee when the waiter came for the bill and Bannerjee fumbled in his pocket, she took a firm grip of his wrist. 'No you don't! I asked you, I pay. When you take me out, I'll let you do it.' She kept her hand on his wrist till the waiter had taken the money from her. Bannerjee felt compelled to ask her out again. And thereafter they had coffee together every day. Martha insisted on paying on alternate days. But this did not prevent Bannerjee from putting his hand in his pocket; nor Martha from holding it and saying, 'no Sir, its my turn.'

Martha took the second step. 'For God's sake stop calling me Miss Stack! I am Martha. What's your first name?'

'My real name is Hiren but at home they call me Gulloo.'

Martha pressed his hand warmly. 'You're Gulloo to me.'

Bannerjee told her that he had given her an Indian name. And once again Martha pressed his hand and said 'that's sweet! I like Yasmeen. And you are going to be the only one in the world to call me by that name'. She came close to him; he felt her breath on his forehead and caught a whiff of the negroid smell he had heard his friends talk of. He found it pleasant—warm and sexy. Much nicer than the sour-milk smell of the white women.

'Suppose I should get back to my French verbs: *J'aime, vous aime, nous aimons . . .*' She laughed and turned away.

Bannerjee wasted many hours day-dreaming the way he would seduce Martha. And yet every time she gave him an opening, he withdrew into himself. Only ten days remained for the closing of the term.

Martha gave him yet another chance. 'Last weekend!' she exclaimed with a sigh. 'So it is', replied Bannerjee laconically. 'How time flies!' Martha seemed determined to force the pace. 'Let's go some place; we may never meet again', she pleaded. 'Let's get out into the open country', suggested Martha. 'Somewhere up the Seine where we could bathe and lie in the sun.'

It was a hot, sunny day in August. They took an early morning train out of Paris. It was practically empty. They sat facing each other in an empty compartment. Martha had brought a pile of American magazines. Bannerjee plunged into them and paid little attention to Martha's enthusiastic prattle about the lessons, students who had made passes at her, Paris and her folks back home. They got to their destination without getting any closer to each other. The *place* on the Seine was crammed with bathers.

Martha became the centre of attraction. Her two-piece swim-suit showed her figure to advantage. Her body seemed to be made of whip-cord. And she had the grace and power of Artemis. A group of young men threw a rubber football to her. She hurled it back at them like a discus thrower. It sailed over the heads of the young men and fell several feet beyond them. Martha swam, went on a ski-board and sunbathed on the sand. Bannerjee sat in the canvas chair turning the pages of American magazines.

The train back to Paris was crowded with returning holiday-makers. They were lucky to find places alongside each other. Within a few minutes people were standing in the corridors and the aisles. The compartment was full of laughter and the acrid smoke of Gaulloise cigarettes. Martha's hand stole over Bannerjee's knee, she twined her fingers in his.

Many people got off at suburban stations. One station before Gare d'Orleans, Martha and Bannerjee were left to themselves still holding hands. Bannerjee was deeply absorbed in the landscape of rows of sooty houses and railway sidings. Martha released her hand, slipped it round Bannerjee's neck and gently kissed him on the ear. Bannerjee put down the magazine he was pretending to read and turned to Martha. She took him in her arms and pressed her thick lips on his. She kissed him on his eyes, cheeks and ears. She bit him passionately on his neck leaving a dark, lipstick-stained tooth mark. Bannerjee surrendered himself to the onslaught. He felt the girl's hot breath all over his face and neck and smelt the wanton negroid body-odour. The train slowed down. Martha released Bannerjee from her grasp. She took a wad of paper-hand-kerchiefs from her bag. 'Here, Gulloo darling wipe your face; I've made such a mess of it.' While Bannerjee scrubbed his lips, chin and eye-lids, Martha repainted her lips and daubed her cheeks with rouge. The train pulled up at Gare d'Orleans.

They had a snack in a students' cafe. Martha stretched her arms and stifled a yawn. 'I am tired! all this bathing and the sun and every-thing else. I must go home. I can fix you a drink in my room to speed you on your way.'

Bannerjee knew what was coming. Could he cope with her?

It was a small room with a bed, an arm-chair and a table. On the table was a silver-framed photograph of Martha's family: her parents, two brothers and two sisters—all large and bony and very negroid. On the floor were heaped different kinds of American magazines. Clothes were strewn on the bed.

Martha poured out two Cinzanos and handed one to Bannerjee. 'Gulloo, here's to us', she said raising her glass—and then kissed him on the lips.

'Here's to us, Martha', replied Bannerjee—and let her kiss him again.

Martha drained her glass in a gulp and placed both her hands on Bannerjee's shoulder. 'Gulloo, I am going to miss you', she said looking him straight in the eyes.

'Me too', replied Bannerjee with some effort.

His eyes dropped to her bosom. 'What are you staring at?' she reprimanded without taking her arms off his shoulders. Bannerjee paid his first faltering compliment. 'You know what Martha, you remind me of the picture of Venus. Know the one I mean? By the Italian—of Venus rising out of the sea!'

'Botticelli's birth of Venus? Why, it's the nicest compliment anyone has ever paid me. That calls for another drink.' She refilled the glasses and gave him a gentle kiss on the forehead. Then she stretched herself on her bed with her hands beneath her head. Bannerjee's eyes wandered restlessly on Martha's body.

'And now what are you gaping at, may I ask? One would think you'd never seen a woman before in your life.'

Bannerjee cleared his throat. 'Well, nothing like this one.'

They fell silent. Martha swallowed what remained in her glass. 'If you promise not to touch me, I will let you see me. I have a nice figure.'

'I promise.'

Martha got up and switched off the light. Bannerjee heard the rustle of clothes and the snap of elastic. 'You can switch on the light now.'

Bannerjee rose from his chair. His eyes remained glued to the nude dimly visible in the glow of the street lamp; his trembling hands caressed the wall. He found the metal knob and pressed it. The light flooded back into the room. He was hypnotized by Martha's large bosom and very black and oversized nipples. With difficulty he forced himself to look lower—the fuzz of her pubic hair and the broad flanks of her muscular thighs.

'Do you like me?' She clasped her hands above her head and slowly pirouetted round on her toes like a ballet dancer. 'How's that?'

Bannerjee gulped the spittle that had collected in his mouth. 'Beautiful', he mumbled. He reclined with his back to the wall.

'Come and kiss me.' Martha held out her arms to him. Bannerjee advanced with uncertain tread and took Martha in his arms. She had made him promise that he would not touch her; and now ... he kissed her passionately on her breast, her flat belly and navel. Martha grabbed him by his hair and turned his face towards her. 'Patience', she commanded. Her legs twined about his and she hungrily took his mouth in her own. Passion welled up in Bannerjee's frame and drained out of his system. He went limp in Martha's embrace. Her breath and the odour of her body began to smell unpleasant to him.

'What's the matter, honey?' asked Martha stepping back.

'This is too much for me. I must go home.'

'All right, if that's what you wish.' She wrapped her dressing gown and lit a cigarette. There was a scowl on her face.

'No, no, Martha, it is not like that', he protested. 'It's best, if you don't wish to ... you know'.

'I suppose so.'

They sat in silence. Bannerjee took her hand. It was cold and unresponsive. She stubbed out her cigarette. 'I am tired, honey', she said getting up. 'Thank you for the nice day.' She kissed him coldly on the forehead and almost pushed him out. He heard her lock her door behind him.

Three days later, he saw her off on the boat train at Gare St Lazare.

That was thirty years ago.

For many years the vision of Martha standing stark naked in the centre of the room had acted like an aphrodisiac. Although he had failed her and was often mortified by the memory, he invoked her assistance to meet his wife's demands. And more often than not it was Martha Stack and not Manorama Bannerjee who received the bounty of his ultimate passion. The tropics and the tedium of an eight-hour day, six days a week played havoc with his constitution. As the years rolled by even the figure of the chocolate nude with its oversized, black protruding nipples and fuzzy pubic hair failed to arouse him. He tried to recall when last he had been cajoled to make love to his wife: months, if not a year; and what a job it had been!

'Don't worry honey, we all get old', that's what Martha had said.

He did not see a Negro woman in the lounge of the Ashoka and rang up Martha's room. 'I'll be down in a second. We've just come back from sight-seeing and I thought I'd change for dinner. Won't be long', she replied.

He watched the elevators come down, disgorge groups of American tourists and shoot up for more. At long last came one with only one passenger; it could not take any more. Filling the entire cage was the form of Martha; six foot tall and broader than any woman Bannerjee had ever seen. She waddled out and held out her fat, fleshy arms to greet him. 'Honey, you've gone fat', she exclaimed pointing to his little paunch. Bannerjee held out a limp hand. 'Martha, I can't say you haven't changed.'

Martha put her arms on her ample waist. 'Now that's not a very nice thing to say to an old friend, is it?' She roared with masculine laughter. 'I've put on a bit of weight, haven't I? I am going to shake it off before I get home. Let me drop my room key.'

She wheezed up to the hall porter's desk. The metamorphosis staggered Bannerjee. Her behind was one enormous mass of hulking flesh; her waist had assumed the same proportions as her bosom and her posterior. Even her neck which had been so slender had accumulated fat. And her once athletic legs were stumpy like those of English charwomen. She was like the picture of Aunt Jemima advertising good, wholesome, instant pudding.

Martha took Bannerjee's arm to walk down the carpeted stairs. Bannerje noticed the sniggers of the bell-boys; the commissionaire turned away and exchanged a lewd remark with the night watchman. Martha's voice was as loud as her dress. She heaved herself into the front seat of Bannerjee's tiny Fiat millicento. 'Not meant for an oversized American', she exclaimed heartily.

At home Martha fared better than Bannerjee had expected. Her unabashed compliment—'Why you old so and so, where did you pick up such a lovely wife?' made her doubly welcome. She handed out gifts: her own lipstick to Bannerjee's daughter, a ballpoint pen to the son, a compact to Mrs Bannerjee. Mrs Bannerjee was kind and condescending; even if her husband had ever desired Martha, there was nothing physically desirable about her now. The evening passed off well.

Martha glanced at her watch. 'I've got to get up early to catch my plane; I think I should be getting back. Can I get a cab?'

'My husband will drop you at the hotel', insisted Mrs Bannerjee.

'Wish you could have stayed longer.' Bannerjee knew that if it had been an attractive woman, his wife would have 'volunteered' to keep him company, or asked one of her children to take a little fresh air.

Martha kissed Mrs Bannerjee and her children and again squeezed herself into the Fiat millicento. 'Nice family you have', she said. 'That wife of yours is certainly pretty. Must have been quite a smasher in her time.'

'She retains her youth better than I', answered Bannerjee, 'some people are made that way.'

He boldly took her arm up the stairs and to the hall porter's desk. Martha again looked at her watch. 'If you like a quick drink, I can fix you one in my room. I can make up for lost sleep in the plane tomorow.'

'For old times sake', replied Bannerjee stepping into the elevator. After the dismissal of Martha as a woman by his family, he felt it was up to him to make up to her.

Martha got two tumblers from the bathroom and fetched a bottle of Scotch from her wardrobe. She held it up against the light. It was almost half full. 'Must finish it, no point taking whisky back with you. Soda or water?'

'A splash of soda for me, please.' Bannerjee got up to take his drink. They clinked glasses; Bannerjee gave her a gentle kiss on the lips.

'This seems pretty familiar to me—except for the follow up. Too fat for that sort of thing', she said smiling broadly. Her gums showed like red rubber. 'Thank you honey, this has made my journey worthwhile. I was wondering if you'd ever kiss me again.'

She poured out another drink, sank into an armchair and waived Bannerjee to the sofa, 'Do sit down'. The gesture was clearly meant to keep Bannerjee at a distance. Bannerjee noticed the gold necklace with a cross dangling between her bosom; perhaps she had become religious—or just like him, old and indifferent to sex. Bannerjee sipped his Scotch; he could hardly bare to look Martha straight in the face. And yet he did not want to do anything which would betray his disappointment and hurt her. He poured himself a third drink and came and sat on the arm of Martha's chair. He put his hand on Martha's forehead. Her skin was greasy. He tried to run his fingers through her hair; it was like tangled wire-gauze. He looked down at her. She had shut her eyes and seemed quite unconcerned. Bannerjee turned up her face and pressed his lips on hers. She sat impassively without opening her mouth. Bannerjee realized that the poor thing had lost all confidence. He slid on the chair in her lap and kissed her more tenderly.

Visions of the Martha he had known in Paris came back to him and a forgotten passion warmed his limbs. Both of them slipped down from the chair on to the floor. Martha lay back—and enormous mound of flesh without any animation. Her eyes remained closed—as if she could not bear to look at herself. Bannerjee's hands went searching for her undergarments. She protested weakly: 'What will your wife have to say'! He knew he could not let her down a second time.

The Bottom-Pincher

I am not a bottom-pincher, but I would like to be one. Like some people are granted freedom of a city I would like to be granted freedom to pinch female citizens' bottoms. Pinching is not the right word. If the bottom is nicely rounded, I would like the freedom to caress it in the cup of my palm. If it is very large or very small, I would like the freedom to run a finger up its crevice. Only if it sags would I want the freedom to take the sagging flesh between my thumb and index finger and tweak it. However, no city has yet conferred such freedom on me.

I am a law-abiding citizen. My employers think well of me. I belong to the best club and am on the governing body of the YMCA. In short I am a respected member of the community. This inhibits me from taking liberties with females' bottoms save with my eyes. As soon as I get close to one I would like to stroke, I warn myself of the consequences. I tell myself that the lady may not like my interfering with her bottom. She may start a shindy. She may collect a crowd and some sanctimonious type though he be a bottom-pincher himself, may take the law into his hands and beat me up. Such thoughts bring beads of sweat to my forehead.

For me bottom-pinching has been a spectator-sport. Again I use a wrong expression. The sport is limited to watching bottoms. Until recently I had not had the privilege of watching anyone pinching them.

A crowded city like Bombay provides ideal conditions for bottom-watching. And the garments in which Indian female bottoms are draped are infinitely more varied than anywhere else in the world; saris, gararas, lungis, skirts (Indian style ghagra as well as the European full lengths and minis), stretch pants, bell-bottom trousers, churidars—you can encounter all varieties in fifteen minutes any time any place. My favourite beat is the half-mile stretch from my office to a conjunction of five roads round a statuary called Flora Fountain. The best time is the lunch hour when it is most crowded. It is not much of a walk, it is more like an ant's crawl, dodging people, bumping into them, brushing off beggars, grinning past whores soliciting for a 'nooner', snarling at touts who want to exchange foreign money. However, I like this bit of the bazar precisely because it is so damnably crowded. There are many roadside book-stalls. The pavements are lined with all variety of smuggled goods: French perfumes, cosmetics and chiffons; Japanese tape-recorders, cameras and transistors playing at full blast. And inevitably a large number of women-shoppers. One has to be very careful not to brush against their bosoms or bottoms. Who wants to be very careful?

It was one such lunch hour that I witnessed a memorable performance of bottom pinching. I was browsing at a pavement book-stall alongside the Dadyseth Parsi Fire Temple. My attention was attracted by a sudden convergence of beggars towards the iron-grilled gate meant to keep out non-Parsis. From the Fire Temple emerged a thin, tall gentleman, in his sixties, wearing a light-blue suit, sola hat and thick post-cataract glasses. He dipped into his pocket and dropped a coin in the hand of every beggar. It was apparent that they knew the gentleman and the time he made his appearance; in the crowd were lepers who had to drag themselves and a blind woman carrying a child on her shoulder. Although I have very strong views on giving money to beggars I could not help admiring one who must by any reckoning part with a small fortune every afternoon.

The gentleman proceeded to walk in the direction of my office. I followed a few paces behind. His charity did not end outside the Fire Temple. He continued to dip in his right-hand pocket and drop a coin in every outstretched hand. Then I noticed that as he passed a group of three women bending over some article at a stall, his left hand brushed the bottom of one of them. By the time the woman straightened up to see who had done it, the gentleman was a few paces ahead in the crowd. He did not look back but walked on, ramrod erect. So it went no. Right hand to give alms to the needy, left-hand to stroke or finger unguarded, unwary female bottoms. What a character! What tremendous risks he ran of being caught, exposed, manhandled!

Next afternoon I was back at the book-stall. I had one eye in a magazine, the other on the gate of the Fire Temple. The beggars had already collected displaying the capital of their trade; lepers their stubby fingerless hands and toes, men on crutches, the blind woman with her babe at the breast. The gentleman emerged from the prayer house; same light-blue suit, sola topee and behind the thick lenses a pale, sexless, expressionless face. He went through the same motions; disbursing his pocketful of coins to outstretched hands. For the blind woman he had more; a rupee note which he insisted on handing to the babe. He said something to the mother which I could at best guess was 'this is for the little one'. In the process he had a nice brush with the young woman's bosom. He was rewarded with a smile. What is a little touch on the breast if you get a rupee for it!

He proceeded on his triumphal march through the milling crowd. It was easy to keep him in sight because of his height, the sola topee bobbing above the sea of heads and the sudden surprise with which women turned to see who had laid a left-handed compliment to their bottoms.

I followed him all the way. He turned in the massive Chambers of Commerce building. The commissionaire saluted him. There was a long queue for the elevator. He went straight into the lift without anyone protesting. He was obviously a big shot.

Some weeks later I was walking back from my office past the Chambers of Commerce building. I saw a cream-coloured Mercedes Benz parked alongside the kerb. Inside were two women—one squat and grey-haired lady bunched up in a corner of the rear seat, the other a teenage girl apparently her daughter. The chauffeur opened both the doors on one side of the car. The commissionaire deposited a brief-case and a stack of files on the front seat. Our hero of the Fire Temple came out trailed by two men who looked like his assistants. The girl bounced out of the car, ran across the pavement and embraced him shouting 'Daddy!' She couldn't have been more than sixteen. Very lovely too! Nut-brown hair falling on her shoulders. Healthy open-air type. And a figure right off the walls of some ancient Hindu temple; large bosom bursting out of her blouse, narrow waist and again a bottom—large protuberant and so provocative as if it were cocking the snook at the world and saying 'I don't give a fart!'

No wonder our hero had such an obsession with bosoms and bottoms. Constant exposure to such temptation! Constant frustration because of not being allowed to touch them!

The next evening I got to know his name. This time the Mercedes Benz was there without its lady passengers. I pretended to admire the car and casually asked the chauffeur who it belonged to.

'The Burra Sahib.'

'Which Burra Sahib?'

'Lalkaka Sahib, who else!' he replied truculently.

There were fourteen Lalkakas in the Bombay telephone directory. All the first names down the list were Parsis—Cyrus, Darius, Framroze, Jal, Jehangir, Nausheer. Then to Ps. One alongside the address Chambers of Commerce Building; the other against 'Residence: Lalkaka Mansion, Malabar Hill.' My repertoire of Parsi first names beginning with P was limited to one, Phiroze. Next morning at eleven when the chances of any member of the family being at home would be minimal I dialled the number. A servant took the call. 'Phiroze Lalkaka Saheb *hai?*' I asked.

The servant replied in a Goan English accent. 'Here no Phiroze Lalkaka. Residence of Pesi Lalkaka. He gawn ophiss.'

'Is Miss Lalkaka at home.'

'Also Missy Baba gawn college. Memsahib awt. No one home. Who calling?'

I hadn't thought of the answer to the question. On the spur of the moment I told the servant to take down my name. I spelt it out slowly for him: 'Mr Bottom-pincher'.

'What number?'

'He knows my number.'

Pesi Lalkaka was not at the Fire Temple the next day. Nor for the whole week following. The beggars assembled at the trysting hour and dispersed with their palms empty. I felt sorry for them. I felt sorry for the good man whose indulgence in a harmless pastime had been put an end to. I had been a spoil-sport.

I wondered how Pesi Lalkaka had reacted to the telephone message. Maybe his wife or daughter had got it first. 'What an odd name! Bottom-pincher! Who is he daddy?' Pesi Lalkaka must have turned pale and stuttered 'I don't know'. They might have questioned the servant. 'He say Sahib know number.' They might have scanned the telephone directory. There wasn't even a Bottom or a Bottomley in the Bombay telephones. They must have dismissed the matter. 'Somebody trying to be funny.' But poor Pesi Lalkaka! What agonies he must suffer knowing that he had been spotted!

A fortnight later Pesi Lalkaka was back at the Dadyseth Fire Temple. He looked uncomfortable. He dropped money in the hands of the few beggars who accosted him. He looked around to see if he could recognize anyone. Then proceeded towards his office. I followed him. He continued to dole out money with his right hand. But this time his left hand was firmly embedded in his coat pocket.

Each time he passed a woman, he turned back to look if he was being followed. Poor, poor Pesi Lalkaka!

He resumed his lunch hour routine of prayer followed by alms-giving on the way back to the office. But now his left hand was always in the coat pocket. And each time he passed by a woman he turned round to look over his shoulder like one pursued by a ghost. So it went on for some time. Pesi Lalkaka seemed to be getting the better of his obsession. He was becoming a commonplace bore.

Not so. It appeared that Pesi Lalkaka had assured himself that the man who had spotted him in *flagrant delicto* once had disappeared from the scene.

One afternoon he was threading his way through the crammed pavement with me trailing a few yards behind him. I saw three women ahead of us examining some merchandise at a stall. Their bottoms presented a tempting variety of sizes and coverings. One was a young girl in blue skin-tight jeans; her buttocks were like two nicely rounded, unripe water melons. Besides her was an older woman in a bright red sari. She was massive like one big pumpkin. The third in the row was a twelve-year Lolita in a white and so mini a skirt that when she bent down it exposed all her thigh and a bit of her bottom as well. I could see Pesi Lalkaka's left arm twitch. The triumverate of bottoms thus served up proved too powerful a temptation to resist. His hand came out of the pocket and caressed the three in quick succession. By the time the women straightened up and turned round Pesi had gone ahead and I was directly behind the three. The old woman glowered and swore '*Badmash*—rascal'. Her younger companion hissed, 'Mummy, don't create a scene'. I had a narrow escape.

I was determined to teach Pesi Lalkaka a lesson. As soon as I got to my office I rang up his residence. It was the same voice at the other end. 'Sahib gawn ophiss. Memsahib resting. Missy Baba gawn college. Who calling?'

'Mr Bottom-pincher.'

'Give number please!'

'Tell him I will ring again in the evening.'

That would fix him! It did.

Pesi Lalkaka was not at the Fire Temple for many days. When ultimately he did appear his left arm was in a sling. He looked paler than ever before. I was sure he had cut himself deliberately. Poor Pesi Lalkaka!

The beggars made solicitous inquiries. He simply waggled his head. As usual I followed him through the crowded corridor. In the few days he seemed to have developed a stoop He plodded on without turning back. Whenever he came to a woman looking the other way his pace slackened. He inclined his head, gave her buttocks a brief, mournful look and proceeded on his way. This time I really felt sorry for him. Or did I? Why didn't he use his right hand to do what his left hand could not? I had read some sociologist's opinion that Indians only used their left hands to caress the genitalia of their women, never the right because they ate with it and did not want it polluted. I wondered if it was that inhibited Pesi Lalkaka. The curiosity got the better of me.

That evening I rang him up. It was the same servant at the other end of the line.

'Hullo! Who calling?'

'The Doctor. I want to speak to the Sahib.'

A few seconds later a voice identified itself 'Pesi Lalkaka this side'.

'How's the left hand, old man?'

'Who is it?' he demanded in a faltering voice.

'Never mind. Try using your right hand. It's more fun', I slammed down the receiver.

I saw no more of Pesi Lalkaka at the Dadyseth Fire Temple for many weeks. Perhaps he had changed his lunch hour place of worship. Perhaps he had found an alternative route where no one trailed behind him. I felt it as a personal affront. I wasn't going to let him get away with it.

The next few days I took my post-lunch hour stroll round the block of the Chambers of Commerce building. I saw Pesi Lalkaka return to the office by different routes. I tried to get him on the phone in his office. He never picked it up himself. I refused to communicate through his secretary. I tried him at home. Here too it was his servant, wife or daughter who took the call. Every time they asked me who I was, I replied I would ring later. It never occurred to me that the fellow might get Bombay Telephones to keep a check on his incoming calls.

Came the Parsi New Year's Day, Navroz. It was a sectional holiday only for Parsis. I had a feeling that Pesi Lalkaka would visit his old haunt, the Dadyseth Fire Temple at his usual hour to be able to give alms to the expectant beggars. I was as usual at the neighbouring book-stall glancing over pages of a magazine with an eye on the temple gate. Standing beside me was a man also turning over the pages of a magazine. He had one eye on me.

There was quite a throng of beggars outside the temple. Parsi gentlemen were dressed in their traditional spotless white muslin caps, starched shirts and trousers. Their ladies wore their saris in the Parsi style, draped straight over their shoulders. The sandal-wood seller beside the doorway was doing brisk business.

My hunch was right; Pesi Lalkaka was there. This time accom-panied by his wife and daughter. He looked very different in his all-white outfit. His arm was not in a sling but both arms were engaged. His right hand rested on his wife's shoulder; his daughter held the left to help him down the temple steps. On Navroz it was Mrs Lalkaka who dipped into her handbag to dole out coins to the beggars. Many complained that they had not seen the Sahib for a long time and made inquiries about this health.

The trio turned their backs towards me to walk in the direction of his office. It was then that I noticed that the Missy Baba was wearing a pleated mini-skirt. Fat thighs, and what a tail! Her but-tocks swayed as if keeping beat to a tango. I cast aside the magazine in my hand and followed them.

Walking three abreast through the crowded pavement was slow business. I walked close behind Missy Baba with my eyes glued to her posterior and languorous music ringing my ears. By the time I came to the parting of ways I was in a high state of exaltation. When would I ever get such a chance again! The desire to caress overcame discretion. I quickened my pace, came alongside the Missy Baba and let my right hand give the silken contour of her behind a loving caress. A voice behind me called 'Mr Bottom-pincher!' I turned back. It was the man I had seen beside me at the book-stall. He took me by the arm, 'Come with me to the police station. Please follow us,' he said to the Lalkakas.

If I had protested the crowd would have given me a rough time. But I could not help pleading innocence, asking my captor what all this was about. 'You will find out. I've been watching you for some days,' he said. I went like the proverbial lamb to the slaughter-house.

What a fool I had been! What would the people say when they read about it in the papers? 'Who could have believed it of him? The old lecher...It often happens to men in late middle-age', etc. I'd be sacked from my job, removed from all committees and expelled from my club. I'd never be able to face the world. Should I kill myself? Or just disappear from Bombay, take the vows of a sanyasi and spend the rest of my days in some sadhu ashram in the Himalayas?

At the police station I was given a few moments to compose myself. The sub-inspector opened a large yellow register to record my statement. I said, 'I have nothing to say. I don't know what it is all about. You have made a big mistake.' It did not impress him. 'No mistake, mister! We checked your telephone calls and what you did I saw with my own two eyes. You better come clean.'

I refused to come clean. I refused to speak to the fellow. He said, 'If you want to consult a lawyer, you can send for one. Otherwise, I'll put you up before a magistrate.'

'I don't want to see any lawyer for anything,' I replied. 'But I would like to see Mr Lalkaka.'

'*Aha*! so you admit to knowing him!' he exclaimed very pleased with himself. He recorded that in his register.

I had put the noose round my own neck.

'Perhaps you would like to see Miss Lalkaka too!' the sub-inspector said with a nasty sneer. 'She will be the material witness to the kind of things you do.'

That was too much for me. I lost my temper and retorted 'Has she eyes behind her head to see who pats her bottom?'

'*Aha*! So you admit somebody did pat her bottom', he replied triumphantly. And wrote it down in his register. I had put yet another noose round my neck. I tried to extricate myself. 'No, I don't want to see Miss Lalkaka. I want to see her father.'

'Why? He has nothing to do with this case.'

'If he has accused me of harassing him, I want to confront him. He has made a terrible mistake.'

'Let's keep Mr Lalkaka out of this. He is a respectable citizen.'

'So am I', I said stubbornly. 'I am every bit as respectable as he.'

We sat glowering at each other. If my reputation was to go down the gutter, I was determined to take Pesi Lalkaka's with me. After a while the sub-inspector gave in. He pressed the bell on the table. A constable came in. 'Ask the Sahib to come in.'

After a while, the constable came back and whispered something in the ear of the sub-inspector. Then left the reporting room. I could hear the voices of the sub-inspector and Pesi Lalkaka, but could only catch a few stray words like confession...water-tight case...not compoundable...Then a long silence. The sub-inspector re-entered and sat down in his chair. He fixed me with his eyes. 'This time I will let you off with a warning. But if I catch you again doing anything or harassing respectable people, you will go to gaol. You can go now.'

I did not want to prolong the agony by protesting my innocence. I got up quietly and left the room.

The cream-coloured Mercedes Benz was parked outside the police station. I turned my face away as I walked past it. I heard a voice call 'Gentleman! Gentleman!' It was Pesi Lalkaka. A very doleful looking Pesi it was. 'Gentleman', he pleaded, 'can I drop you anywhere?'

A Bride for The Sahib

'**W**hat can I do for you, gentlemen?'

Mr Sen asked the question without looking up. He pushed the cleaner through the stem of his pipe and twirled it around. As he blew through it, his eye fell on the rose and marigold garlands in the hands of his callers. So they knew that he had been married that morning! He had tried to keep it as quiet as possible. But as he had learned so often before, it was impossible to keep anything a secret for too long in his nosey native land.

He screwed on the bowl to the stem and blew through the pipe again. Through his lowered eyes, he saw his visitors shuffling their feet and nudging each other. He unwrapped his plastic tobacco pouch and began filling his pipe. After an uneasy minute of subdued whispers, one of the men cleared his throat.

'Well, Mr Bannerjee, what is your problem?' asked Mr Sen in a flat monotone.

'Saar,' began the Superintendent of the clerical staff, 'Whee came to wheesh your good shelph long liphe and happinesh.' He beckoned to the chaprasis: 'Garland the Sahib.'

The chaprasis stepped in front with the garlands held aloft. The Sahib stopped them with a wave of his pipe. '*Mez par*—on the table,' he commanded in his gentle but firm voice. The chaprasis' hands came down slowly; their fawning smiles changed to stupid grins. They put the garlands on the table and stepped behind the semicircle of clerks.

'If that is all,' said Mr. Sen standing up, 'we can get back to our work. I thank you, gentlemen, for your good wishes.' He bowed slightly to indicate that they should leave. 'Bannerjee, will you look in later to discuss the redistribution of work while I am away?'

'Shuttenly, Saar.'

The men joined the palms of their hands, murmured their 'namastes' and filed out.

Sen joined his hands across his waistcoat and watched the smoke from his pipe rise in a lazy spiral towards the ceiling. A new chapter in his life had begun. That's how Hindus described marriage—the third of the four stages of life according to the Vedas. It was alarming, he reflected, how his thought processes slipped into cliches and how Hinduism extended its tentacles in practically every sphere of life. His father had not been a particularly orthodox Hindu and had sent him to an Anglo-Indian school where the boys had changed his name from Santosh to Sunny. Thereafter he had gone to Balliol. He had entered the Administrative Service before the Independent Indian Government with its new-fangled nationalist ideas had made Hindi and a vernacular language compulsory. His inability to speak an Indian language hadn't proved a handicap. As a matter of fact, it impressed most Indians. Although his accent and mannerisms made him somewhat of an outsider, it was more than compensated by the fact that it also put him outside the vicious circle of envy and back-biting in which all the others indulged. They sought his company because he was an un-Indian Indian, because he was a brown British gentleman, because he was what the English contemptuously decribed as a Wog—a westernized oriental gentleman.

Sen's main contact with his country was his mother. Like an orthodox Hindu widow she shaved her head, only wore a plain white sari and went in bare feet. He was her only child so they both did the best they could for each other. She ran his home. He occasionally ate rice, curried fish and sticky over-sweetened confections she made on special occasions. Other times she had the bearer cook him the lamb chops and the shepherd pies he liked better. She had converted one of the rooms to a temple where she burnt incense and tinkled bells to a diminutive image of the black-faced, red-tongued goddess, Kali. But she never insisted on his joining her in worship. Although he detested Indian movies, he made it a point to take her to one every month. She, at her end, did not object to his taking his evening Scotch and soda or smoking in her presence. She never questioned him about his movements. They got on extremely well till she started talking about his getting married. At first he had laughed it off. She became insistent and started to nag him. She wanted to see him properly settled. She wanted to fondle a grandson just once before she died, she said with tears in her eyes. At last he gave in. He did not have strong views on marriage or on whom he would marry. Since he had come back to settle in India, he could not do worse than marry one of his countrywomen. 'All right Ma, you find me a wife. I'll marry anyone you want me to marry,' he said one day.

His mother did not bring up the subject again for many days. She wrote to her brother living at Dehra Dun, in the Himalayan foothills, to come down to Delhi. The two drafted an advertisement for the matrimonial columns and asked for insertions in two successive Sunday editions of the *Hindustan Times*. It read: 'Wanted a fair, good-looking virgin of a high class respectable family for an Oxford-educated Bengali youth of 25, drawing over Rs 1,000 p.m., in first class gazetted Government Service. Applicant should be conversant with H.H. affairs. C and D no bar. Correspond with horoscope. P.O. Box No. 4200.'

The first insertion brought over fifty letters from parents who enclosed not only the horoscopes of their daughters but their photographs as well to prove that they were fair and therefore good-looking. A fortnight later the applicatons were sorted out and Sunny's mother and uncle triumphantly laid out nearly a hundred photographs on the large dining table. Their virginity and capacity to deal with household affairs had, of necessity, to be taken on trust. But despite the professed indifference to C and D, the applicants selected for consideration were of the same caste as the Sens and those whose fathers had made offers of substantial dowries. Now it was for Sunny to choose.

This was the first time that Sunny had heard of the matrimonial advertisement. He was very angry and acutely embarrassed as some anxious paarents had travelled up all the way from Calcutta, bribed the clerks concerned at the newspaper office and called on him at the office. He told his mother firmly that if it did not stop, he would call off the whole thing. But as he had given his word, he would accept anyone chosen for him. His mother and uncle quickly settled the matter by selecting a girl whose father promised the largest dowry and gave a substantial portion of it as earnest money at the betrothal ceremony. The parties took the horoscopes of the affianced couple to a pandit who consulted the stars and, having had his palm crossed with silver, pronounced the pair ideally suited to each other and the dates that suited the parties to be most auspicious. That was as much as Sunny Sen could take. He told them quite bluntly that he would be married at the Registry or not at all. His mother and uncle sensed his mounting irritation and gave in. The bride's parents made a nominal protest: the cost of a wedding on the traditional pattern, which included feasting the bridegroom's party and relations, giving presents and paying the priests, could run into thousands of rupees. The registrar's fee was only Rs 5.00. That was how Srijut Santosh Sen came to marry Kumari Kalyani, the eldest of Srijut Profulla and Srimati Protima Das's five daughters. Mr Das was, like his son-in-law, a first class gazetted Government servant.

The honeymoon also created difficulties. His mother blushed as if he had said something improper. The Das's were outraged at the suggestion that their daughter should go away for a fortnight unaccompanied by a younger sister. But they resigned their daughter to her fate. Her husband had been brought up as a Sahib and she must follow his ways.

Sen's thoughts were interrupted by his colleague Santa Singh bursting into the room. The Sikh was like the rest of his race, loud and aggressive: 'Brother, you think you can run away without giving us a party?' he yelled as he came, 'we insist on having a feast to welcome our sister-in-law.'

Sen stood up quickly and put his hand across the table to keep the Sikh at arm's length. Santa Singh ignored the proffered hand, came round the table and enveloped his friend in his arms. He planted his wet and hirsute kisses on the Sahib's cheeks. 'Congratulations, brother, when are we to meet our sister-in-law?'

'Soon, very soon,' replied Sen, extricating himself from the Sikh's embrace and wiping his cheeks. And before the words were out of his mouth, he knew he had blundered: 'As soon as we get back from our honeymoon.'

'Honeymoon!' exclaimed Santa Singh with a leer; he took Sen's hands in his and squeezed them amorously. 'I hope you've had yourself massaged with chameleon oil; puts more punch into things. You should also add crushed almonds in your milk. Above all, don't overdo it. Not more than....' There was no stopping the Sikh from giving unsolicited advice on how to approach an inexperienced virgin and the proper use of aphrodisiacs. Sen kept smiling politely without making comment. When he had had enough, he interrupted the Sikh's soliloquy by extending his hand. 'It was very kind of you to have dropped in. We will call on you and Mrs Singh as soon as we are back in Delhi.'

Santa Singh took Sen's hand without any enthusiasm. 'Goodbye. Have a nice time,' he blurted and went out. Sen sat down with a sigh of relief. He knew he had not been rude. He had behaved with absolute rectitude—exactly like an English gentleman.

A minute later the chaprasi raised the thick curtains to let in

Mr Swami, the Director of the Department. Sen again extended his hand across the table to keep the visitor at arm's length: the native's desire to make physical contact galled him. 'Good morning, Sir.'

The Director touched Sen's hand with his without answering the greeting. His mouth was full of betél saliva. He raised his face to hold it from dribbling out and bawled out to the chaprasi: 'Hey, spittoon *lao.*'

The chaprasi ran in with the vessel which Sen had ordered to be removed from his room and held it under the Director's chin. Mr Swami spat out the bloody phlegm in the spittoon. Sen opened his table drawer and pretended he was looking for his match box. The Director sat down and lit his bidi. 'Eh, you Sen, you are a dark harse. By God, a pitch black harse, if I may say so.' Mr Swami fancied his knowledge of English idiom. 'So quietly you go and get your-self hitched. My steno says "Sir, we should celebrate holiday to celebrate Sahib's marriage!" I say, "what marriage, man?" "Sir, Mr Sen got married this morning." "By God", I said, "I must get the truth, the whole truth and nothing but the truth right from the harse's mouth—the dark harse's mouth."' The Director stretched his hand across the table. 'Clever guy you eh?' he said with a smirk. Sen touched his boss's hand with the tip of his fingers. 'Thank you, Sir.'

'What for thank you? And you come to the office on the day you get married. Heavens won't fall if you stay away a few days. I as your boss order you to go back home to your wife. I will put in a demi-offical memo. What do you say?'

The Director was pleased with himself and extended his hand. Sen acknowledged his boss's wit by taking his hand. 'Thank you, Sir. I think I will go home.'

'My God, you are a Sahib! I hope your wife is not a Memsahib. That would be too much of a joke.'

The Director left but his betel-stained smirk lingered on like the smile of the Cheshire Cat and his last remark began to go round and round in Sen's head with an insistent rythmic beat. 'I hope your wife isn't a Memsahib, not a Memsahib, not a Memsahib. I hope your wife is not a Memsahib.'

Would his wife be a Memsahib, he mused as he drove back home for lunch. It was not very likely. She claimed to be an M.A. in English Literature. But he had met so many of his countrymen with long strings of firsts who could barely speak the English language correctly. To start with, there was the Director himself with his 'okey dokes' and 'by gums' who, like other South Indians, pronounced eight as 'yate', an egg as a 'yagg', and who always stumbled on words begining with an 'M'. He smiled to himself as he recalled the Director instructing his private secretary to get Mr M.M. Amir, Member of Parliament, on the phone. 'I want Yum Yum Yumeer, Yumpee.' The Bengalis had their own execrable accent: they added an airy 'h' whenever they could after a 'b' or a 'w' or an 's'. A 'virgin' sounded like some exotic tropical plant, the 'vharjeen,' 'will' as a 'wheel,' and the 'simple' as a 'shimple.'

There was much crying at the farewell and the bride continued to sniffle for a long time afterwards in the car. She had drawn her sari over her forehead down to her eyes and covered the rest of her face with a silk handkerchief into which she blew her nose. When Sen lit his pipe, she firmly clamped the handkerchief on her nostrils. 'Does the smoke bother you?' was the first sentence he spoke to his wife. She replied by a vigorous shake of the head.

They stopped at a mango orchard by the roadside to have lunch. His mother had made two separate packets with their names in Bengali pinned on them. The one marked 'Sunny' had roasted chicken and cheese sandwiches. The other contained boiled rice and pickles in a small brass cup with curried lentils. His wife poured the lentils on the rice and began to eat with her fingers.

They ate without speaking to each other. Within a few minutes they had an audience of anxious passers-by and children from a neighbouring village. Some sat on their haunches; others just stood gaping at the couple or commenting on their being newly married. Sen knew how to deal with the rustic. 'Are you people hungry?' he asked sarcastically.

The men turned away sheepishly; but the urchins did not budge. 'Bugger off, you dirty bastards,' roared Sen, raising his hand as if to strike. The children ran away to a safe distance and began to yell back at Sen, mimicking his English. 'Buggeroff, Buggeroff,' they cried. 'Arey he is a Sahib, a big Sahib.'

Sen ignored them and spoke politely to his wife. 'Pardon the language,' he said with a smile. 'Would you like to sample one of my sandwiches? I don't know whether you eat meat; take the lettuce and cheese; it is fresh cheddar.'

Mrs Sen took the sandwich with her curry-stained fingers. She tore a strip off the toast as if it were a chapatti, scooped up a mixture of rice, curry and cheddar and put it in her mouth. She took one bite and stopped munching. Through her thick glasses she stared at her husband as if he had given her poison. She turned pale and, being unable to control herself any further, spat out the food in her mouth. She turned her face the other way and brought up the rice and curry.

'I am dreadfully sorry,' stammered Sen.'The cheddar upset you. I should have known.'

Mrs Sen wiped her mouth with the end of her sari and asked for water. She rinsed her mouth and splashed it on her face. The lunch was ruined. 'We better be on our way,' said Sen, standing up. 'That is if you feel better.'

She tied up her brass cup in a duster and followed him to the car. They were on the road again. She fished out a silver box from her handbag and took out a couple of betel leaves. She smeared one with lime and catechu paste, put in cardamom and sliced betel nuts, rolled it up and held it out for her husband.

'I'm afraid I don't touch the stuff,' he said apologetically. 'I'll stick to my pipe if you don't mind.' Mrs Sen did not mind. She slipped the leaf in her own mouth and began to chew contentedly.

They got to the rest-house in good time. The rest-house bearer took in the luggage and spread the bedding rolls. He asked Mrs Sen what they would like for dinner. She referred him to her husband. 'Just anything for me,' he replied, 'omelette or anything. Ask the Memsahib what she would like for herself. I will take a short walk before dinner.'

'Don't go too far, Sahib,' continued the bearer. 'This is wild country. There is a footpath down to the river which the Sahibs who come to fish take. It is quite safe.'

Sen went into the bedroom to ask his wife if she would like to come out for a walk. She was unpacking her things. He changed his mind. 'I'll go for a short stroll towards the river. Get the bearer to put out the Scotch and soda in the verandah; there's a bottle in my suitcase. We'll have a drink before dinner.'

His wife nodded her head.

The well-beaten fishermen's footpath snaked its way through dense foliage of sal and flame of the forest, ending abruptly on the pebbly bank of the river. The Ganges was a magnificent sight; a broad and swift-moving current of clear, icy-blue water sparkling in the bright sun. It must have been from places like where he stood, he thought, that the sages of olden times had pronounced the Ganges the holiest of all the rivers in the world. He felt a sense of kinship with his Aryan ancestors, who worshipped the beautiful in nature, sang hymns to the rising sun, raised goblets of fermented soma juice to the full moon and who ate beef and were lusty with full-bosomed and large-hipped women. Much water had flowed down the Ganges since then and Hinduism was now like the river itself at its lower reaches—as at Calcutta where he was born. At Calcutta it was a sluggish expanse of slime and sludge, carrying the excrement of millions of pilgrims who polluted it at Hardwar, Banaras, Allaha-bad, Patna and other 'holy' cities on its banks, and who fouled its water by strewing charred corpses for the fish and the turtles to eat. It had become the Hinduism of the cow-protectors, prohibitionists—and chewers of betel leaves. That must be it, he thought cheerfully. His was the pristine Hinduism of the stream that sparkled before him; that of the majority, of the river after it had been sullied by centuries of narrow prejudices. He walked over the pebbled bank, took up a palmful of the icy-cold water and splashed it on his face.

The shadows of the jungle lengthened across the stream and the cicadas began to call. Sen turned back and quickly retraced his steps to the bungalow. The sun was setting. It was time for a sun-downer.

Tumblers and soda were laid out on the table in the verandah. The bearer heard his footsteps and came with a bunch of keys in his open hand. 'I did not like to open the Sahib's trunk,' he explained. 'Please take out the whisky.'

'Why didn't you ask the Memsahib to take it out?'

The bearer looked down at his feet. 'She said she could not touch a bottle of alcohol. She gave me the keys but I don't like to meddle with the Sahib's luggage. If things are misplaced . . . '

'That's all right. Open my suitcase. The bottles of whisky and brandy are right on the top. And serve the dinner as soon as the Memsahib is ready.'

It was no point asking his wife to sit with him. He poured himself a large Scotch and lit his pipe. Once more his thoughts turned to the strange course his life had taken. If he had married one of the English girls he had met in his University days how different things would have been. They would have kissed a hundred times between the wedding and the wedding night; they would have walked hand-in-hand through the forest and made love beside the river; they would have lain in each other's arms and sipped their Scotch. They would have nibbled at knick-knacks in between bouts of love; and they would have made love till the early hours of the morning. The whisky warmed his blood and quickened his imagination. He was back in England. The gathering gloom and the dark, tropical forest, accentuated the feeling of loneliness. He felt an utter stranger in his own country. He did not hear the bearer announcing that dinner had been served. Now his wife came out and asked in her quaint Bengali accent, 'Do you want to shit outshide?'

'What?' he asked gruffly, waking up from his reverie.

'Do you want to shit inshide or outshide? The deener ees on the table.'

'Oh I'll be right in. You go ahead. I'll join you in a second.' Good lord! What would his English friends have said if she had invited them in this manner! The invitation to defecate was Mrs Sen's first communication with her husband.

A strong sweet smell of coconut oil and roses assailed Sen's nostrils as he entered the dining room. His wife had washed and oiled her hair; it hung in loose snaky coils below her waist. The parting was daubed with bright vermilion powder to indicate her status as a married woman. He had no doubt that she had smeared her body with the attar of roses as her mother had probably instructed. She sat patiently at the table; being a Hindu woman, she could not very well start eating before her husband.

'Sorry to keep you waiting. You should have started. Your dinner must be cold.'

She simply wagged her head.

They began to eat: he, his omelette and buttered slice of bread with fork and knife; she, her rice and lentil curry mushed in between her fingers and palm of her right hand. Sen cleared his throat many times to start a conversation. But each time the vacant and bewildered look behind the thick lenses of his wife's glasses made him feel that words would fail to convey their meaning. If his friends knew they would certainly have a big laugh. 'Oh Sunny Sen! How could he start talking to his wife? He hadn't been properly introduced. Don't you know he is an Englishman?'

The dinner was eaten in silence. Kalyani Sen emitted a soft belch and took out her betel-leaf case. She rolled a leaf, paused for a split-second and put it in her mouth. Sunny had promised himself the luxury of expensive Havana cigars over his honeymoon. He took one out of its phallic metal case, punctured its bottom with a gold clipper and lit it. The aromatic smoke soon filled the dining room. This time his wife did not draw the fold of her sari across her face; she simply clasped her hands in front of her mouth and discreetly blocked her nostrils with the back of her hands.

They sat in silence facing each other across the table; she chewing her leaf—almost like a cow chewing the cud, thought Sen. He, lost in the smoke of his long Cuban cigar. It was oppressive—and the barrier between them, impassable. Sen glanced at his watch and stood up. 'News,' he exclaimed loudly. 'Mustn't miss the news.' He went into the bedroom to fetch his transistor radio set.

Two beds had been laid side by side with no space between them; the pillows almost hugged each other. The sheets had been sprinkled with the earthy perfume of khas fibre and looked as if they also awaited the consummation of the marriage performed earlier in the day. How, thought Sen, could she think of this sort of thing when (they hadn't even been introduced! No, hell) barely a civil word had passed between them? He quickly took out his radio set and hurried back to the dining room.

He tuned in to Delhi. While he listened in to the news, the bearer cleared the table and left salaaming, 'good night, Sir.' Mrs Sen got up, collected her betel-leaf case and disappeared into the bedroom.

The fifteen minutes of news was followed by a commentary on sports. Sen had·never bothered to listen in to it. He was glad he did because the commentary was followed by the announcement of a change in the programme. A concert of vocal Hindustani music by Ustad Badey Ghulam Ali Khan had been put off to relay a performance by the Czech Philharmonic Orchestra from New Delhi. Ghulam Ali Khan was the biggest name in Indian music and even the Anglicized natives had to pretend that they admired the cacophony of gargling sounds he produced from the pit of his stomach. Members of the diplomatic corps were known to sit through four hours of the maestro's performance lest they offend their Indian hosts or be found less cultured than staffs of rival embassies. The Czech Philharmonic had come to India for the first time and the wogs who ran Delhi's European Music Society had got away with it. Pity, thought Sen, he wasn't in town; he could have invited the right people for dinner (tails, of course!) followed by the concert. How would his wife have fitted in a party of this sort?

The sound of applause came over the air, followed by an announcement that the opening piece was a selection from Smetana's 'The Bartered Bride'. Sen was transported back to the glorious evening at Covent Garden and the Festival Hall. Smetana was followed by Bartok. The only thing that broke the enchantment was the applause between the movements. How could one expect the poor, benighted natives to know that the end of a movement was not the end of the symphony!

There was an interval of ten minutes. The last piece was Sen's favourite—Dvorak's Symphony No. 5 in E minor. He poured himself a liqueur brandy (V.S.O.P.), drew a chair and stretched his legs on it. He had never heard Dvorak as well performed even in Europe. A Cuban cigar, an excellent Cognac and the world's greatest music, what more could one ask for! He gently decapitated the cigar of its ashy head, lay back in the armchair and closed his eyes in complete rapture. By the final movement he was fast asleep with the cigar slowly burning itself out between his lips.

Neither the applause, at the end of the concert, nor the silence and the cackling of the radio woke Sen from his slumber. When the cigar got too hot, he opened his mouth and let it drop on his lap. It slowly burnt through his trouser and then singed the hair on his under-belly. He woke with a start and threw the butt on the ground.

Although the cigar had only burnt a tiny hole near a fly button, the room was full of the smell of burning cloth. That was a narrow escape, thought Sen. He switched off the transistor and glanced at his watch. It was well after midnight. He blew out the oil lamp and went to the bedroom.

An oil lamp still burned on the table. His wife had fallen asleep— obviously after having waited for him. She had not changed nor taken off her jewellery. She had put mascara in her eyes. Her tears had washed some of it on to her cheeks and the pillow had a smudge of soot.

Sen changed into his pajamas and slipped into his bed. He stared at his wife's gently heaving bosom and her open mouth. How could he? In any case, he didn't have the slightest desire. He turned the knob on the lamp. The yellow flame turned to a blue fluting on the edge of the wick, spluttered twice, then gave up the struggle and plunged the room into a black solitude.

The bearer came in with the tea-tray and woke him up. 'Sahib, it is after nine. Memsahib has been up for the last four or five hours.

She has had her bath, said her prayer and has been waiting for you to get up to have her chota hazri.'

Sen rubbed his eyes. The sun was streaming through the verandah into the room. His wife had made a swiss roll of her bedding and put it away on the top of her steel trunk. 'I'll have my tea in the verandah,' he replied, getting up. He went to the bathroom, splashed cold water on his face and went out.

'Sorry to keep you waiting. I seem to do it all the time. You should really never wait for me.' He stretched himself and yawned. 'I am always . . . what on earth.'

His wife had got up and, while his face was still lifted towards the ceiling, bent down to touch his feet. He was her husband, lord and master. He looked down in alarm. She looked up, tears streamed down both her cheeks. 'I am unworthy,' she said half-questioning and half-stating her fears. And before he could reply, she drew the flap of her sari across her eyes and fled inside.

'What the hell is all this?' muttered Sen and collapsed into an armchair. He knew precisely what she meant. He sat a long while scratching his head with his eyes fixed in a hypnotic stare on the sunlit lawn. He had no desire to go in and make up to his wife.

The bearer came, looked accusingly at the untouched tray of tea and announced that breakfast was on the table. Sen got up reluctantly. She would obviously not have anything to eat unless he cajoled her. And he was damned if he was going to do it. Again he was wrong. She was at the table. He avoided looking at her.

'Tea?' he questioned and filled her cup and then his own. Once again they ate their different foods in their different ways without saying a word to each other. And as soon as the meal was over, she went to her betel leaves and he to his pipe. She retired to her bedroom. He took his transistor and returned to the verandah to listen in to the morning news.

The arrival of the postman at noon put the idea in his head. It was only a copy of the office memorandum sanctioning him leave for a fortnight. He walked in waving the yellow envelope bearing the legend—'On India Government Service Only.'

'I am afraid we have to return at once. It's an urgent letter from the Minister. He has to answer some questions in Parliament dealing with our department. I'll get the bearer to help you pack while I give the car a check up. Bearer, bearer,' he yelled as he walked out.

Half an hour later they were on the road to Delhi; a little before sunset, Sen drove into his portico. The son and mother embraced each other and only broke apart when the bride knelt down to touch her mother-in-law's feet. 'God bless you, my child,' said the older woman, touching the girl on the shoulder, 'but what ...'

Her son pulled out the yellow envelope from his pocket and waved it triumphantly. 'An urgent summons from the Minister. These chaps don't respect anyone's private life. I simply had to come.'

'Of course,' replied his mother, wiping off a tear. She turned to her daughter-in-law. 'Your parents will be delighted to know you are back. Why don't you ring them up?' A few minutes later Mrs Sen's parents drove up in a taxi. There were more tears at the re-union, more explanations about the letter from the Minister. There was also relief. Now that the bride had spent a night with her husband and consummated the marriage, she could return to her parental home for a few days.

Sen spent the next morning going round the local bookshops and coffee houses. The weekend followed. On Sunday morning, when his mother was at prayer, he rang up the Director at his home to explain his return and ask for permission to resume work. 'My mother has been keeping indifferent health and I did not want to leave her alone for too long.' He knew this line of approach would win both sympathy and approval. The Director expressed concern and spoke warmly of a Hindu son's sacred duty towards his widowed mother. 'And we must celebrate your wedding and meet your wife ... as soon as your mother is better.'

'Yes, Sir. As soon as she is up to the mark, we will invite you over.'

The mother being 'a bit under the weather' and 'not quite up to the mark' became Sen's explanation for cancelling his leave and not having a party. It even silenced Santa Singh who had planned a lot of ribaldry at Sen's expense.

Days went by—and then weeks. Kalyani came over with her mother a couple of times to fetch her things. She came when her husband was in the office and only met her mother-in-law. It was conveyed to Sunny Sen that, under the circumstances, it was for the husband to go and fetch his wife from her home. Sen put off doing so for some time—and then had to go away on a tour of inspection to southern India. It was a fortnight after his return that his parents-in-law learnt that he was back in town. The relations between the two families became very strained. Nothing was said directly but talk about the Sens being dowry-seekers and Sen's mother being a difficult woman started going round. Then Sunny got a letter from his father-in-law. It was polite but distinctly cold. From the contents it was obvious that it had been drafted and written on the advice of a lawyer with a carbon copy made for use if necessary. It referred to the advertisement in the matrimonial columns and the negotiations preceding the marriage, the money given on betrothal and in the dowry, the wedding and its consummation in the forest rest house on the Ganges. Sen was asked to state his intentions.

For the first time, Sen realized how serious the situation had become. He turned to his mother. A new bond was forged between the mother and son. 'It is a matter of great shame,' she said firmly. 'We must not let this business go too far. You must fetch her. I will go away to my brother at Dehra Dun for a few days.'

'No, Ma, I will not have anyone making insinuations against you,' he replied, and pleaded, 'in any case you must not leave me.'

'No one has made any insinuations and I am not leaving you. This will always be my home; where else can I live except with my own flesh and blood. But you must get your wife. Let her take over the running of the house and become its mistress as is her right. Then I will come back and live without worrying my head with servants and cooking and shopping.'

Sen flopped back in his chair like one exhausted. His mother came over behind him and took his head between her hands. 'Don't let it worry you too much. I will write to my brother to come over to fetch me. He will go to your father-in-law's and bring over your wife. Before we leave, I will show her everything, give her the keys and tell the servants to take orders from her. When you come back from the office you will find everything running smoothly.' She kissed her son's hair. 'And do be nice to her, she is only a child. You know how much I am looking forward to having a grandson to fondle in my lap!'

Sen found the whole thing very distasteful. He felt angry with himself for allowing things to come to such a pass. And he felt angrier with his wife for humiliating his mother and driving her out of her home. He would have nothing to do with her unless she accepted his mother. He instructed his cook-bearer about the arrangements of the bedrooms. If the new mistress asked any questions, he was to say that those were his master's orders.

On Monday morning, when the bearer brought him his morning

tea, he told him not to expect him for lunch and to tell his wife not to wait for him for dinner as he might be working late in the office. He had breakfast with his mother and uncle. He promised to write to his mother every day to tell her how things were going. 'You must try and understand her point of view,' admonished his mother. 'She has been brought up in a different world. But love and patience conquer all.'

Sen was the last to leave his office. He drove straight to the Gymkhana Club. For an hour he sat by the bathing pool, drinking ice-cold lager and watching the bathers. There were European women from the diplomatic corps with their children; there were pretty Punjabi girls in their pony tails and bikinis; there were swarthy young college students showing off their Tarzan-like torsos as they leapt from the diving board. This surely was where he belonged—where the east and the west met in a sort of minestrone soup of human limbs of many pigments, black, brown, pink and white. Why couldn't he have married one of these girls, taught her proper English instead of the Americanized chi-chi which they thought was smart talk.

The bathers went home. Sen got up with a sigh and went to the bar. He was greeted by several old friends. 'Hi, Sunny, you old bastard. What's this one hears about you?'

Sunny smiled. 'I don't have to proclaim everything I do from the house tops, do I?'

'Like hell you do. You stand drinks all round or we'll de-bag you and throw you out in front of all the women.' Three of them advanced towards him.

'Lay off, chaps. Bearer, give these B.Fs. what they want. What's the poison?'

They sat on the high stools and downed their drinks with 'Cheers,' 'here's mud in your eye' and 'bottoms up.'

'Where's your wife?' asked one. 'Don't tell me you are going to keep her in the seclusion of the purdah like a native!'

'No ruddy fears,' answered Sen. 'She's gone to her mother's. Would you chaps like another?'

One round followed another till it was time for the bar to close. One of the men invited him home for dinner. Sen accepted without a murmur.

It was almost 1 a.m. when Sen drove back into his house. He was well fortified with Scotch to gloss over any awkwardness. He switched on the light in the hall and saw trunks piled up against the wall. His wife had obviously come back. There was no light in her bedroom. She must have gone to sleep many hours earlier. He switched off the hall light, tip-toed to his bedroom, switched on the table-lamp, went back and bolted the door from the inside. A few minutes later, he was fast asleep.

The bearer's persistent knocking woke him up. His head rocked as he got up to unfasten the bolt. What would the bearer think of the Sahib bolting his door against his wife? He couldn't care less. The throbbing in his head demanded all his attention.

'Shall I take tea for the Memsahib?' he asked.

'She does not have bed-tea,' replied Sen. 'Isn't she up yet?'

'I don't know Sahib; she had also bolted her door from the inside.'

Sen felt uneasy. He swallowed a couple of aspirins and gulped down a cup of strong tea. He lay back on his pillow to let the aspirins take effect. His imagination began to run away with him. She couldn't. No, of course not! Must have waited for him till midnight, was scared of being alone and must have bolted the doors and was sleeping late. But he had been nasty to her and she might be over-sensitive. He decided to rid himself of the thought. He got up and knocked at the door. There was no response. He went to the bath-room and then tried her door again. There was no sound from the inside. He went to the window and pressed it with both his hands. The two sides flew apart and crashed against the wall. Even that noise did not waken her. He peered in and caught the gleam of her glasses on her nose.

With a loud cry Sen ran back into the house and called for the bearer. The master and servant put their shoulders to the door and battered against it. The bolt gave way and they burst in to the room. The woman on the bed didn't stir. A white fluid trickled from her gaping mouth to the pillow. Her eyes stared fixedly through the thick glasses. Sen put his hand on her forehead. It was the first time he had touched his wife. And she was dead.

On the table beside her bed was an empty tumbler and two enve-lopes. One bore her mother's name in Bengali; the other was for him. A haunted smile came on his lips as he read the English address:

'To,

    Mr S. Sen, Esq.'

Maiden Voyage of the Jal Hindia

I had seen many ships go out to sea but had never experienced as much excitement as I did at the embarkation of the *Jal Hindia*. That was strange because it wasn't really her maiden voyage. As a British ship she had carried cargo across many seas. She had been bought by an Indian firm of shippers and converted into a cargo-cum-passenger vessel. The Indian High Commissioner's wife had come all the way from London for her second christening. She had smashed a discreetly cracked coconut on her bow and pronounced, 'I name thee *Jal Hindia*. May God bless thee and all those that sail on thee.' A naval band had struck up the Indian National Anthem as a massive tricolour slowly went up the flagstaff. It was a proud moment, a moment which brought tears in the eyes of many Indians. 'Our first passenger ship...' They could say no more for emotion. A fortnight later, the *Jal Hindia* was docked in Liverpool. Her holds were bursting with cargo; each one of her 150 berths—both in the first and the tourist classes—had been taken. I had a tiny cabin on the port side all to myself.

A printed passenger list lay on the dressing table. I was surprised to find a large number of English names among them. There was also a Pakistani diplomat and his family. The rest of the first class passengers were Indians except for one whose name indicated that she must be a foreigner married to an Indian—Mrs Magda Braun Singh. She was obviously travelling alone. Among the tourist class passengers was a Pakistani hockey team returning from a triumphant tour of Europe. Then there were nearly two dozen Singhs. From their first names I could guess that they were Sikh pedlars of the Bhatra community who have become a familiar sight in the suburbs of London and the Midlands. One name in the tourist list attracted my attention because the academic distinctions at its end spread right across the page: Dr Chakkan Lal, M.A.(Alld.), D.Litt. (Eng. Lit., Leeds).

It was an interesting crowd—Europeans, Pakistanis and Indians:

an auspicious beginning for an Indian ship to be carrying people of diverse races and religious creeds. Could also be a source of tension! I went up on the deck to see what was going on. It was not difficult to identify the different groups. At one end were the Sikh pedlars— the greybeards in a huddle looking very morose; the younger ones, armed with transistors, looking very pleased with life. Alongside them were the hockey players in green blazers with the crescent-moon crest of Pakistan. The Pakistani diplomat was immaculately dressed in a Saville Row suit and with a Jinnah cap on his head. A group of subordinates, similarly attired, were fawning around him and his family. Then there was a dapper little man, barely five feet high, wearing thick horn-rimmed glasses, darting forward and backward in the crowd, introducing himself and handing out his visiting card. Who could this be but Dr Chakkan Lal, M.A. (Alld.), D.Litt. (Eng. Lit., Leeds)! The Europeans were at the other end: obviously box-wallahs and tea-planters. They did not look a pleasant crowd although some of the women in their midst were attractive. The group which attracted most attention were Indian Army officers surrounding a European woman dressed in a peacock-blue sari with a broad gold border. She was tall—almost a head taller than her officer friends. She was blonde and full-bosomed as only Nordic women can be. A steward brought a tray of champagne glasses. The men raised their glasses to the blonde and burst into: 'For she's a jolly good fellow,' in the pucca 'wog' style of the Indian Army.

'Attention please!' crackled the loud-speaker impatiently. 'This is the final call. The *Jal Hindia* is about to sail. All visitors are requested to leave the ship immediately.' The warning was accompanied by two blasts from the siren. People embraced each other in the Punjabi style; shook hands in the English fashion; the blonde kissed her friends on both sides of their cheeks like a European. The officers made a feeble effort to sing 'Auld Lang Syne,' but gave it up after whining the opening bars.

The visitors went ashore and resumed shouting and waving from the wharf. The gangway was drawn up and the ship began to edge away from the dock. Old Sikh pedlars formed a semicircle and said a prayer of thanksgiving. Tears trickled down their beards as they watched the shores of the land that had given them sustenance over the years recede. Within a few minutes the ship cleared the docks. She gave another blast of her siren and headed for the open sea. It was a bright May afternoon. Hundreds of gulls followed in the wake, diving and screaming in the blue sky. They looked like bits of confetti at a wedding. A thought crossed my mind. It wasn't after all a maiden voyage; it could be more appropriately called the honey-moon trip of the *Jal Hindia*.

As I turned to go back to my cabin, I caught sight of the blonde. She was looking down at something with a benign expression on her face. I passed by her and noticed the object of her attention. It was the little man in horn-rimmed glasses who, I had already decided, was Dr Chakkan Lal. I was not wrong. I heard him repeat the name as he handed a visiting card to the lady. 'You can keep this,' he said, generously, as if he was offering a box of chocolates. 'I am in the tourist class, but I will be coming over to see you, surely.'

At tea-time I had another chance to give the first class passengers the once-over. We were allotted our tables for meals. The elite were given the place of honour at the Captain's table. It consisted of an English couple—a coarse-looking man (who I later learned was John Tyson, manager of a shipping firm in Calcutta) and his wife, a slender woman with feline agility in her movements. Included in the same category were the Pakistani diplomat, his wife and daughter, and the massive blonde. I found myself at a table near the kitchen with a South Indian couple and a young barrister from Bombay. I noticed the look of dismay on the faces of my table-mates when they saw me; they had been put at the bottom of the social ladder—for what else could I be but a pedlar who had money and developed fancy notions! I turned on my special haw-haw accent of English to impress them. The young barrister, Minoo Patel, decided the issue in my favour. He was a shrewd judge of men and rightly guessed that I would be willing to pay for the privilege of his company by signing for all the drinks.

The first evening there was an after-dinner dance in the first class lounge. The Europeans wore their dinner-jackets; some of the Indians wore sherwanis. The blonde appeared in a bright red sari with a blue blouse cut low down in the centre. Mrs Tyson was in a snow-white dress sparkling with sequins. The contrast between the two women was remarkable. One looked like a sexy Juno, the other like a marble statue of Diana.

After dinner, we thronged up to the lounge for the dancing. Except for the rectangular space in the middle, the room was packed. The Pakistani hockey team, still in their green blazers and grey flannel-trousers, occupied the sofas on one side; the young Sikh pedlars, now in multi-coloured turbans, salwar and kurta, sat cross-legged on the other. The remaining seats were occupied by other passengers from the tourist class. They were attired in a variety of styles, ranging from dhotis to striped pajama suits. There was no use protesting. In a socialist state, there could be no class distinctions (at least on the dance floor) and the *Jal Hindia* was the first passenger ship of socialist India. 'You can go to the tourist class whenever you like; there'll be no objection,' we were told.

The band struck up a quick-step. No one ventured on the floor. They tried a waltz, a samba and then a tango. The French chalk on the floor remained untrod. The would-be dancers huddled round the bar, fortifying themselves like timid matadors before entering a bullring. The Captain looked dismayed. 'Somebody should break the ice,' he said loudly to the crowd at the bar and then gestured to the band. The strains of a slow English waltz floated across the lounge. A thin, piping voice rose from about waist-level, 'May I have the pleasure?'

It was Professor Chakkan Lal, looking very spruce in his dinner-jacket. He had addressed the invitation to the Junoesque blonde. Before she could reply, the Captain accepted the invitation on her behalf by shouting, 'Bravo—come along, everyone on the dance floor.'

Professor Chakkan Lal strutted across the open rectangle and waited for his partner threading her way through the chairs and sofas. As she arrived on the floor, he bowed to her and held out his arms like one about to send a semaphore signal. The blonde took one of the Professor's hands in hers and put the other on his shoulder. The Professor slid his right arm round the lady's ample behind, laid his head sideways on her equally ample bosom, closed his eyes in a beatific smile and with a jerk took her systematically across the floor: long-long short; sideways. Long-long, short . . .

The crowd gaped in amazement; the sheer audacity of the little man stupefied them for some time. But by then other couples, including the Tysons, had taken the floor.

The slow waltz and the quick-step went off nicely. Then came the tango. Professor Chakkan Lal had by now established a mono-poly over the blonde. She was delighted, too, having previously experienced only reluctance from men to dance with a woman taller than themselves. But the tango was a disaster. The Professor's amorous movements sent the pedlars and the hockey players into giggles. The distinct beat of the music encouraged them to keep time by clicking their fingers and slapping their thighs. The Tysons left the floor in disgust. Other couples followed them, leaving only the Professor in his closed-eyed dream world and his partner on the floor. He was shaken out of his reverie by the tremendous applause that followed. He was too much of a gentleman to take notice of vulgarity. He led his partner by the hand to the bar and offered her a drink.

Next evening the dancing was in the tourists' lounge. The blonde accepted the Professor's invitation and danced with him despite the ill-mannered clicking and giggles of the onlookers. Thereafter one saw them together alternating their evenings between the first and the tourist, wherever the dancing was. The Professor ignored all the witticisms about his size and the bawdy jokes about a monkey in love with a she-camel. The blonde also cultivated a sense of protection towards her diminutive admirer and turned down other people's invitations. By the time the *Jal Hindia* rounded the Straits of Gibraltar, everyone had got used to seeing the two together. The men smiled, the women whispered. The Professor and his dancing partner treated the rest of the passengers with contemptuous disdain.

The *Jal Hindia* entered the Mediterranean—its perennially blue and sparkling waters. The men changed from grey flannels to shorts: the women into cotton dresses. Mrs Tyson, whose figure was meant for it, and the blonde, whose figure was not, began to appear in bikinis. There was shuffle-board, deck-tennis and bathing in the canvas pool. The calm sea and balmy air were loaded with romance, particularly for those romantically inclined, of whom Professor Chakkan Lal was one. He had a large repertoire of amatory verse which he produced on appropriate occasions. The blonde's English was not very good, but she understood the emotions behind these poetic outbursts and nodded appreciatively.

One night, the Professor took the blonde to the deck to get a little fresh air after a sweaty waltz. It was a moonless night but the 'vault of heaven,' quoted the Professor, 'was thick with patines of bright gold.'

'You know somsing about zee stars?' she asked.

'Not much,' replied the Professor modestly. 'I recognize Hesperus, the evening star sacred to lovers.' Then added hoarsely, 'Of course, it is too late for it now.'

'Zen you must show it to me tomorrow,' said his companion, putting her hand on his shoulder. The gesture sent a thrill through the Professor's little frame. 'With pleasure. That is the cluster of the Pleiades,' he said, pointing above his head. 'If you can count six, you have good eye-sight.'

'Where?'

'There,' he replied, taking her hand and raising her index-finger towards the sky. 'How many can you count?'

He held her hand while she counted: 'One, zoo, sree, four, faive… zat's all.' He did not let go her hand. She seemed to have forgotten that he was holding it. He entwined his fingers in hers. The declaration had been made and not rebuffed.

Music floated up from the bowels of the *Jal Hindia* to the upper deck. The Professor showed no impatience to go down. The blonde squeezed his hand in a friendly way and said, 'Come along, Prof… one last danz and zen to bed.'

The Professor's head went round in a whirl. What did she mean by that last sentence? He followed her to the lounge, he danced in a daze. Sweat came on his forehead, froze, and broke out afresh. Did she mean what she had said? The music stopped. There was a weary applause. The dancers trailed off the floor. The Professor mopped his forehead with his handkerchief. He couldn't ask her in the glare of the lights. But, as they passed the bar into the dark side of the room, he quietly slid his hand in hers. She turned and smiled. 'No more danz,' she said firmly. 'Sank you very much for ze iffening.'

It was now or never. And she hadn't said good night. He looked around to reassure himself that no one was overhearing. He summoned up all his courage and asked her in a whisper, 'What's the number of your cabin?'

'Twenty-one, boat deck.'

Professor Chakkan Lal lay on his back and stared at the bunk above him. He was still in his dinner-jacket. He switched on his bed light and tried to read. Every few minutes he looked at his wrist watch. From above the rim of his book he saw that two of his cabin mates, who were students, had also got their bed lights on and were reading. One of them switched off his light. 'Professor, aren't you going to change?' he asked. Chakkan Lal grunted, without making a reply.

'Professor Sahib has a date,' ventured the other. The boys sniggered.

How did they guess? The Professor dismissed the observation with another contemptuous grunt. He shouldn't have been travelling tourist with this bunch of students, pedlars and hockey players. But what could he do with a salary of Rs 350.00 per month!

He glanced at his watch again. It was only five minutes past eleven. He got up from his berth, picked up his tooth-brush and paste, saw from the corner of his eyes that the boys had noticed what he was doing, and slowly walked out of the cabin. He put the tooth-brush and paste in his pocket and went up on the deck. He was dismayed to find quite a number of people about. Some had brought their pillows and were looking for places where they could sleep in the open. Would the first class passengers be doing the same?

He looked up at the sky. It was cluttered with stars. He saw the Pleiades and secretly blessed the constellation for bringing him good luck. Even with his glasses he could count only three. Then there was the Great Bear, the Scorpio and the Cassiopeia. That was all he knew of astronomy. But it was enough to sustain the legend of his all-round learning. And weren't the Pleiades going to pay off a handsome dividend? He blessed them again.

The sea was a sheet of black without a ripple. A ship was passing by at a distance. The radio operators of the two ships were flashing signals across the water. The Professor let the ship disappear into the vast nothingness. The curious passengers retired to sleep. He cupped his palm on his wrist watch. The radium needles glowed, one on top of the other. It was midnight, the trysting time for lovers.

With his heart wildly aflutter, the Professor made his way to the first class deck. He tried to look as casual as he could. What would he say if someone questioned him? That he was taking aspirin for someone? No! That might entail: who for? Ah, yes, 'I dropped my gold cuff-links while dancing.' That would work. But the stewards he passed were too engrossed in their own work to question him, and he found himself in the first class lounge.

The Professor now suddenly realized that he did not know the plan of the first-class deck, and that if someone caught him in the maze of the corridors, he would be hard put to explain. He mounted the stairs and came on the boat-deck. The Professor was assailed with doubts and fears. Hadn't she said, 'Twenty-one'? She may have just given him the information. Almost as if he had asked, 'How old are you?' and she had replied, 'A lady never tells her age, but I will tell you as a special favour. I am twenty-one.' Had she realized what he had in mind when he had asked her the number of her cabin? How could one be sure with these foreigners! Her English was so poor.

The Professor dismissed these cowardly thoughts from his mind. He had crossed the Rubicon, the barrier which said 'First Class Passengers Only.' He had thrown down the gauntlet for an amorous escapade and it had been picked up without hesitation. There was no turning back now. But how to go forward? There were two rows of cabins with their portholes opening on the deck. The corridor which separated the two rows and into which the doors bearing the numbers of the cabins opened had the main light switched off. Only a dim blue bulb lit the way for those who knew their destination. The Professor had to know the exact location of Cabin 21 before he could take liberties with its door. He decided to peep into the portholes as he passed.

He took a few deep breaths of the warm sea-breeze, looked up for the blessings of his patron constellation—the Pleiades—then started from one end.

Despite the dark interior, it was not difficult to see the berths in the cabins. And he knew that his blonde had a single-berth cabin to herself. Besides, many had their bed lights on. A quick glance at the figures sprawled in different stages of disarray was enough to eliminate the first half. Nobody had stirred and, even if some of them were awake, they had taken scant notice of his presence.

The Professor came to a four-berth cabin bathed in the blue of the light. His first casual glance changed into a stupefied stare. There were two children on the upper berths. On one of the lower berths lay sprawled a mass of what looked like the putrefying flesh of a male, clad in shorts. On the other was a life-size painting of Velazquez's 'Venus'—an exquisitely beautiful nude lying with her face towards the wall. Professor Chakkan Lal's eyes traced the outlines of the figure from its tousled head, the shoulders, down the faintly perceptible bosom to the very narrow waist; then meandered about the thighs, the legs and the feet—and back over the torso to the tousled head.

The nude turned on her side and lay now on her back. The Professor's academic mind interpreted it in terms of another famous painting, 'Maja Nude,' by Goya. But he recognized her mortal frame. It was Mrs Tyson. He gaped in speechless wonder. His feet lost their mobility, his heart its amorous pursuit.

The hypnotic spell was broken by the screaming of a child. The hulking mound of male flesh on the lower berth suddenly came to life. The Professor quickly stepped back into the dark. He heard a gruff voice ask, 'What's the matter, Mary?'

'Daddy, there was somebody at the porthole.'

'At the porthole?' repeated Mr Tyson. 'I can't see anyone. You must be dreaming.'

'What time is it, dear?' asked Mrs Tyson.

'12.30.'

'Go to sleep, Mary. There is no one about at this hour. If you feel scared, you can come down to Daddy's bunk. Good night, dear.'

'Good night, Mummy.'

Professor Chakkan Lal did not stir. That was a narrow escape and he wasn't going to take any more chances.

Suddenly the main fuse blew off and the lights went out. The ship was plunged in absolute darkness. After three minutes, which seemed to the Professor like three hours, the lights came on. The Professor had by now lost track of the cabins he had already examined and eliminated, and had to start all over again. And once again his feet came to a halt in front of the Tysons' porthole, for inside, under the haze of the lapis lazuli blue, lay in recumbent pose 'Venus de Milo'—this time on her belly, with her hands clutching a pillow.

The Professor realized the hazards he was exposing himself to, but his feet had turned into lead and refused to move. His eyes caressed the contours of the marble statue until the spell was broken again by the screaming of a child. This time it was accompanied by a gruff masculine oath. Mr Tyson had woken up and seen the face in the porthole before its owner could withdraw into the dark. He switched on the bright light, sprang out of his bunk and rushed out of the door, shouting, 'I'll teach the swine a lesson.'

Professor Chakkan Lal did not know which way to run, and fear made his already leaden feet heavier. In his confusion, he turned round, went up to the rails and began to look out towards the sea.

Tyson caught the Professor by the collar and hauled him into the beam of light coming out of the porthole. 'I saw you! You dirty nigger! What the hell were you up to, peering through the porthole?'

'I...I...I...' stammered Chakkan Lal. 'It wasn't me. I...I... I... was just standing here.'

'Oh no, you weren't, you bloody liar,' roared Tyson, and landed a sharp slap on the other's face. Professor Chakkan Lal's glasses fell on the deck, followed by the sound of splintering glass.

Lights began to go up in the neighbouring cabins. A murmur of questioning voices rose from all sides. The Professor felt he had to make a stand. 'How...how dare you hit me?' he demanded, weakly.

'I've a mind to throw you into the sea, you dirty little rat!' roared Tyson.

'Leave him alone, John,' pleaded Mrs Tyson.

'What's the matter?' demanded some people, coming up. The Pakistani diplomat and some Europeans appeared in their dressing-gowns. Before Tyson could explain, the Professor pleaded: 'I was just standing here and this man started beating me.'

'You bloody liar!' muttered Tyson, clenching his teeth. 'You asked for it.' He sent his fist smashing into the Professor's face. The Professor staggered backwards and fell on his back. His head hit the edge of a capstan. He lost consciousness.

'You've no business to hit a man like that,' spoke the Pakistani, angrily. 'You can report to the Captain, but you cannot take the law into your own hands.'

'Oh, haven't I?' demanded Tyson, menacingly. 'And what business is it of yours, may I ask?'

Another group of Europeans joined the party. 'What's up, John? What's going on here?' they asked.

'That rat was peeping through the porthole at Jenny...who, who...'

'Oh, was he!' exclaimed a hothead and grabbed the Pakistani diplomat by the collar. 'You fancy yourself, don't you, you smart Alec!' he said. –

'Lay your hands off me,' raged the Pakistani. 'I'll have you gaoled if you dare to do violence to me.'

John Tyson grabbed the man's hand before it could find its mark. 'Not him, you fool, this chap,' he said, pointing to the figure lying sprawled on the floor.

The young man let go the diplomat and stammered an apology. 'Sorry, mister,' he said, 'How was I to know who had been up to mischief.'

'Sorry's not enough,' roared the Pakistani. 'I'll haul you before the Captain and teach you chaps how to behave. You…you scamps!' His anger had lent his voice a tone of authority. Somebody whispered in the young Englishman's ear, 'Jack, you silly ass, the chap's an ambassador of some sort.'

'Awfully sorry, old chap,' repeated the young man. 'I didn't mean any harm to you. Just a simple mistake.'

The attention of the people was diverted by the appearance of Mrs Tyson, who came out wrapping her dressing-gown about her. The blonde, who was in the next cabin, joined her. Mrs Tyson knelt down to see the damage her husband had done. Her fingers felt the ooze of warm, sticky fluid. She held them against the light, saw blood and cried, 'John, you've killed him.'

'Mein Gott, Mein Gott,' screamed the blonde, clutching her face with both her hands.

The quarrel between the Pakistani and the Englishman subsided. Someone flashed a torch. The Professor lay like an etherized patient on the operating table. A trickle of blood, flowing from under his head, had skirted past the capstan and ran down the deck.

'Somebody get zee doktor,' cried the blonde, 'quickly, zee doktor.'

The Englishman, who had almost hit the Pakistani diplomat, utilized the oportunity to get out of his predicament. He extricated himself from the circle. 'I'll get him,' he cried, as he ran.

'And the Captain, if you don't mind,' ordered the Pakistani, in a tone that became an ambassador.

John Tyson's temper cooled down as suddenly as it had boiled up. The angry looks of the brown-skinned Asiatic unnerved him. He clutched his hair and moaned, 'What have I done! God, what have I done.'

The Pakistani was relentless. 'I will tell you what you have done,' he replied, pronouncing each word distinctly. 'You have murdered an Indian national. Your friend has insulted the Pakistani flag. And both of you have made insulting references to coloured people. At Karachi, your friend will learn his lesson. At Bombay, I trust, you'll learn yours.' He turned round to the Europeans and said, in an oratorical manner, 'It is time you realized that times have changed.'

The ring around the prostrate Professor opened to admit the Captain and the doctor. The clamour of explanations was silenced by the Captain's uplifted hand. 'Please do not disturb the doctor. We will go into this business later.'

The doctor flashed his torch in the Professor's face. There was a red patch on one side where Tyson's fist had caught him. The doctor raised the Professor's eyelids and also felt his pulse. There was plenty of sparkle in the eye and the pulse was beating merrily. He turned the Professor's head and with his fingers felt the contusion caused by the impact of the capstan. The skull was intact; the blood had stopped flowing. The doctor stood up and said with a tone of relief, 'Could have been worse. Can I have some cold water?'

'He is all right, doctor, isn't he?' inquired Mrs Tyson nervously. 'There isn't any danger, is there?'

The doctor replied, lighting his cigarette, 'He'll come round in a minute. Where's that cold water?'

'Sank Gott!' exhaled the blonde loudly.

Tyson brought a flask of iced water from his cabin. The doctor took several palmfuls and sprinkled it on the Professor's face. 'Can we have a little fresh air, please,' he requested, turning to the crowd.

'Will all of you please go back to your cabins?' commanded the Captain. 'The Professor is all right. We will discuss this matter tomorrow morning. Back to your cabins, everyone,' he repeated, clapping his hands.

The crowd retreated a few steps. The Professor had begun to moan and shake his head to avoid the water dripping on his face. The doctor gave him a few gentle slaps on the cheeks. 'You are all right. Wake up.'

Professor Chakkan Lal opened his eyes and turned them like the beam of a searchlight on the people around him. The beam stopped at the blonde. She clutched at her dressing-gown and covered her bosom. She tried to step back into the anonymity of the crowd, but the Professor's eyes transfixed her, like the pin through a butterfly. He raised his hand slowly, pointed an accusing finger at her and drawled like a drunk: 'You are responsible for this.' He closed his eyes and fainted again.

'I…I…don't know vat he iss talking about,' stuttered the blonde. 'I have nossing to do vit eem,' she proclaimed and ran back to her cabin.

Next morning the passengers of the *Jal Hindia* found themselves divided according to their races—the Europeans on one side, the Pakistanis and Indians on the other. The Captain was like a caged animal pacing between the two groups, pleading with them to end the quarrel and let his ship sail into Bombay without any other untoward incident.

The racial conflict produced new attitudes and leaders. Tyson was utterly deflated and willing to pay for the damage he had done— the broken glasses and the doctor's bill. He was even willing to apologize. So was Jack Wilson, who had unwittingly embroiled himself with the Pakistani diplomat. But the consensus among the European group was that Chakkan Lal had deserved what he got—a thrashing was a mild punishment for a chap who came sneaking around and peeped at naked women through the portholes. And as for the Pakistani diplomat, what was he getting so hoitytoity about? Wilson had made a mistake, as anyone might have in the dark, and he had apologized straightaway. What more was required now? These Orientals expected everyone to crawl on their knees, as was their custom. It was a point of honour. These brown-skinned upstarts had to be shown their place. 'You give them an inch and they'll take a yard,' said one of them, using a time-worn cliché. The Europeans foregathered in one corner of the lounge.

The Pakistanis and Indians assembled in another corner to plan their campaign. The young Sikh pedlars were there—some still with their transistors slung on their shoulders like Stenguns. The Pakistani hockey players were also present, some carrying their hockey-sticks. They clustered round the diplomat, who explained the previous night's incident to them in detail. The barrister, Minoo Patel, sat beside him, making an occasional note in his diary. A cigarette glued to his lower lip sent up a wisp of smoke, which made him blink his eyes and so gave his countenance a semblance of acute concentration. Occasionally, he interrupted the diplomat's narrative with sentences like, 'Just a minute. What exactly were the words used by Mr So and So?' or 'Would you mind repeating that?' People craned their necks when Patel interrupted and were deeply impressed with whatever he was putting down on paper. When the diplomat had finished his story, Patel slapped his pencil into his diary and asked, 'Well, where do we go from here?'

That one question made the Pakistani hand over the sceptre of leadership to the barrister, 'That's for you to decide,' he conceded to Patel. 'But we mustn't let the incident go unquestioned.'

'I think we are all agreed on that,' remarked Patel, looking around at his audience. They indicated their agreement. 'Right,' he said, slapping his pencil again. 'If I have your permission to act on your behalf, I shall first send notice to the Captain, asking him to put the two white men concerned under arrest on charges of assault and attempted murder. I shall send a copy of the notice to these men at the same time.'

These brave words made Patel the hero of the India-Pakistan group. There were, however, a few dissenters. One was a young lady from Oxford. She asked in her very refined English, 'I am sorry to interrupt, but I do think we should first find out the truth about this affair. It wasn't the right thing to do, was it?'

'No, it wasn't really the gentlemanly thing to do,' agreed some of them. A young pedlar spoke in support of the Oxford Miss, giving her speech a Punjabi twist. 'If a white chap peep at our mothers or sisters changing saris, what we say? We give him a mukka in his bloody face.'

Patel sensed the chink in the united front of the coloured passengers. He held up his hands. 'Gentlemen, gentlemen, if we are going to start disputing between ourselves, we may as well call the whole business off. We don't know whether Professor Chakkan Lal was peeping—that is the Tyson version. In any case, you don't go about killing people because they happen to pass by a window when your wife is changing. Why didn't she draw the curtains over the porthole if she wanted to sleep naked?' asked Patel triumphantly.

The Oxford Miss was persistent. 'I don't want to sound a note of dissent; I am all for demanding an apology from both these men. But I would like to know what Professor Chakkan Lal was doing at that hour of the night on the first-class deck when he is a tourist passenger.'

Patel rose to the occasion again. 'I will find out from the Professor in the surgery. But I don't think it is very relevant at this stage. All we are concerned with is an unwarranted insult to a senior diplomat, and a violent onslaught accompanied by words which indicate homicidal intent. We take up these issues. The rest is marginal detail.' That silenced the Oxford Miss and everyone else. It recreated the united front against the whites.

Minoo Patel called on the Professor in the surgery. One side of his face had turned blue and he could barely open his left eye. The injury at the back of his skull did not justify the yards of bandage which turbaned his head. The Professor gave his version of the incident. He had simply happened to be passing by the porthole when Tyson had pounced on him. Patel asked him: 'If I am not being curious, Professor, what exactly were you doing there after midnight?'

Professor Chakkan Lal remained silent for a long time, and then said quite blandly, 'That does not concern anyone. That is my own business.'

Patel drafted the legal notices. Before lunch when the passengers had gathered in the lounge—the Europeans in one corner, the Indians and Pakistanis in the other—Patel got a steward to take his two letters across the room to Messrs Tyson and Wilson.

The European group got into a huddle. The notices were read and discussed in whispers. After some consultation, the womenfolk got up and left. The leader of the group took out his pen, scribbled a few words on Patel's letters and put these on the silver platter for the steward to take back to the sender. The steward had a broad grin on his face as he offered the platter to Patel. On it lay the two notices rolled up to give them a phallic semblance.

Not all the Indians or Pakistanis understood the offensive gesture. The diplomat and the barrister did. So also the Miss from Oxford, whose face coloured. The doubts about the rights and wrongs of the conflict vanished and she exploded in anger: 'If you are men, now is the time to give them a suitable reply!'

The Pakistani boys clutched at their hockey-sticks; the Sikh pedlars muttered choice Punjabi abuse. Even Patel felt his temper rise. But he was not a man of violence; he also knew that the Europeans would get the better of the Indians and Pakistanis in a brawl. He help up his hands again and demanded silence. 'Please, please,' he said impatiently. 'Give me just one more chance. I'll bring these rascals to their knees. If I fail, you can do what you like.' The meeting dispersed. Patel and the Pakistani diplomat got down to drafting another notice.

Patel spent the afternoon hammering on his typewriter. A look of triumph hovered on his face. The new notice was not addressed to Tyson or Wilson or the Captain, but to the Egyptian Chief of Police at Port Said. (Messrs Tyson and Wilson and the Captain were served with carbon copies.) It stated that while the ship was on the high seas, assault with intent to murder and insult the dignity of the State of Pakistan had been made by two Englishmen. It further stated that the Captain of the ship had been remiss in not taking action against the culprits and there was serious danger of a breach of peace on board the ship when it entered Egyptian waters. The *Jal Hindia* was due to touch at Port Said two days later and go through the Suez Canal.

Patel circulated the original for signatures. The Indian and Pakistani passengers signed it with great enthusiasm. Copies of the notice with the names of over one hundred signatories typed underneath were handed to Messrs Tyson, Wilson and the Captain.

The Captain begged Patel and the diplomat to stay their hand. They promised to do so, if the culprits made a public apology in the lounge and paid compensation to Professor Chakkan Lal.

The harassed Captain went to the European group and found them in a state of dither. They did not know the law, but had assumed that Patel, being a barrister, knew what he was talking about. They also realized that, no matter what the law was, the Egyptians were not likely to take a kindly view of the Europeans and might detain them at Port Said. There was, however, the question of face. After what had happened, a one-sided apology would be eating humble pie. Gloom descended on their faces. Some were for pocketing their pride and apologizing; others were for holding out (Tyson and Wilson were not in this group). Jennifer Tyson rose to the occasion: 'I will handle this. You leave it to me.'

Mrs Tyson called on the Professor in the surgery. His wound had healed and he was simply prolonging his stay there to avoid questioning by his fellow passengers. Mrs Tyson's visit was more than he could resist. He took the hand she had put out to him and clasped it with great warmth. She ran her fingers through his hair and asked him if it hurt. 'No,' replied Chakkan Lal gratefully. 'Do you want this sordid business to go on, Professor?' she asked him at last. He didn't answer. How could he, without consulting Patel? She continued: 'I was very much flattered that I should have diverted your attention from your object. It wasn't me you wanted to see that night was it, Professor? It doesn't pay to be fickle. Your friend is most offended by your disloyalty.'

Professor Chakkan Lal was embarrassed and he blushed like a woman. He held out his hands to Mrs Tyson. 'Forgive and forget. We are friends.'

Mrs Tyson proceeded to call on Patel and the diplomat. She told them that her husband would not make any apology. But, if it was agreeable to them, she would make amends to the Professor on behalf of her husband, and Wilson would apologize to the Pakistani. She made one condition—that the apologies would be made only after they had passed through the canal and were out of Egyptian territory. Mrs Tyson's terms were accepted. The battle was virtually won.

That evening there was jubilation in the tourist lounge. The Indians and Pakistanis drank to each other's health in unhealthily large potions of liquor. Professor Chakkan Lal was hauled out of the surgery and treated like a hero. The bandages round his head made him look like one.

The *Jal Hindia* stopped for six uneasy hours at Port Said. The Pakistani and Indians went ashore to look around and buy duty-free goods from the stores. The Europeans did their buying from the bum-boats that clustered round the ship. The ship entered the Canal at night and by morning was sailing past Port Tewfik into the Red Sea. The passengers waited for the great day. They were also eager to know the answer to the mystery: 'What had taken the Professor to the first-class deck at midnight?'

The *Jal Hindia* bunkered at Aden and proceeded eastward through the Arabian Sea to Karachi. The Captain announced a fancy-dress ball in the first-class lounge and he invited competitors from the tourist class. He invited the Pakistani diplomat, Patel, Chakkan Lal, the Tysons and Wilson and the blonde to be his guests. Patel and the blonde were to act as judges.

With one stroke the Captain dissipated the racial ill-will that had poisoned the atmosphere aboard the ship. The passengers were themselves a little ashamed of their conduct and were eager to make up to each other.

The competitors came in the costumes usually seen at fancy-dress balls—as maharanis, sadhus, bandits, bewigged seigneurs, Marie Antoinettes. The dancing went on till midnight. The band struck up The Blue Danube and out of a dark corner Jennifer Tyson appeared, leading Professor Chakkan Lal by the hand. Tremendous applause followed and continued right through the performance. The passengers, however, noticed John Tyson get up and leave the hall. Obviously, he could not take it. When the dance ended, Jennifer Tyson said loudly, 'Now, I will make up to the Professor in the way we all know he likes best.' Without warning she kissed the Professor on both his cheeks. There was a deafening roar of appreciation.

The Captain called for a break to judge the fancy-dress competitors. They came in, one by one, and were greeted with appropriate hand-claps. Once more, Jennifer Tyson got up and went up to the microphone. 'Mr Captain, ladies and gentlemen, before the judges give their verdict I would like to announce that there is one more entry, which might also give you the answer to the question that has been plaguing our minds.'

John Tyson made his entrance. He had a black eye and his shirt was torn. He hobbled in on a pair of crutches and came to the centre of the dance floor. Then, he slowly turned round on his heels. On his back was a placard with the legend in bold letters: 'Wrong Cabin'.

India is a Strange Country

This story could also be entitled 'From Babar to Kenneth Tyson' because its theme is the reaction to India of foreigners, starting with the sixteenth- century Mongol invader to the present-day European 'box-wallah'.

Babar did not like India. In his memoirs, the famous *Babar Namah*, he set down his views in no uncertain terms:

'Hindustan is a country that has few pleasures to recommend it; the people are not handsome. They have no idea of the charms of friendly society, of frankly mixing together, or of familiar intercourse. They have no genius, no comprehension of mind, no politeness of manner, no kindness of fellow-feeling, no ingenuity or mechanical invention in planning their handicrafts, no skill or knowledge in design or architecture; they have no horses, no good flesh or bread in their bazars, no baths or colleges, no candles, no torches, not a candlestick ...'

The English translators of the memoirs went out of their way to echo Babar's animus against India. The footnote beneath the passage quoted above reads: 'Babar's opinions regarding India are nearly the same as those of most Europeans of the upper classes, even at the present day.'

Fortunately, there were some foreigners who loved India with as much passion as that with which Babar and 'most Europeans of the upper classes' hated it. It is a curious fact that few countries of the world have aroused as much loathing or affection—it is one or the other—as India. This was as true five hundred years ago as it is today. It is not very surprising that Indians have become sensitive to other people's opinions about them.

Indians usually divide foreigners into three different categories. Most numerous are the haters who dislike both India and the Indians. Next come the 'half-haters' who dislike Indians but like the Indian landscape and the conditions of living: big bungalows, servants, shikar, polo etc. The only natives they can suffer are the Gunga Dins of Rudyard Kipling—faithful as their dogs and who know their place. They particularly dislike educated Indians who are either babus (clerks) or, if Anglicized, wogs—wily oriental gentlemen. The third category consists of lovers who like everything about India and the Indians. They find Indian mysticism more satisfying than Christianity; Indian ragas more melodious than Beethoven's symphonies; the dhoti more sensible dress than trousers; hot curries tastier than European food. They disdain mixing with their own nationals. They learn Indian languages. They eat with their fingers; their women wear saris, put a red spot on their foreheads and say namaste with the palms of their hands joined together. This third category is very small. Indians treat them as the lunatic fringe.

There remains, however, a fourth category—those whose reactions are uncertain. It is the fourth category which arouse the most lively speculation in Indian circles. Kenneth Tyson belonged to this category.

I first met Tyson in the bar of the Gymkhana Club some time in the autumn of 1947—a couple of months after India had gained independence. I was in a party of friends, a Bengali, a Punjabi and their respective wives. Tyson attracted attention as he entered. He towered over the crowd. He was bald. He limped. And he was the first Englishman seen in the place since the Club had passed into Indian hands.

'First white man in darkest Hindustan!' remarked the Punjabi who fancied his wit.

'Who is he?' I asked.

'Don't you know Kenneth Tyson?' he demanded. 'A box-wallah of the pucca Sahib variety. One of the haters, a species becoming very rare in this country.'

Tyson limped up to the bar. The bearer greeted him with an effusive salaam and served him a brandy and ginger ale.

'What is he doing in India when all his ilk have fled?' I asked.

'To have one last chota peg before he puts in his resignation,' suggested the Punjabi. 'Too many natives about the place for the likes of Kenneth Tyson.'

The Punjabi's wife took up the theme with greater vigour. 'You should meet his wife—a real British Memsahib if there is one!' She mimicked Mrs Tyson's accent. 'M'deah, must keep the black man in his place. Give him an inch and he will take a yard, Wot!'

Everyone laughed.

'I think you've got Tyson wrong,' protested the Bengali. 'I had dealings with him when he was posted in Calcutta. Although he did not mix very much with us, he quite obviously liked living there because he never went home on leave.'

'Half-hater!' remarked the Punjabi lady. 'A half-hater married to a full-hater. Jennifer Tyson does not mince her words. "My deah, I'd rather scrub the floors in me own bed-sitter in Tooting Bec than live in one of them ruddy oriental palaces waited on hand and foot by a horde of black flunkeys!"'

'Poor woman, she's had a hard time with somone of the other in her family going down with amoebic,' pleaded the Bengali's wife.

'Occupational disease of the hater,' replied the Punjabi. 'Ever known a lover go down with it? No. It's always these chaps. They boil their drinking water and drown their vegetables in "pinkie" but the amoebae gets them. It's the "Delhi belly" or the "Bombay belly" or the belly of whatever place they happen to be in. Then like the Mullah who runs from his home to his mosque five times a day, the hater's beat is between his bedroom and the lavatory. It is on the antiquated thunder box that the white man has the blackest thoughts about India.'

Tyson turned round; he had obviously sensed that he was being discussed. The Bengali waved to him. Tyson picked up his drink and limped towards our table. 'May I join you?' he asked as he pulled a chair from the next table.

'With pleasure! May I introduce you to my friends...'

We shook hands. We pressed drinks on him. He accepted without fuss. 'I don't mind if I do; a last one for the road. The same for me, bearer, please.' He had three double brandies before he stood up. 'Now if you'll forgive me, I've got my little girl friend waiting for me in the car. I must get her home.'

As soon as he left, the discussion on Tyson was resumed with even greater animosity. 'Not a bad chap, is he?' demanded the Bengali who had introduced us. 'One must not make facile generalizations about people. He is quite willing to make friends with Indians.'

'Now, perhaps,' hissed the Punjabi lady. 'And with suckers who will go on offering him drinks. He didn't bother to return one.'

'Now really!'

'Oh shut up!' exploded the lady. 'Your kind make me sick. Not a bad chap Tyson; he accepts drinks from the blacks.'

No one took up the challenge. The lady continued her tirade,

'His woman is worse than him. She graciously accepts gifts from her Indian acquaintances who keep fawning on her. But she will not allow her children to mix with their's. "My deah, it is not the colour of their skin I mind—my God I am not that narrow!—But I cannot bear to have my kids speaking their awful chi chi sing song!"'

'I think you've got a chip on your shoulder about this black-white business,' protested the Bengali. 'If they do not like it, what is it that keeps them here?'

'Hasn't found a good job in England,' retorted the Punjabi lady. 'His wife is out there on a reconnoitring expedition.'

The analysis continued. Someone quoted Tyson's opinion on Indian sculpture: 'Them eight-armed monstrosities, you can have them, and with my compliments!' As to Indian literature, Tyson echoed the views of his distinguished compatriot—'One shelf of a library in Europe is worth more than the entire learning of the East. I did not say that, Lord Macaulay did.' Indian music 'bores me to tears.' He could not play polo or go out to shikar. What then kept him in India? And why did he forgo his home leave year after year? Did he have a native mistress tucked away somewhere?

I found the answers a few months later. I shall narrate the circumstances which led to their discovery. I was in the habit of taking my dog for a walk every evening. Our favourite promenade was through a beautiful park in which there were many tombs of the Lodhi dynasty. We used to return home before sunset to avoid running into jackals who were known to become vicious during the mating season—and often rabid. One evening we were later than usual. It had got dark; only the domes of the Lodhi mausoleums could be seen silhouetted against the twilight. I quickened my pace and called my dog. The smell of tobacco wafted across the green. I saw the figure of a tall man smoking a pipe and twirling a leash in his hand. When I came closer I noticed his companion; it was a dachshund. Its front half was inside a hole in the ground; its rear was marked by a rat-like tail swishing in the air. The sound of my feet distracted the dachshund. It backed out of the hole, shook the earth off its nose with a loud snort and came yapping towards me.

'Stop it, Martha! Stop it at once!'

'Good evening, Mr Tyson.'

'Oh, hello.' He had not recognized me, but seeing I was a Sikh, added, 'Good evening, Mr Singh. Taking a stroll in the park? Lovely this time of the evening, isn't it? Oh, stop it, Martha!'

Martha scampered back and plunged into the rat hole. 'She's quite happy as long as she has some place to stick her nose into,' remarked Tyson, looking proudly at his dog. 'All dogs are like that. My last one—I lost her two months ago—she used to do exactly the same.'

'I am afraid mine's a little more demanding in the way of exercise. He's rather large and we live in a small flat,' I explained. The words were barely out of my mouth when Simba, my German shepherd, loomed out of the dark. He saw Martha's wiggling tail and applied his inquisitive nose to her posterior. Martha shot backwards, ticked off Simba with a few effeminate yaps and then began to circle round him at break-neck speed.

'Too big for you, girlie! Leave him alone. Come along now, it's getting very late,' he ordered. 'Sweet, isn't she?'

'Very cute,' I replied. I sensed that he did not want to linger on. 'Good night, Mr Tyson. Come along, Simba.'

Thereafter I saw Tyson almost every evening in Lodhi Park. I exercised Simba by doing several rounds of the park. Tyson preferred to stay in the one part which had many rat holes. His dachshund busied itself ferreting for rodents while her master waited patiently by smoking his pipe and twirling the leash in his hand. There they stayed long after sunset. Some evenings I saw his tall figure against the dusk; sometimes the smell of tobacco indicated that he was still somewhere on the lawn. His parting words were always the same. 'That's enough for the evening! Time to go home. Come along Martha sweetie.' The bitch would extricate herself, cock her head at her master as if pleading for 'just one more rat'; then have a quick sniff inside the hole, a loud snort outside and scamper off happily at her master's heels.

The years passed without Tyson taking his home leave. 'I can go when I like, you know,' he explained. 'My leave will accumulate and then I will have a couple of years at one go. Wouldn't that be nicer?'

'But you can't accumulate the passage money.'

'Oh that! Who cares for a piddling passage!'

After some years people stopped asking why Tyson did not go home. During the winter months when his wife was in Delhi, they did a certain amount of entertaining. In the summer when she was away, people asked Tyson over for supper because they thought he was lonely. He always took Martha with him. He left her in the car: the leash was always in his hand.

The years added layers of fat to Martha. Like all ageing dachshunds, Martha, who had never been mated, began to look chronically pregnant with a belly that barely cleared the ground. Tyson became more solicitous in his address.

'Nice old gal; she's getting on you know. She's thirteen—which makes her over eighty if she were human. Mustn't tire yourself out, lady.'

After letting her ferret for a while, he would pick her up and take her back to the car. Martha grunted and sighed in the arms of her adoring master.

One summer evening I happened to be visiting an English friend when Tyson dropped in for a drink. He let Martha out of the car. Our host had an equally aged bull terrier bitch. The two waddled about in the flower beds while we sipped our Scotch in the garden.

'Bet you'd like to get out of this now if you could,' remarked our host referring to the stillness and the heat; the thermometer had been touching 112° every day of the past week. 'Think how nice it would be in a country pub somewhere along the Thames near Richmond! I'd give my left arm to be back in old Blighty.'

Tyson had been through this before. 'I don't mind it, you know! The dry heat agrees with me. Anyway there are all the remaining years of one's life.'

Tyson did not answer. We relapsed into silence. The only sounds were the tinkling of ice in the tumblers and the chirping of crickets. Tyson lit his pipe.

Martha sneezed in the flower bed. The bull terrier bitch joined her. The two snorted in unison, then began to squeal with excitement.

'A bandicoot, I bet,' exclaimed our host, turning back. 'Get it, Flossie! They are a damned nuisance. Come creeping into the house and leave droppings as large as snails. Get it, Flossie!' he commanded.

The dogs redoubled their efforts, yapping and squealing. Every now and then they looked up at their masters for instructions.

A bandicoot ran out of the hole—crying tikkee, tikkee, tikkee. It ran across the lawn towards us. The dogs chased it yapping at a higher and higher pitch. We put up our legs on the table and shouted encouragement to the dogs. 'Here Martha! Here, Flossie!'

The bandicoot turned sharply and made for the road; its shrill tikkee, tikkee marking a sound trail. The dogs ran after it as fast as they could; the bull terrier led the chase by a few yards. The rodent crossed the road and ran down a dry storm-water drain on the other side. The bull terrier was hot on its scent. Martha got to the middle of the road when the headlights of a car diverted her attention. She stopped and turned her large brown eyes towards the glare. A second later the car had gone over her.

Tyson leapt up from his chair and ran out. Martha's back was broken; she wriggled like an earthworm cut in half. Tyson picked her up in his arms and brought her in. His eyes were blurred with tears.

His host rang up for the vet. The vet drove up a few minutes later. He examined Martha and shook his head. He took out a syringe from his bag, loaded it with a fluid and jabbed the needle into the dachshund. 'That will put her out of her misery,' he explained.

Martha died with her large eyes fixed on her master. Tyson broke down and wept like a child.

I did not see Tyson in Lodhi Park again. A few days later notices appeared on the boards of local clubs announcing the sale of his crockery, cutlery, and furniture. He was not going on leave; he had resigned his job and was leaving India for good.

A fortnight later he was at the airport. His English friends and the Indian staff of his office came to see him off. He was his usual quiet, phlegmatic self. He made polite conversation and bowed his head to let the Indians put garlands round his neck. When the loud-speaker announced the departure of his flight, he shook hands without any trace of emotion an his face.

'Well Tyson, you are off at last,' remarked one of his English friends. 'We almost believed you were going to settle down here and take on Indian nationality.'

'No ruddy fear!' replied Tyson, waving his hand in farewell. 'It's these damned uncivilized laws England has for animals. How can you leave a dog you love in quarantine for six months, I ask you?'

Mr Kanjoos and the Great Miracle

Someone asked Lord Krishna, 'what is the greatest miracle in the world?' Mr Kanjoos* turned the tumbler of whisky in his hand and gave us the Lord's reply. 'Krishna said, "the greatest miracle is that although man knows his end is certain, he never entertains the thought of death."' He drained his whisky in a gulp and looked inquiringly into the depths of his tumbler.

Mrs Kanjoos took up the theme. 'As my husband is always saying, you cannot take it with you. Eat, drink and be merry is our motto.' She too drained her whisky and looked at me for confirmation of their views. I had stood them their first drink, I ordered the second round. And why not? I couldn't take my money with me! We had a second each; and then a third. I signed for the lot. The Kanjooses got up to leave.

'You must come and have a meal with us,' said Mr Kanjoos shaking me warmly by the hand. 'Yes, you must drop in whenever you like and have pot-luck,' added his wife.

How absurd that a man as generous should have a name like that! How many people invite a stranger for a meal? That was thirty years ago. During the last three decades I have had the invitation to have pot-luck extended to me many hundred times. Somehow I have never been able to make it. On the other hand the Kanjooses have had pot-luck many times with me. They are a most thoughtful couple. They drop in to call when we are having our pre-dinner drink. They allow themselves to be pressed to have 'one for the road.' And then since it is dinner-time, it doesn't take very much to over-rule Mrs Kanjoos's protest that 'everything is ready at home' and get her to ring up her servant to say that they will be dining out. (The Kanjooses' servant has obviously developed a telepathic communication with his master and mistress. Whenever I do the ringing up, he replies: 'I know'—or does not reply at all—having taken the evening off.)

* Kanjoos is the Hindi word for 'miser'.

Although I haven't had a meal with the Kanjooses, I have got to know their dietary and other habits very well. What's there in a measly chapatti or two when they have given me such a rich feast of their minds and their methods?

Soon after my first meeting I discovered that the Kanjooses were members of the same Golf Club as I. I had not known this despite the fact that the Kanjooses were regular club-goers. This was not altogether surprising: for me the club meant the fairways and the greens and for the Kanjooses it meant the bar. He showed his usual expansiveness by inviting me over. 'Come along and join us, what's your drink?'

'I'll join you in whatever you are having,' I replied, before I noticed that the Kanjooses were not having anything. 'Perhaps a small beer,' I said, 'And what about you?'

'I don't mind,' she murmured coyly.

The bearer came and Mr Kanjoos ordered: 'One beer for the Sahib, a small whisky for the Memsahib, a large one for me.'

The drinks arrived. While they sipped their Scotch, the Kanjooses told me of the many parties they had at their house and of the many people who had got drunk on their whisky. 'If you offer a drink, you must be generous,' remarked Mr Kanjoos sticking his thumbs inside his braces. 'I'd rather have a tomato juice than the sort of whisky people serve you these days—a tumbler full of soda spiked with a few drops of some undrinkable Indian concoction.'

I agreed heartily. And after the hearty agreement I couldn't but order two double Scotches and a beer when it came to my turn. Mrs Kanjoos protested mildly. 'I don't drink very much you know,' she said, 'but if you insist ...'

I insisted. Mrs Kanjoos warmed to the theme of generosity. She lamented the passing of the good old days of the Raj when hospitality was not mean and calculated. 'I remember this club in the 1930s,' she said. 'There were a dozen parties every night. Why, we used to have at least one or two every week ourselves, didn't we, darling?'

Mr Kanjoos nodded his head in agreement.

'Now,' continued Mrs Kanjoos, 'no one entertains. Everyone is willing to accept hospitality. It is all a one-way traffic. Quite honestly one doesn't want to mix with the kind that come to the club these days. We hardly know anyone here any more. We have our drink or two and go home.'

Mr Kanjoos and I nodded agreement.

I noticed the bearer getting the cashier to make up our bill. Just then Mr Kanjoos excused himself to go to the lavatory. When the bearer came I had to sign for the two rounds we had. Mr Kanjoos came back and beckoned the bearer. 'What! You've signed for the whole lot!' he exclaimed indignantly. Then he forgave my rashness. 'All right, next time it will be on us. Then you come home.'

'And have pot-luck,' added Mrs Kanjoos.

The next time we met at the club we had a few rounds of Scotch. When the bearer came with the bill, Mr Kanjoos had gone to make an urgent telephone call. And on our third drinking encounter when the bill arrived Mr Kanjoos was busy talking to a friend. I turned mean and began to avoid the Kanjooses. I began to suspect the Kanjooses of sponging. In the club people described them simply as 'pencil shy'.

Fate had ordained that the Kanjooses and I should tread the same path. We were nominated members of an Indian delegation to an international conference in Germany. The conference was to last several months. So we were thrown together a great deal.

Mr Kanjoos was more generous than I. He decided to take at his own expense his wife and two children. He persuaded the delegation to employ his wife as a Secretary; she was a very competent woman. And he was able to pass off his younger child, a boy of fifteen, as under twelve and so travel at half-rates. None of this occurred to me. I could not even afford to pay my wife's fare to Europe. ('What is the point of carrying coals to Newcastle!' one of my friends remarked somewhat indelicately.)

The Kanjooses and I were lodged in the same hotel. He took a single bedroom. His wife shared it with him. He bought a car at diplomatic rates and parked it on the road outside the hotel. The children spent the day in the hotel and slept in the car at night. They came up early in the morning, used their father's bathroom and dressed there. Then Mr Kanjoos ordered his breakfast—the entire menu ranging from fruit juices, porridges, eggs, bacon, sausages, fish, coffee and fruit, and the four filled themselves on a repast meant for one.

During the day while Mr Kanjoos attended meetings and Mrs Kanjoos looked after the delegation's correspondence, the little

Kanjooses imbibed European culture by visiting picture galleries and museums where there was no charge for admission. Once a week the elder child, a girl of eighteen, came to see me. She usually rang up about noon to ask me whether she could come for advice— and on my replying in the affirmative (she was an uncommonly pretty wench) turned up with a pocket book and pencil to take notes. This flattered my vanity. Consequently when she had had her fill of my wisdom, I would ask her for lunch and other members of our delegation were similarly approached once a week for advice—and compensated Miss Kanjoos for listening to them by giving her lunch.

The Kanjooses were always together in the evenings. In the conference building there were a series of reception rooms for the use of delegations. Most of the time they were monopolized by leaders of the delegations or Directors who only invited other leaders and Directors. It was very seldom that invitations percolated down to people like us or the Kanjooses. But the Kanjooses were not deterred by this kind of class discrimination and made it a point of principle to be present at one or the other reception.

The Kanjooses' entry into the cocktail reception fell into a pattern. Mr Kanjoos would wander into the corridor like one who had lost something and approach one of the hosts at the door with an honest query: 'Have you seen my wife anywhere?' No, they hadn't seen Mrs Kanjoos but wouldn't Mr Kanjoos join them for a drink! After a mild protest Mr Kanjoos allowed himself to be prevailed upon to accept a drink—and be lost in the crowd of guests. A few minutes later Mrs Kanjoos would wander in the corridor looking as lost as her husband had been before her and approach the host: 'Have you seen my husband anywhere?' Of course, he had. He was some-where in the milling crowd of guests. Wouldn't Mrs Kanjoos stay on and have a drink before taking her husband away? Mrs Kanjoos agreed—very reluctantly. A few minutes later the two children would come in looking for their parents. Thus was the family united and seen doing full justice to the caviare and smoked salmon sandwiches and meat patties.

It was later reported that every evening when the children joined her, Mrs Kanjoos recited a *mantram* in some ancient Indian language. It was also noticed that only after these magic words had been uttered did Miss and Master Kanjoos proceed to devour the deli-cacies laid out on the table. After much research and evesdropping the *mantram* was deciphered by an Indian member of the delegation to be a sentence in a rustic dialect of Punjabi to the effect: 'My little rubies, eat all you can. We won't have to go to a restaurant.'

It was hardly surprising that everyone came to know the Kanjooses. This was partly due to the family's ready acceptance of hospitality and partly due to the burgeoning beauty of the eighteen-year-old Bhooki Kanjoos. Foreigners fell like nine pins before her. Their enthusiasm was contagious enough to infect the Indians who had hitherto dismissed her as just a nice little girl who would one day make a nice-little-wife to a young IFS or IAS or a firm-job-wallah (or failing all that a tea-estate type). As a matter of fact, from the number of lecherous foreigners who had taken to kissing Miss Kanjoos's hand it was obvious that unless a patriotic Indian was forthcoming to make her a Shrimati, Bhooki Kanjoos might end up as a Signorina or a Frau or a Madam. It is fortunate that in such situations our countrymen are never found wanting in patriotism. A young member of the foreign service who had eluded the pursuit of many an ambitious mamma in India made a pass at Bhooki. Whether the young diplomat's intentions were honourable or not Mamma Kanjoos took good care that they became so. Budhu Sen—that was his name—made some attempts to wriggle out but he had little chance against the machinations of the Kanjoos family. Budhu Sen pretended to give in and agreed to the marriage in India when he came on home-leave. Mamma Kanjoos saw the hazards of leaving the eligible Budhu in Europe and, acting on the principle that a bachelor in the foreign service abroad was worth two in the I.A.S. in India, resolved to clinch the issue at once. She announced that the horoscope of Bhooki and Budhu required the union to take place across the seven seas.

We wondered how a Hindu wedding could take place in the non-Hindu climate of Europe. And where was the foreign exchange to buy a dowry or pay for the wedding reception to come from? Our hearts went out to the Kanjooses. We talked of pooling our savings and handing them over to the family. All this proved unnecessary.

Mamma Kanjoos again consulted her astrologer (how she found one in Bonn, still remains a mystery). Her astrologer was reported to have pronounced that for their future happiness, Budhu and Bhooki must be married (by Hindu rites) on the 15th of August at 3.00 p.m. at a particular spot—which on closer scrutiny of the map turned out to be the building of the Indian Embassy. Mamma Kanjoos called at the Embassy and poured out her sorrowful predicament to the Indian Ambassador and his wife. Between her sobs Mamma Kanjoos also suggested the way out. If she would have the use of the Embassy reception room for half an hour, she promised to have the whole business over and her wedding guests (five or six at the most, she said) out of the building well before 4.00 p.m.—the time of the Ambassador's reception—she as a patriotic Indian had not forgotten that the 15th of August was Independence Day.

The Ambassador and his lady were moved by Mrs Kanjoos's tale of woe. In any case, Budhu Sen was a member of the staff and a Hindu bridal pair would add flavour to their formal reception. They agreed and as Mamma Kanjoos had foreseen, insisted that the wedding guests be asked to stay on for the reception. 'A few more or less does not make much difference,' assured His Excellency.

Papa Kanjoos spent a considerable sum in having the wedding invitation cards printed. They were on thick ivory paper with a suitable invocation in Sanskrit. Bhooki took it upon herself to deliver them to the more important people—heads of delegations and many ministers of the central and state governments who were in the habit of migrating to Europe during the summer recess of the Lok and the Vidhan Sabhas. Mamma Kanjoos coyly informed the recipients that by Hindu custom a bride was looked upon as a daughter and had to be sent off with a gift—'It doesn't matter how trifling it is—even a sugar cube will do, but it is inauspicious to come empty-handed.'

So was Saubhagyavati Bhooki Kanjoos wed to Srijut Budhu Sen of the I.F.S. Wedding guests—well over a hundred—turned up at 3 p.m. and stayed on for the Independence Day reception. There were so many presents that Master Kanjoos had to be bribed with money to stand guard on the pile.

It was a wonderful party. After the foreign guests had departed His Excellency sent for champagne to toast the newly married couple. Corks popped like fireworks at Diwali and the frothy nectar flowed like the waters of holy Ganga. The Kanjooses, both well fortified with bubbly, were in their element. Papa Kanjoos stuck his thumbs in his braces and began to orate: 'One is so happy when one can do one's duty by one's child. What else does one live for, I ask! You can't take your money with you. Spend it, I say, spend it while you live. Arjuna once asked Lord Krishna what he thought was the greatest miracle in the world. Lord Krishna replied . . .'

Mr Singh and the Colour Bar

'If you ask me, I would say our countrymen are to blame,' explained Mr Singh stroking his glossy beard. 'Every single case of colour prejudice you examine closely you will see that some Indian or the other has gone and misbehaved.'

Mr Singh had been in the country only a couple of weeks but he knew a great deal about its people and had examined the problem of race prejudice minutely.

'Take this matter of boarding houses,' he continued. 'I've been to several which would not take coloured people. I asked the landladies the reason—of course after getting to know them. Every time it started by some act of misbehaviour. Our boys stretch their hands across the table to help themselves before even the ladies have taken anything. They belch loudly. They sit on their haunches on lavatory seats and make them dirty. They splash water in the bathrooms by pouring it over themselves with a lota instead of lying gently in the long baths. These things cause unpleasantness and unpleasantness causes prejudice. Our boys must be taught European etiquette before they leave India. Don't you agree?'

Most of us agreed; it did not do to disagree with Mr Singh. It was resolved that a school to teach European etiquette should be set up in Bombay where Indians could be put through a six-week course of table and bathroom manners.

'But,' blurted someone who did not know Mr Singh, 'educated negroes know all these manners and yet there is prejudice against them.'

'In some countries they are known to lynch and hang negroes without trial for raping women,' added another.

Mr Singh was indignant. 'Anyone who rapes anyone should be hanged. Hanged ten times,' he roared with a menacing stab of his finger. 'Don't you agree?'

We thought ten times a bit much but we murmured approval.

'Actually you have hit upon the cause of the trouble,' he said. 'It is sex.'

We agreed that most of the world's troubles were due to sex.

'It is this business of girls which causes most of the complication,' he announced pompously. 'Cheap looking girls you know! That is why no decent family mixes with our boys.'

'We should import our own girls to go about with.'

'That is not funny,' admonished Mr Singh. 'I mean it seriously. Our boys come here and look at women as a hungry dog looks at food. I know lots of men give up their studies in pursuit of women and return home with nothing better than an LLD. You know about LLD, don't you?'

There was no point in saying one did. Mr Singh would repeat his joke in any case. He had a genius for repeating old jokes and emphasizing platitudes with an air of originality.

'You don't know the one about LLD?' he repeated excitedly. 'Then you must hear it. It is so funny, so funny.'

He clasped his hands across his paunch and leaned back in his chair.

'A chap spent five years in a foreign university and all he acquired was a wife. When he got home and his father asked him what he had done, he replied LLD.

"LLD? What's that?' asks the father. The son presents his wife saying this is the LLD, my landlady's daughter. Hee... hee... hee, wasn't that funny? Put your hand there.'

Mr Singh put out his right hand which we smacked in turns to acknowledge his joke. He slapped his thighs and laughed till tears came into his eyes.

Mr Singh wiped off his tears and regained his composure. 'Jokes apart,' said he, dismissing hilarity with a stern wave of his hand, 'we must do something about it.'

He stuck his thumbs in his braces and spoke as if he was addressing a multitude.

'As I was saying to a group of students the other day, we are all ambassadors of our country. We should behave like ambassadors. I was discussing the subject with Mrs Wilkins—Mrs Wilkins is the lady I am staying with. She said, Mr Singh, if there were more Indians like you...'

'There'd be none of this ere prejudice,' we added.

'Yes, that's what she said. You know Mrs Wilkins, then?'

'No, we don't know Mrs Wilkins. But we know Mrs Jones and Mrs Henry. They sai the saime. You are O. Kai. But some of them!

Mind you, I don't 'old against coloured folk like Mrs Mackintosh 'oo won't taik them. But I do 'ave to 'ave a little extra cos then I don't get the others. But no goings on with girls! Once I sees me lodger with a girl, out e' goes. Money or no money.'

'That's how it should be,' said Mr Singh warmly. 'Bringing girls to boarding houses is not decent.'

Mr Singh loved the word 'decent.'

'Where should we take them? The police nab you in the parks.'

'Parks!' exploded Mr Singh. 'In front of everyone! That is not decent. Not at all.'

'What do you do with your sex problems, Mr Singh?'

'You can't get sex off your minds. You are obsessed with it,' replied Mr Singh taking the offensive again. 'Now look at me. I don't find it a problem. And mind you being a married man ...'

We looked at Mr Singh; at his gorgeous silk turban and his glossy black beard neatly rolled under his chin; at his bright black eyes, his betel-stained lips, his dear little paunch begging to be caressed. Besides the appearance, there was his name which had acquired several honorifics since his arrival. These were only meant for foreigners to whom Mr Singh modestly communicated their noble import—as he did of the significance of the gold on his turban and his ornate Indian shoes. He had also become a bit of a palmist. In fact he had all the esoteric learning of the Orient with its glamorous facade.

'I would have brought my wife along but all these exchange control regulations make it so hard. I am very anxious to get back to her now. No women like Indian women you know! Indian women are like *devis* and we are like devils. We should try to prove ourselves worthy of them. I never forget what the priest told me when I got married. "As from today," he said, "you shall regard all women other than your wife as mothers, sisters or daughters." I always bear that in mind. You should, too. In fact make it a principle to address them as such according to their ages. All girls who are more or less of my age I address as sisters. Once you've called a woman your sister, you can't do anything wrong with her can you?'

We could. However!

'Is it a sort of verbal chastity belt?' we asked.

'I don't know what that is, but you try. It will work.'

Mr Singh left on his ambassadorial goodwill mission smashing all bars of colour and race. We did our best with Mr Singh's watchwords 'mother, sister or daughter—as the case may be.' And we did say 'please' and 'thank you.' We did not stretch our hands across the table. We did not belch. We sat on lavatory seats as if they were armchairs. We even used toilet paper instead of water. We bathed in long tubs with our own filth floating around. It was all for the cause of the coloured races.

Some months later we happened to be at a sea-side resort staying at a very large fashionable hotel. It was almost like a city in itself, with a dozen lounges, dining rooms, beauty parlours, chemists, booksellers and lots of chromium and glass. It had many lifts which worked all hours of the day and night. The lifts were operated by young girls dressed like boys—just a mass of brass buttons and behinds.

One night we went out celebrating. The celebrations lasted till midnight and since there was no prohibition, we returned some-what unsteady in mind and step. But we got back to the hotel—and the lifts. We were welcomed by a dark brunette. She almost looked Indian but for her dress. She wore a short waistcoat with a glittering row of buttons and tight-fitting trousers displaying a figure which would melt an iceberg if she sat on one.

'Eleventh floor, Sir?' she asked, slamming the lift gate.

'Ye yes—please.'

We watched the numbers of the floors light up on the panel and then looked at the girl.

'Jai Hind,' said the *devi*, putting her hands together in the manner of an Indian greeting.

We shut our eyes hard. They opened on the same brunette in the tantalizing waistcoat and pants. Mr Singh's words came to our lips and stuck there.

'Jai Hind,' repeated the *devi* with a saucy smile and another folding of hands.

'You know my country?'

'No! But I knew a countryman of yours. He was staying here. He also wore a turban and a beard. His turban was much nicer than yours—it was made of gold. He was ever so nice, too!'

The *devi* closed her eyes in ecstasy. 'He took me out dancing and we used to have drinks in his room after that. He was also on the eleventh floor.'

Floor eleven arrived.

'You wouldn't like to come and have a drink?'

The *devi* smiled. She whispered, 'I am on duty till one o'clock. I'll look in after that if that is O.K. by you.'

'Sure, sister.'

The Morning After the Night Before

It was the proverbial morning after the night before. One of those rare experiences which live up to the reputation which makes them proverbial. It seemed as if all the liquor that I had consumed had solidified and stuffed into my skull to make it burst. I dare not get up. No, not even move. Each little move would set the artery on the temples throbbing and produce a dull, heavy headache.

It was a Sunday morning and I could lie in bed as long as I liked—or rather as long as my wife would let me. So I decided to postpone the agony of getting up and undoing my dinner jacket. I first loosened my stiff collar sticking into my underchin, flung the bow on the floor and buried my face in the pillow to resume my sleep. In a few moments my magic carpet mind transported me back to the pleasant world of the evening before—with its cool green lawns surrounded by trees lit up with coloured lights; with its soft music wafted in gentle gusts of summer breeze; with its lovely women looking lovelier under the influence of alcohol.

We had gone dancing in a party of five couples. All the men were friends. All their wives friendly. The men generally admired their friends' wives more than they did their friends. We all knew that but the rules of our group strictly forbade admitting it. On the contrary, it was a recognized convention to be frivolously critical of the friends' wives and profess admiration for their husbands. It was humbug—but it worked—and it kept us closely knit together.

I had determined to get drunk that evening. I was not particularly fond of drink and even find it distasteful. But in our group the capacity for drink was the recognized test of a good fellow and a he-man. I had an obsession for popularity. I had also to prove my manliness since insinuations had been cast on me on that score. So I emptied several tankards of beer with nonchalance and matter-of-factness. At any party of our group, the motto of the he-man was 'bottoms up'. And I was determined to be the he-man par excellence. So 'bottoms up' I did. Several times and with several kinds of liquor.

I must have had a lot of beer inside me when the effects began to register. I had to excuse myself several times. In the solitude of my many communions with the herbaceous borders of the lawns I warned myself to go steady. 'You're drunk, old man,' I said to myself, 'don't make an ass of yourself—you know very well you can't do a thing if you've had too much—half drunk's best drunk— Chinese but good sense—Can't do a thing.'

As soon as I returned to the table, my weak protests about having had enough had to be abandoned to answer the taunts of my friends. 'Can't take it you blighter,' they shouted, 'Can't drink for nuts.'— 'Can't I half?' I heard myself say—and I took full doses.

The liquor was beginning to get the better of me. The girls were eyeing us suspiciously. Could they see we were drunk? I was going to prove that I was not. So I smiled back at all of them and at the inebriated menfolk. One of them, a slim, sallow-looking youth had his arms round my neck. He was singing and exhorting people to pickle parts of their anatomy. I extricated myself from his hold and patted him on the head with sympathetic understanding. I was going to dance. A couple of continental waltzes and I would sweat it out. A little unsteadily I went on to the floor. I couldn't recall who my partner was. But she began to look dangerously attractive to my inebriated person. She was smiling and laughing all the time and her face was lit up by the sparkle from her pearlwhite teeth. She would toss her head back with an abandon and laugh at the moon. I was beginning to feel unsafe. I wanted to dig my fingers into the dimples in her cheeks and to smother the curls that she had let loose on her cheeks with studied carelessness. The desire seemed to be over-powering—but I was determined to resist. I bit my lips till they bled and burst. That was symbolic of the resistance. Then the dance was over and I was back in the company of others, still undisgraced.

I decided to dance with someone safer. Dancing was now for the sake of exercise and not fun. My eyes wandered round the circle looking for a suitable partner. They rested on the most unsuitable one. She wasn't particularly good-looking. Just fair and buxom. She had been slimmer but had refused to recognize the accumulation of fat on various parts of her system. The size of her clothes remained what it had been when she was in college. She had tried to squeeze all her protrusions in tight-fitting clothes. But her flesh had voluptuously overspread its narrow confines. Her bulbous breasts were ever on the verge of escaping from the narrow strap of cloth which held them down. One couldn't keep one's eyes off them.

She was conscious of the object of men's attentions and hung her head down in an attempt to cover them. Her chin rested in the Centre of the protrusions and she looked bashful—and bashfulness enhanced her desirability. She was vulgarly desirable. I knew I should not dance with her, but I did.

My will-power yielded to the gentle and persuasive pressure of her contact. Even if I had held her as far as I could, I could not have avoided her person touching mine. And I did not keep her as far as I could. I held her so close that the fleshy folds of her breasts flattened against my chest and mounted up to my neck. My head began to be completely befogged. When I had first gone dancing, my friends had warned me that dancing was not suited to the Indian temperament. I had taken note of their warning and strapped myself so that disagreement with the Indian temperament should not become too obvious. After several warnings and practice I had discontinued the precaution as offensive to the refined art of ballroom dancing. I was now regretting my mistake. I became embarrassed at my own reactions. The one was to take her off the dance floor behind the herbaceous border. The other to divert my vulgar intentions towards legitimate channels and seek my wife's company.

I didn't now what I did. I was too drunk to remember. But I knew what I would like to do within the safe confines of a morning dream. I would have undone the little strap that held her bust in subjection and put it in my trouser pocket. My hand involuntarily carried the imaginary article into my trouser pocket. Suddenly I stopped dreaming. My hand encountered a foreign object. It was soft and silken. It couldn't be a handkerchief. No! it had edges and stitches. I gently pulled it out—a silk brassier, straps and all—and held it aloft with both my hands. There could be no mistake. There was a tell-tale lable sewn on with the inscription 'KESTOS—high line'. The headache vanished and gave way to consternation. Cold sweat mounted my forehead. Had I really gone that far in drink? What would my wife say when she discovered it? She had warned me that the one thing she would never condone was physical disloyalty. Had I ruined my home life by one senseless fling? She had often threatened. 'If you do it once—I'll do it a hundred times.' Was my home going to be invaded by fellows who were going to outbalance my score of one by 99? No! my wife must never know.

I heard my wife shouting for me. She did not sound friendly. I thrust the incriminating article back into my pocket and pretended to be in the throes of a hangover, groaning piteously. 'For heaven's sake get up,' she said coarsely—'It serves you right after the way you behaved last night.' She couldn't know how far I had gone? So I groaned again and holding my head in my hands proceeded to the bathroom. In the bathroom I decided to destroy the evidence of my amorous escapade. I pulled it out and tore it up bit by bit. Then I tied it in a bundle and flushed it down the water-closet. Now I could face my wife and find out how much she knew.

'I must have had a lot too drunk last night,' I said.

'You certainly did,' she snapped back.

'Did I misbehave much?' I inquired apologetically.

'You certainly did,' she snapped again.

'What did I do,' I asked again.

'What do you do when you are drunk. I have to put up with it. And you are so brutally rowdy. Where are my what-nots? You put them in your pocket.'

My headache vanished as if someone had bored a hole in the head and pulled it out. I went back to my bed—and dug my face in the pillow and dreamt the sequel to my interrupted dream—that's the only amorous adventure a married man undertakes without recriminations.

A Love Affair in London

'May I have your attention, please! We shall be landing at London airport in another fifteen minutes. Please fasten your belts and do not smoke. Thank you.'

The panel above the door was more peremptory. 'Fasten seat belts. No smoking'—it flashed in red letters.

Kamini looked out of the window. They were still flying above the clouds which stretched beneath her like a vast sea of fluffy cotton. She could hardly believe she was going to be in England in another quarter of an hour: an England she had read about, heard about from friends and relations, seen in pictures, but an England she never believed she would ever visit herself. The age of miracles had not passed. After a month of agonizing indecision about her scholarship, followed by difficulties in getting her passport, visas, foreign exchange and income-tax clearance and health certificates, there she was actually flying into London!

'Your seat belt, madam,' reminded the air hostess gently.

'Oh, yes, sorry,' mumbled Kamini fixing the belt about her waist.

She wondered if she was going to enjoy her stay in England. From what she had read and heard it was a beautiful country. It was about the people that she had her doubts. Her family had suffered at their hands. Her father and brothers had been imprisoned during the passive resistance movements and had been beaten in jail. She herself had done a spell of seven days' detention while she was still in her first year at the University. She had never met an Englishman, unless her encounter with the magistrate, Robert Smith, could be described as a meeting.

It had been a curious affair.

It was during the 'Quit India' movement of 1942. Along with a batch of college girls she had gone round the streets singing patriotic songs and shouting the slogan 'Quit India' whenever they came across a foreigner. They had been rounded up by the police and put up for trial. All the girls except her had pleaded guilty and been let off with a warning. She had been taken to a police lock-up and later in the day produced before Robert Smith, I.C.S., who was the district magistrate.

Kamini remembered the scene well. The monsoon was spending itself in all its fury. A damp odour of sweat, paper and ink pervaded the court-room. It was dark except for two circles of light shed by lamps on the magistrate's table, and on the clerk's who sat on one side fumbling with files of yellow paper. The magistrate was a youngish man with light red hair. He wore a short-sleeved shirt and his tie was loosely knotted halfway down his chest. There was an aura of the Universities, boat races and rugger matches about him. He was engrossed in reading a book and did not even look up at the people being tried.

The clerk read out Kamini's name, her father's name and the nature of the offence.

'Guilty or not guilty?' asked the clerk in Hindustani.

'Not guilty.'

'Ask her how old she is,' drawled the magistrate without looking up.

'Seventeen,' replied Kamini without waiting for the translation.

'Tell him to go back to England and mind his country's business.'

The magistrate looked up. His steel-grey eyes wandered from her face framed by masses of raven hair down to where they fell in profusion about bare shoulders; to her long neck and youthful figure, and back again to meet her eyes sparkling with defiance.

'Incredible,' he mumbled. 'Incredible coincidence. What was the name?' he asked the clerk without taking his eyes off her.

'Kamini... Kamini Garve.'

'Miss Garve, do they teach you any poetry at school?'

'Yes... no,' stammered Kamini. 'What has that got to do with the case?' she added aggressively. 'Do they pay you to read fiction in court?'

'Not fiction, young lady, poetry. I'll lend you the book to read in jail. Seven days, "A" class. And if you continue to be rude you will get another seven for contempt of court.'

The next day Kamini received a copy of a beautifully bound volume of the collected works of Hilaire Belloc inscribed: 'Pleasant reading in jail. With compliments from the man who sent you there.' A slip of paper marked a page where a verse had two lines under-lined in red. Alongside the lines were the initials 'K.G.' They read:

Her face was like a king's command,
When all the swords are drawn. ·

Kamini had resolved to tell the newspapers of Smith's behaviour in court. She was certain it would cause his dismissal. But before her seven days were over, she began to be less sure of herself. When she came home she, heard that Smith had resigned. A few days later he had returned to England.

Kamini had not quite understood what the lines meant except that they were some sort of compliment to her looks. And it was the first time anyone had paid her one. Thereafter, every time she looked at herself in the mirror, the words came back to her and she had the odd sensation of Smith staring at her, making her embarrassingly conscious of her young womanhood. The incident had not made any difference to her opinion about the English people, except that she no longer believed they were as shy as they were made out to be.

Kamini was shaken out of her day-dreaming by a series of bumps. The plane had descended through the layer of clouds and was flying over a mass of red-roofed houses and criss-cross of tarmac-roads with rows of cars crawling along like beetles. A few minutes later it touched down on the runway and taxied up to the Customs sheds.

For a long time Kamini sat by the window taking her first look at England. It was a warm autumn afternoon and the park opposite her hotel was full of people strolling about in the amber sunlight. The grass was a lusher green than she had ever seen before and there was a rich variety of gladioli along the fence. At the entrance of the park an old beggar was grinding a long forgotten melody on his barrel organ. It looked peaceful and friendly. Kamini decided to step out herself.

Kamini was a little apprehensive of people staring at her because of her sari, but no one took any notice. She watched children sailing boats in the pond, women feeding ducks and boys wheeling noisy toy aeroplanes amid circles of spectators. She saw couples strewn about the grass oblivious of the world about them. She joined the crowds around the soap-box orators and listened to their speeches and the heckling.

When she turned her footsteps back to her hotel a sense of loneliness came upon her. She realized that this was perhaps the first afternoon in her life that no one had spoken to her. Everyone had someone to talk to except her. Why, she asked herself, had she come to this unfriendly land?

Kamini did not find the answer to her question in the days that followed. Her life fell quickly into a routine of penny-half-penny bus rides to the underground station, strap-hanging in an over-crowded train for half an hour, another bus ride, lectures, lunches in the cafeteria, more lectures, and once more the bus rides and strap-hanging back home, if the hotel could be called one—a home where no one spoke except to exchange a banal greeting, where the necessary conversation was carried on in whispers and where the pervading funeral hush was only broken by the crackle of news-papers.

Ever since she had left India, Kamini had harboured a vague hope that she might run into Robert Smith. She knew it was silly. For all she knew he might be living in Africa or America. Even if he was in England the chances of meeting him by accident in London's milling population of eight million were not very bright. And if she did meet him, would he recognize her? What would she say to him? Or he to her? She had tried to look up his name in the telephone book, but the number of Smiths that filled page after page of the directory was disheartening. There were several with the initial 'R'. And if she did ring him up, she would not know what excuse to make for doing so.

Nevertheless the thought persisted and grew into an obsession. She believed that if she willed it, somehow, somewhere, she would run into him. She had read in books that people who were attracted to the same thing were often drawn together. She had the details of the meeting all settled in her mind. He would raise his hat and ask: 'Miss Garve, I do not suppose you recognize me?'

'Mr Smith, if I am not mistaken? Yes, of course, we have met; although I am not sure if I could call it a pleasure. How do you do, Mr Smith?' And one thing would lead to another.

The polytechnic term began to draw to a close and neither her will-power nor any coincidence brought Kamini face to face with Robert Smith. One day, like all other days, she took her bus to the tube station. When she came out of the underground at the other end to catch the next bus she found the pavements crowded and the roads cleared of traffic. From a distance she heard the whining of bagpipes and the thudding of big drums. She glanced at the paper in her hand and discovered that the Queen was due to drive past with some visiting monarch. She decided to give her lectures a miss, and joined the crowd.

The Highlanders went by with the band-leader tossing his mace high into the air. They were followed by the Guards marching at a slow, majestic pace. Their enormous black busbies, scarlet coats with bright brass buttons and rifles with bayonets, all agleam like a forest of spears, sent a thrill through her. The Guards came to a halt in front of her and lined both sides of the road. A little later came a troop of Cavalry and then the Queen's gold coach drawn by a dozen black horses. The Guards came to attention and sloped. The Queen and her royal guest went by, gently waving to the crowd which had joined the band, singing lustily.

The crowd began to break up as soon as the procession had passed. Kamini remained rooted to the spot as if in a trance, jostled by people hurrying to their offices. Only the woman just in front of her stayed where she was. Kamini heard her sob and when she turned round saw her dab her eyes with the back of her hand and then rummage in her handbag for her handkerchief. The woman noticed Kamini looking at her and was embarrassed.

'I am silly when it comes to soldiers and processions. They always make me cry.'

'It was very moving. And so beautiful. Don't you think a lot of soldiers together look beautiful?'

'It's odd you say that. My friend used to say that a beautiful woman looked like thousands of soldiers with drawn swords. As a matter of fact he was always saying that to me. He had been in India too and liked it.'

The woman found her handkerchief and put it against both her eyes. Kamini felt as if her feet had turned to lead.

'Where is your boy friend now?' She knew she had no right to ask a question like that of a stranger, but something had forced it out of her.

The girl turned up her tear-stained face.

'He was killed in the war. D-Day.'

Rats and Cats in the House of Culture

' Should be of the same sex.'
        Director Langford pondered over his final noting on the
'rats' file. In one brief sentence he had summed up ten pages
of budgeting minutiae penned by a host of subordinates from
different departments. The only other noting made by him in the
file was on page five—exactly half-way through the maze of
proposals, counter-proposals, facts and figures. That noting was
also characteristic of the brevity and commonsense for which he
had become famous, 'Why not cats?'

Langford threw the 'rats' file in the 'out' tray. He took a cigar out
of its metal container, licked its bottom with his tongue before clip-
ping it. He put down the cigar and picked up the file again. He opened
the first page to see the date. It had been started almost two years
ago—in the time of the French director. And in between there had
been an Italian. Both had written long notes on the subject—
undoubtedly after many confabulations with heads of departments
and the staff actually concerned. It was in this sort of situation that
American commonsense scored over the long-winded erudition of
the European. Ten pages of flatulence punctured by two pithy
sentences: 'Why not cats?' and 'Should be of the same sex.'

Langford flung the file back into the 'out' basket and lit his cigar.
Rats, he recalled, were a part of his inheritance when he took over
as Director of the House of Culture at Paris. The first thing he had
done was to examine the budget of every department over the
previous years. When he was looking over the expenses of administration he came across the incongruous entry in the accounts
of the canteen. Although meant to be non-profit-making it had
shown some profit in the first two years. Then the profit had been
evened out by an entry which read 'depredation by rats.' In the
subsequent entries the figure against depredations had more than
doubled and the canteen had become a heavy liability. He had sent
for the Englishman who was head of administration and asked for
an explanation. The Englishman had brought the 'rats' file giving

the details. The canteen was in the basement which consisted of seemingly endless corridors ending in iron grills beyond which were sewers which ran into the river. It had not taken the sewer rats very long to discover the stores of food which began to be stocked in the corridors. They ate up the bread and the butter, the meat and the vegetables. They gnawed through the wood of the crates and even punctured cans of fruit juice. It was then that the French director had asked for plans for the destruction of rats and the 'rats' file was started. There were schemes for poisoning, names of various brands of rat poison and the cost of operations. The danger of disease from dead rats had finally put an end to the poisoning project. The Italian director had considered plans for using traps. Varieties of rat traps, bait, services of trappers, disposal of trapped rats etc. filled a couple of pages in the 'rats' file. The size of the sewer rats (said to be bigger than cats) had put the lid on the trapping proposal. Meanwhile, the rats continued to invade the cellars in greater numbers and the loss to the canteen assumed proportions which were bound to arouse hostile comment at the annual general session which was due in a couple of months. It was at this stage that Langford had taken over.

'I would like to see one of these rats,' he had told the caretaker. This was arranged. One night, two guards who had been armed with ·22 pistols to defend themselves against the rats went down into the cellar. One man flashed his torch on a moving mass of rodents. The beam dazzled the rats to a momentary stillness. The guard picked out two of the largest and fired in quick succession. Next morning the carcasses were laid out on a table near the entrance. They were bigger than the biggest neutralized tom cats and more sinister-looking to boot. They were hairy; their fangs jutted out from beneath whiskers larger than those of Salvador Dali. Blood still oozed from the holes bored by the ·22 pellets. Girls coming in to the office screamed. Langford had stared at the carcasses in cold disdain and remarked: 'Monstrous, aren't they?' He had sent for the 'rats' file and having convinced himself that the beasts were too big to be poisoned or trapped, penned the sentence, 'Why not cats?'

Once more the departments concerned got to work. A scout was sent out to find out the price of kittens. Apparently they could be had for nothing. For budgetary purposes a nominal franc was affixed to each. Provision was made for feeding them while still young; the job description of the manager of the canteen was amended to include 'care and feeding of cats.' On his own initiative the head of the administration decided to have six kittens. The file was scrutinized by the budget department before being put up to Langford. He penned his approval with the sentence, 'Should be of the same sex.'

The manager of the canteen was charged with the buying of the kittens. He performed the duty with dispatch. The neighbour's cat had a litter of eight. They were planning to drown seven and keep only one. The manager relieved them of seven; one more, he said with a Gallic shrug of his shoulders, would not bring down the House of Culture. He did his best to examine their sex. But the sex of a week-old kitten is largely a matter of speculation—and the portions he examined looked equally sexless. The kittens arrived in a little basket. For many days they were the chief attraction in the canteen.

When they were two months old, the saucer-feeding and the cuddling was stopped. They were let loose in the cellars to fend for themselves. They suffered terribly in the beginning. Several mornings they were found huddled together on tops of dining tables piteously meauwing for milk. But they were given neither milk nor sympathy. Five days later they made their first kill. Their character underwent a sudden change. Their eyes sparkled fiercely. They growled if anyone came near their kill. Instead of scratching themselves between the legs of diners, they arched their backs and spat venomously. Within a matter of some weeks they changed from furry, cuddlesome kittens to ferocious little tigers.

Thereafter, though the cats were seldom seen, they were often heard disputing the game or gnawing at the bones of the sewer rats.

Half-yearly estimates proved the experiment to have been a complete success. There were no depredations whatsoever. The non-profit-making canteen showed handsome profits. Langford had reason to stick his thumbs behind his braces and let the ash from his cigar drop on his complacent belly.

For six months there was peace in the House of Culture. Then the cats started to become a nuisance. They invaded other parts of the building. Lady stenographers shrieked with terror when they ran past. They meauwed and fought in the corridors like their well-known Kin from Kilkenny. Rumours began to float around that they were courting. Some swore that they had seen them in the act of copulation. The meauwing and the fighting ceased as mysteriously as it had started. A few weeks later a cat was reported to have been seen carrying a kitten in her mouth. And a few months later people swore that there were many more cats in the House than the seven that had been introduced.

Langford was not the one to lend an ear to irresponsible gossip. His fears were however confirmed when he was examining the end of the year budgets of the different departments. Profits of the canteen had once again been evened out by the losses. The losses were explained by one sentence, 'depredation by cats.'

This is how the 'cats' file was started. The General Conference was due to meet in six months and it was necessary to have everything ready for the delegates. The House of Culture had inherited a certain tradition. First an attempt was made to get a census of the cats. The Department for the Dissemination of Science prepared a note on the known methods for the destruction of cats. Bureau of Budget made a complete breakdown of the resources available in Paris with an estimate of costs. The whole thing was translated into the working languages of the House: English, French, Russian and Spanish—and then printed.

Langford kept his patience. The staff was used to doing things in a certain manner; and he did not want to upset the pattern unless absolutely necessary. But in the case of the cats, as it had been in that of the rats, weeks went by without any action. Matters came to a head at the MACOO Conference.

The Conference for the Mutual Appreciation of the Cultures of the Orient and the Occident was convened to draw up a programme for the interchange of cultures of the East and the West which would then be put to the General Conference. Eminent scholars from many parts of the world had come to Paris. The Department of Information had done a good job placing articles on the subjects to be discussed in the local press. Langford allowed himself to be pressed to inaugurate the proceedings.

The conference room was packed. In the front were the delegates seated behind placards announcing the country they represented. Behind them were their alternates and observers. The press had one corner all to itself. Visitors and secretarial staff filled the remaining chairs. Arrangements had been made for simultaneous translation in the three languages. There was an air of seriousness: chandeliers, cigarette smoke, decanters with tumblers atop, ear-phones and the whirring of newsreels and television cameras.

Langford opened the conference with a short address stressing the importance of a cultural rapprochement between the East and the West. He invited the delegates' comments on the proposals drawn up by the secretariat which had been printed and circulated earlier. He called upon the seniormost of the delegates, the Minister of Education of the Government of India, to be the first speaker.

The Minister, an elderly gentleman with a French-style beard and dark glasses, came up to the rostrum amid loud applause. He was accompanied by his secretary. The Minister neither understood nor spoke any of the working languages. He had not bothered to read the proposals of the secretariat nor listened to the Director's introductory remarks. Nevertheless he proceeded to propound his views with great eloquence in the most florid Hindustani. After every few sentences he paused to let his secretary translate his words into English. The translation then came over the ear-phones in Russian, French and Spanish. It slowed down the tempo of the conference.

The crisis came as the honourable Minister was winding up his speech. 'Culture knows no frontiers,' he roared as he pounded the desk. 'It knows no barriers of race, religion, caste or creed.' He paused to give his secretary time to put the immortal words in English while he turned to the newsreel cameras and twirled his moustache. The secretary opened his mouth but no translation issued into the microphone. Instead a loud *meauw* came down from one corner of the balcony. It was answered by a louder *meauw* from the other end. Delegates and visitors turned back to see what was going on. The *meauws* were followed by a head-on clash between two tom-cats. Women in the balcony screamed and stood upon their chairs. Stewards rushed up to drive away the warring cats. The assembly burst into laughter.

Langford did not show any ill-temper. On the contrary he forced a smile on his face as he called the meeting to order. He apologized to the delegates and requested the speaker to continue. But the honourable Minister brusquely ended his oration and marched down to his seat followed by his secretary. The conference adjourned for coffee. Langford asked his senior deputy to take his place at the conference and went back to his office. He sent for the Head of Administration and asked him to bring the 'cats' file with him.

'Mr Smith, you heard what happened at the meeting?' Langford demanded, doing his best to control his temper.

'Yes Sir; I am awfully sorry, Sir,' stuttered Smith. The Director usually addressed him by his Christian name, John. 'But, Sir, we have been considering the matter for quite some time. Budget were not sure if they had provision for this sort of thing; they wanted to consult Audit before committing themselves.'

'So there is no provision for this sort of thing! Lemme have a look at that,' said Langford snatching the file out of Smith's hand.

Langford dumped the file into his waste paper basket. 'To hell with the Budget and the Audit,' he exploded. 'I want those darned cats out of the House by the week-end; every single one of them. Get hold of some cat-catcher, give him what he wants. If Budget create any difficulties, tell them to see me. If there is a cat found in the House on Monday, there will be hell to pay.'

'I'll do my best, Sir,' replied Smith as he fled from the Director's room.

'You'd better.'

Smith got out the duplicate copy of the 'cats' file and scrutinized the various proposals for the disposal of the cats. There was an estimate from a firm of cat-catchers. He picked up the telephone and rang the number indicated. A woman's voice answered. Yes, that was the right number, but her man was out on work and would not be back till lunch. Smith emphasized the urgency of his commission and hinted that he could pay more if his commission was executed with dispatch. Would her husband come over as soon as he could after his lunch?

Raoul Colin had heard about the generosity of the House of Culture in matters of payment from many functionaries who had dealings with it. He quickly swallowed his lunch, washed it down with a carafe of *vin ordinaire* and drove his truck to the House of Culture.

Smith presented the problem to M. Colin with the precision he would have used in addressing a full meeting of the Board of the House. '*Voila, monsieur, C'est notre probleme*', he said and then summed it all up in three sentences: Can you handle the job? Can you complete it over the week-end? What will be your terms?

'*Combien de chats, monsieur?*'

'30, 40, may be 50. Not more.'

'*Alors!*' exclaimed Colin morosely shaking his head. He fumbled in his pocket. Smith pushed his silver box towards him and lit his cigarette. Colin began to scribble figures on a piece of paper.

		Francs
1.	Trapping (50 or more cats)	300
2.	Hire of truck	150
3.	Wages of three assistants	75
4.	Three course lunch with wine for four persons	55
	Total:	580

He borrowed another piece of paper from Smith, and while Smith had his nose in his files, re-wrote his estimate in fair hand doubling all the figures (the House of Culture was largely financed by American money). He re-checked the total and then pushed the paper across the table.

Smith scrutinized the estimate and rang up Budget. He put down the telephone. '*Bon*, Mr Colin. This is quite reasonable. We can pay you a small advance if you like. Full settlement will be made when the last cat is out of the premises. And it has to be by Monday as the big Conference begins on Tuesday. Is that agreed?'

'*D'accord, Monsieur*' replied Colin, putting out his hand. 'Advance will not be necessary. The House of Culture has a good reputation in the market. We will get to work straightaway. *Au revoir, Monsieur.*'

Smith grabbed the proffered hand. 'Good! and *bonne chance!*'

The House of Culture was usually closed over the week-ends. Only the Director and some heads of departments were in the habit of coming in on Saturday mornings to do their personal correspondence. Special arrangements were made to serve them beverages. They met for a few minutes at eleven, sipped their coffee and sighed at the amount of work they had to get through. On the Saturday in question, arrangements for coffee were cancelled. A notice at the entrance explained that the canteen had to be sealed off for '*l' operation chats*' and that on Sunday the entire building would be closed so that every room could be scoured in turn. Heads of departments hurried through their letters and returned to their homes to take their families out into the country.

Raoul Colin and his friends got down to their business. They placed tiger-sized traps with wire meshing in different parts of the canteen and the corridors. Inside the traps they put saucers of milk generously spiced with powdered dope. They went from room to room driving stray cats and locking the doors behind them. They shared their sandwiches and flagons of wine with the night-watchmen and slept for a couple of hours on the benches. A little after midnight they went to inspect the result of their operations. The beams of their torches fell on cats in different states of stupor. Some slept in the cages; others were curled up outside in blissful slumber with smiles on their faces. Some were able to stagger away; others glowered and arched their backs as the light dazzled their eyes. Colin's men picked the sleeping ones up by the scruff of their necks, dropped them in one cage and bolted it. By the time one cage was full, many other cats were discovered asleep in the corridors and were similarly dumped into the second cage. It was a satisfactory haul, perhaps a complete one. Colin and his mates celebrated their success with generous swigs of cognac before returning to their benches of the night.

On Sunday morning, the men did a *grand tour* of the House of Culture. They went to every room, looked under every sofa, chair, table and other pieces of furniture, locked the door from the outside and then chalked a cross on it. They came back and with the help of the watchmen hoisted two cages full of cats into the truck parked in the portico. The cats had woken from their stupor; but there was no fight left in them. It seemed that they had resigned themselves to their fate. They cowered in the corners of the cages too frightened to even squabble among themselves. Colin and his mates argued about the pros and cons of giving them something to eat, then decided against it. If they opened the door, some cats might escape out. They would in any case fight each other for the food. And what was the point of feeding animals you were going to destroy!

In the afternoon they undertook another round of the House; this time to inspect the canteen and the corridors. They did not see any cats but heard lonesome *meauws* in the cellars. Once more saucers of doped milk were placed at strategic points. One man stayed on the premises; others took a few hours off to see their families. A final tour of inspection was made at midnight. It yielded another five cats. They were accommodated in the more spacious quarters of a third cage which was gently put alongside the other two in the truck. This surely was the end of the cats! They emptied their bottle of cognac and stretched themselves on the benches. The only sounds that broke the stillness in the House of Culture were the snores of four contented Frenchmen.

The General Conference was due to open on Tuesday morning. But arrangements had to be completed a day earlier. On Monday morning janitors came in to put up the flags of 101 nations on the masts that flanked the entrance like an avenue. They swept the floors and rolled out the carpets.

At nine o'clock Langford's Cadillac drove in and came to a halt behind the truck. 'What the hell is this truck doing here?' he demanded of his chauffeur who had opened the door for him. 'Tell them to remove it at once.'

'*Oui, Monsieur. Je vais chercher le chauffeur.*'

Langford's eyes fell on the cages. He went up and saw the mass of cats—striped grey and black and marmalade—heaped on top of each other. He recalled the fiasco of the meeting and thought how much more embarrassing it would be if the same thing were to happen in the plenary session. His thoughts were interrupted by the chauffeur, who had brought out Colin and his mates. He was turning on the Director's heat on the cat-catchers.

'That's all right, Jacques,' interrupted Langford. 'I'll deal with this. *Combien de chats avez vous attrape?*' he asked in his politest French. Colin shrugged his shoulder. '*Je ne les ai pas comptes,*' he replied in a huff. He did not stand for rudeness from anyone, least of all from a liveried lackey driving a Cadillac.

Langford sensed Colin's temper. He patted the Frenchman on the back. '*Ca, c'est excellent, monsieur.*' He fished out his cigar case and held it out. '*Pour la victoire contre les chats.*' Colin's anger vanished. '*Merci monsieur.*' His mates also took a cigar each and put them in their pockets.

'Have you caught all of them?' asked Langford.

'*Jel'espere beaucoup, monsieur le Directeur Nous attendons* Mr Smith,' he explained.

'*Tres bien!*' Langford told them that the delegates would be arriving in a short while so it would be best if they parked their truck on a side street. He would see that they were paid their fee as soon as the office opened. He shook hands with all the cat-catchers and went in to inspect other arrangements.

Smith came in soon after Langford. Cats were on the top of his check-list and he hurried from his office to the side street to see the catch for himself. '*Combien?*'

Colin again shrugged his shoulders in the Gallic style, '*C'est impossible de compter, monsieur, peut-etre cinquante,—peut-etre plus.*'

'Are you sure you have got them all?'

'*Oui, oui, certainement, monsieur.* We have spent two whole days and nights at the job. We've searched every nook and corner of the building. There isn't one left. If you hear of one later, it will have come from outside.'

'*Bon!* I will send a note to the accounts department to make the payment at once. I hope you don't mind waiting a little; the office opens at 9.30.'

The accountant turned up a little after 10. Colin was paid his fee in full and sent off with many expressions of gratitude.

Colin and his mates drove off towards the river. The crates rattled but no sound of protest issued from the inmates. At a traffic signal in the Bois de Bolougne where there was no traffic and no other noise save the gentle purring of the truck engine, one of the men remarked: 'How silent they are! as if they knew what is coming to them.'

'How many do you think they are?' inquired Colin to divert his mate's line of thought.

'Hard to tell. Thirty, forty, fifty, may be more.'

The traffic lights changed. The truck lurched forward towards its destination. They came to a bridge and turned right along the Seine. They had to get well clear of habitation before they could carry out their final assignment. They pulled up at a bistro at the edge of the Bois. It was a pleasant spot with orange-coloured umbrellas, and chairs and tables on the pavement. 'We deserve a drink or two,' said Colin cheerfully.

They ordered four absinthes. Colin ducked a sugar cube in the green liquid and began to suck. 'Jean, there is something in what you said; they do seem to know what is coming to them. Not a *meauw.*'

They heard the shuffling about in two crates. No, not a *meauw.*

'How many did you say they were?' asked Jean.

'I didn't say: you said may be fifty or ...'

'Sixty or more I would reckon,' ended Jean.

'*Merde!*' exclaimed the third man, Auguste, and spat on the ground. They topped their absinthes. Colin called to the waiter.

'*Garcon! Rencore la meme chose.*'

The waiter filled their glasses. He heard the shuffling in the truck and looked in . '*Jiens; tiens!* What a cargo! Who are you going to sell the livestock to?'

'The butcher, who else?' Auguste spat again and again swore '*merde!*'

The waiter understood. 'Are you going to drown them in their cages? Cats can swim.'

Colin looked up. They hadn't thought of that problem. They couldn't very well transfer them into gunny sacks. And they had not brought anything to weigh down the gunny sacks.

'*Oui,*' he replied nonchalantly.

'How many have you there?' inquired the waiter.

'How the hell should we know,' roared Jean.

'*Merde!*' swore Auguste for the third time and banged his beret on the table. 'Fifty innocent cats!'

Colin raised his empty glass. The waiter refilled it and then refilled the others.

By the time they had downed six absinthes each, the problem of drowning the cats had assumed weighty proportions. They could not afford to lose the cages; and they could not possibly put them in bags without being clawed and bitten. Anyway, they hadn't brought any bags with them.

'How far are we from the House... of whatever it is?' asked Colin.

'Five, six or seven kilometres,' replied Jean.

Colin walked up to the rear of the truck and eyed the cages with their writhing mass of fur. He took the key out of his pocket and clambered in. He unlocked one cage, opened the door and jumped out.

One wary cat peered from the side of the camion and leapt lightly on to the road. It looked either way like a trained pedestrian and bolted towards the Bois. Then there was a rush. Some followed the leader to the green of the Bois, others ran across the road to the pavement on the side of the river.

The men downed their seventh absinthes and ordered some sandwiches. 'Bad, drinking on empty stomachs.'

Jean took the keys from Colin and opened the other two cages. They watched the remaining cats leap out of the camion and likewise seek the paths of life and liberty.

They stood the waiter a drink. They munched their sandwiches. 'I couldn't have eaten with the blood of fifty innocent cats on my hands,' remarked Auguste examining his hands.

'Nor me either,' agreed Jean.

The General Conference opened on Tuesday as scheduled. It was a bright May morning. A blue sky with a few fleeting clouds ambling along with a gentle breeze. God was in His Heaven.

Cars began to arrive. Langford welcomed the delegates in his usual expansive manner. He knew most people by their first names. 'How are you Philip.... Nice to see you, Signor... welcome! its good to have you in Paris again, Mr Ali.' The revolving door swallowed up the delegates.

The Indian Minister of Education arrived in a Rolls Royce with the tricolour fluttering on its bonnet. Langford stepped down to open the door. 'Your Excellency, how very nice to see you again!'

His Excellency extended a thin, cold hand without saying a word in reply. Langford had wanted to apologize to him for the earlier incident but decided to put it off till after the Minister had made his inaugural speech at the plenary session: he would then be more receptive and charitable.

Langford accompanied the Minister to the crowded hall. As they entered, the delegates rose to welcome them. The way the Indian bowed to acknowledge the applause convinced Langford that the worst was over.

Langford opened the proceedings by introducing the Minister. He spoke with great warmth regarding the honour of having the Minister of Education of a great country and a scholar of repute give the inaugural address. He invited the Indian to the dais.

Once again the Minister, impeccably dressed for the occasion in white sherwani went up to the dais followed by his interpreter. Arc lights were switched on; newsreel cameras whirred; camera bulbs flashed. There was a renewed burst of applause.

Two microphones had been fixed; one for the Minister, the other for his aide. The Minister unfolded the text of his speech and removed his dark glasses to read. His translator unfolded the translation in front of the other microphone and took off his long-distance spectacles and put them in his pocket. He nodded to his boss to indicate that he was ready.

The Minister cleared his throat. The audience fell silent. An air of expectancy hung in the smoke-filled room gently lit with a glitter of chandeliers.

'Mr Director General, Your Excellencies, Ladies and Gentlemen. I deem it a great privilege to have been invited to open the 7th General Conference of the House of Culture,' he said in Hindustani and turned to his interpreter.

The interpreter cleared his throat and adjusted his tie. He opened his mouth. From the balcony issued a strange sound: '*meauw.*'

The Red Tie

Chishti leaned back resting his elbow on the mantelpiece above the fireplace. He had his legs stretched wide to let the warmth envelop his behind from the ankles to the bottom. We only saw the fire between the inverted V of his legs. But we did not matter. Only Chishti mattered. He had dined well and was full of genial warmth. We stood around him in a semi-circle—some admiring, some amused, some envious.

The dinner was over but the ladies had not left the dining room as was conventional in anglicized Indian circles like ours. Wherever Chishti went conventions had to be overlooked. The hostess herself had her hands resting on Chishti's elbow and was bubbling with laughter. Chishti was a great draw. He was always talking. Whenever he came, there were no moments of silence which sometimes descended in her other parties and chilled her to the marrow. At the slightest sign of an approaching silence one heard Chishti's voice: 'I must tell you about an incident which happened to me,' or, 'Have you heard my latest joke? I think it is a good one.' It was so much nicer than her husband's laboured attempts: 'I had rather an interesting case in the court today'—a case which was always the same for every party and rarely interested anyone.

'Have you heard Chishti's definition of marriage?' asked the hostess looking around. 'I think it's damned good.' We had all heard it and knew it wasn't Chishti's. But that didn't matter. The hostess had twined her arms round Chishti's and was pressing him to let us know of his opinions on matrimony. Chishti smiled condescendingly and agreed that it was a good one—a damned good one. 'Let me see.... Oh yes, I remember now. Marriage is like chewing gum, sweet in the beginning, sticky in the end. Ha! ha!' Chishti was always the first to laugh at his jokes. His laughter was contagious and the women joined him enthusiastically. Some men smiled politely—others just sat in frigid silence.

Men's reactions never bothered Chishti. The poor devils were plain and simple jealous of his success with women. Most of his colleagues had gone bald and obese and dull. Chishti was full of *joi de vivre*. He had fought back his forty years with persistent exercise. When he was eighteen a woman had described him as 'something like a Greek-God', and ever after his life had become one long effort to look and behave like one. In the thirties the battle had become a losing one. The forehead which had once been just broad had became broader with the hair receding backward. His broad chest had begun to show slight protuberances about the nipples and the once flat belly had a convex curve which Chishti tried to hold back by a stomach belt.

Looks were not the only Hellenic thing about Chishti. There was the fig leaf aspect; in this Chishti's endeavours and achievements had always remained as much a mystery as the nature of the object covered by the leaf on the Greek statues. Stories of his miraculous seductions were enviously narrated by men and hungrily listened to by women. How he had just held a woman's hand under the dinner table and started an affair; how he had enticed rich men's wives, bureaucrats' wives, clerks' wives, old women, young women, college girls and even school girls. Some people had suggested that the stories were an exaggeration. But you had to see Chishti at a party and know that it must all be true. Chishti himself answered queries in this direction with a contemptuous smile meaning 'what do you think.' No, there was no denying that Chishti got what other men only dreamt about. That is why they did not like him.

The ladies left the dining room reluctantly and the men settled down to their coffee. Chishti still stood with his back to the fire and surveyed the company. 'I must tell you about rather a good one that I pulled off on my last tour. Absolutely unbelievable. Had a woman in the railway train at a junction station while she was waiting for her connection. She gave me this tie, too.' Chishti held aloft his somewhat smudged red tie. 'Probably her husband's. Wonder what story she went and told him. Ha Ha!' We also wondered.

Chishti had been detailed to go to a district town for the day. He caught the morning train from the city and found himself alone in a first class compartment. He put his attache case on the table and stood before the mirror to look at himself. He took off his red tie and hung it on a peg. He ran his hands across his neatly combed hair. He knew he·was handsome. Why the devil didn't he have the guts? Some ugly men got away with it; hardly anything had come his way. Women talked about him and yet he had never succeeded in seducing one. Ever since his college days he had carried contraceptives in his wallet hoping some day someone would compel him to use one. He fished into his inner pocket for his wallet. Yes, there it was as usual. It made him feel good and manly to have it with him. That was all. Chishti sank into his seat and began to read a magazine.

The train left the city and passed through a number of noisy stations where villagers clamoured to get on the train. Chishti who was left peacefully alone in his first class compartment surveyed the squabbling crowds with serene indifference. At a junction station the train pulled up alongside another going in the other direction. His own compartment came to a halt opposite a very crowded third class of the other train. Eager faces leant out to inspect the upper class with its leather seats, its cane chairs, its three fans—and above all its well-dressed Sahib stretched on a seat in solitary splendour. Why, he could be just feeling as if he was at home with his coat hung on a peg, his red neck tie on another and his little attache case on the table. Chishti was eminently well bred and disliked vulgar curiosity. With an air of boredom he pulled himself up to let down the shutters. He looked out of his window to give the train opposite a brief 'dekho'. A few compartments behind the one facing him was a zenana third class equally full but more colourful. At one window sat a woman staring blandly at Chishti. Chishti who had just released the catch of the shutter and was slowly letting it down put it up again. He changed his position and took his seat by the window to see the woman better. The woman continued to stare at Chishti without blinking. Chishti felt nervously agitated. Was she a . . . ? She must be. Her hair was done in fantastic perms with several multicoloured celluloid clips stuck all over. The antimony in her eyes! the bright red lipstick! and the constant chewing of betel nut! and the stare! There could be no doubt. But Chishti was a bundle of nerves. The woman produced a cigarette and began to smoke. Not the way other people do. It was held between the fingers in a clenched fist while she sucked at it noisily near the thumb. She sent two streams of smoke pouring out of her nostrils. Now there could be no doubt whatever and Chishti boldly stared back at her—a mixture of bravado, desire and fear. What fun if she were on his train! He felt the blood rushing to his face at the very thought. He continued looking on.

The engine of the opposite train gave a long blast and the train began to move. The zenana compartment started moving towards Chishti. Chishti's face coloured up. He felt he must do something... something appropriate for the occasion. The woman was now almost opposite him. With one surge of superhuman endeavour, Chishti shut his left eye in a lecherous wink and sank back into the safety of his solitary compartment. His heart beat wildly. He was utterly exhausted.

Chishti got up in a state of frenzy. There was shouting and tumult on the platform opposite. There was a screeching of brakes and the neighbouring train came to halt.

Chishti looked out at the zenana compartment. It had pulled up just a few yards beyond his own. The woman looked back at him and then disappeared from the window. A galling thought came to Chishti's mind. Perhaps the woman was coming over to his compartment. Would she have him beaten up? Perhaps she wasn't a... Chishti made a dash for the lavatory and bolted it from the inside.

Some minutes later Chishti heard the door of his compartment open and the sound of feet quite close to the lavatory door. Chishti held his breath and sat still. It seemed like an age. At long last the guard blew his whistle. Chishti heard the sound of feet going out and the door of the compartment slam. Another whistle—this time the engine's—and the train began to move.

Chishti got up from the commode seat, opened the lavatory door just a little and looked into the compartment. It was empty. His coat and attache case were gone. His red tie still hung on the peg but saliva trickled down its broad end on to the floor. Nevertheless, he was relieved and triumphant. Someone—a woman—had taken his wallet with its contents.

'And,' ended Chishti triumphantly with his hands inside his trouser's pockets. 'She left me this tie as a memento. Let's join the ladies.'

My Own My Native Land

On a sultry April afternoon, the *Stratheden* moved into Bombay harbour. In the dining room some three hundred Australians and Englishmen with half a dozen Indians were eating an early lunch and having their last alcoholic beverages before entering the three-mile limit. At our table many bottles of sickly sweet Australian champagne had been emptied before the order to stop drinking came over the loud-speaker. An Englishman rose from his seat and proposed a toast 'to prohibition'. Many responded with polite good humour. I rose unsteadily from my seat, filled my glass with water and raising it aloft, recited to an embarrassed audience:

> *'Breathes there a man with soul so dead*
> *Who never to himself hath said*
> *This is my own my native land,' etc. etc.*

Six Indians rose to answer the toast which was drunk to a loud 'Jai Hind.' Half an hour later we were alongside the pier.

Within a few minutes the boat was full of visitors. At no other port did we come across such generosity in allowing people to greet their folk on board. But then we were a warm-hearted people. 'B' deck was an animated mass of flowers, dhotis and saris. A large number of wrist-watches changed wrists; shiny little compacts disappeared in friendly handbags and many other articles of smaller dimensions were safely tucked inside coat pockets. Then we moved down lighter in worldly possessions but paradoxically light-hearted. We arrived at the Customs shed at 1.30 p.m.

The Customs shed was seething with humanity. Cordoned off from us was the counter behind which sat a number of handsome men in naval uniforms. Facing them were long queues of passengers having their declaration forms scrutinized. I did not know which queue to join, so I joined the one which trailed off a board marked 'Inquiries'. After a couple of minutes I faced the lady on the other side with a grin and asked her where I ought to be.

'See the number on the board above the Customs Officer,' she snapped efficiently.

I went round the hall looking at the boards. There were no numbers on them. So I rejoined the Inquiry queue. Without another grin I announced my discovery to the lady. That upset her. She armed herself with several pieces of chalk and waded through humanity to inscribe the numbers of the boards. Several queues had a quick game of ducks and drakes. I found myself at the tail end of mine. Half an hour later I was at the counter and announced myself to the harassed official. He looked over his papers and informed me that my declaration form was not with him. Before I could protest he was dealing with the man behind me. The Customs clock stood at 2.30.

I rejoined the Inquiry queue. This time the lady was certain I was being unnecessarily tiresome. But she walked briskly over to the Customs Officer, looked at his file of papers and then picked up one from the floor and triumphantly waved to me. I went back to my queue.

Some time later I found myself facing the Customs official with my declaration form lying open in front of him.

'Are you claiming exemption for transfer of residence?'

'Yes, I have been away for four years.'

'Fill in this form and come back.'

I retired to a corner of the hall to fill in the form and then I was back at the tail end of my queue. Forty minutes later, I was again facing my Customs Officer with my form of exemption duly filled.

'You cannot claim exemption. You came home for a fortnight in between,' he announced.

'But,' I protested, 'that was not transfer of residence. I was sent on official duty. My wife and children stayed abroad.'

'Sorry, the rule is clear. If you insist, see the Inspector.' I found him surrounded by a throng. When my turn came I explained my position. He tore up the form I had filled and with an understanding smile said, 'Just say you never came home. That'll be all right.'

I filled in another form and came back to my queue. In twenty minutes I was up at the counter once more with the harassed official in an uneven temper.

'Who asked you to fill in this form?'

I looked round the hall and pointed to the Inspector. He went over to the Inspector and an argument with much gesticulation followed. Apparently the Inspector triumphed. I was granted an exemption. But the declaration form had to be filled in again. So back I went to my corner to fill it and for the last time joined the queue. When I left the Customs Officer, the clock struck five.

Thereafter, there were other queues. The one where one paid the customs levy on new purchases and another where one paid the port trust charges. In half an hour one was through all that to face the ordeal of a customs inspection. With eleven packages consisting of crates, steel trunks and revelation cases packed to bursting, the prospect of a thorough examination was galling.

Then appeared my guardian angel in the form of an unkempt middle-aged man full of obsequiousness and grease. He had an umbrella tucked under his arm.

'*Arrey Bhai*,' he whined. 'What phor you bother so much. Give me ten rupees and it will be hokay and my children will bless you too.'

'But I have an exemption. Diplomatic, you know?'

'*Arrey, arrey*, I know all that. But I have to eat and my children, too. Ten rupees is not big sum and you will have no trouble. What say you?' He gave me a friendly dig in the ribs and bared his betel-stained teeth.

I saw my neighbour tucking in dirty socks and handkerchiefs in the corners of one of his many suitcases. That was enough. I put myself in the hands of the angel. My packages were marked without an inspection and I was the richer for all the blessings my guardian angel heaped on me.

Then I faced the hordes of coolies who claimed to have carried my luggage till the relays of claimants exhausted my goodwill towards the working class. I battled and emerged victorious with my packages on a truck and myself on top of the packages. I had only a little change left in my wallet. We shot out of the pier as the clock struck six.

At a wayside restaurant I begged the driver to stop for a minute and join me for a drink. We raised our glasses to a 'Jai Hind'.

It was iced lemonade, but strangely enough it tasted better than Australian champagne.

The Convert

'One spade.'

Mr Sethi's mind was somewhere else.

'One heart,' called Mrs Robinson.

Mr Sethi continued staring at the cards he held in his left hand like a Japanese fan. With his right hand he beat time on his knee to the tune he was humming. A thin wisp of smoke rose from the pipe in his mouth.

'Darling,' hissed his wife Sarla. 'Its your call; do wake up!' She bared her teeth and smiled apologetically to the Robinsons.

'Oh, sorry, sorry, sorry,' he sang good humouredly as he put his pipe on the table and rescrutinized his cards. 'Lets see. What did you call Mrs . . . Mrs . . .?'

'Mrs Robinson,' added his wife fiercely. 'Mrs Robinson called "One spade".' She was just able to control her temper.

'Ah yes, one spade, one spade,' chimed Mr Sethi. He put the pipe back in his mouth and began to chant 'one spade, one spade'. 'What can you do with one spade?' He examined his cards. 'One spade didn't you say, Mrs . . . Mrs . . .' 'Robinson,' snapped Mrs Sethi. Her voice was hoarse.

'I beg your pardon Mrs Robinson. Your most humble pardon. One no trump,' he added and triumphantly banged his pipe on the table. The tobacco fell on the green tablecloth. He pressed his hands on the embers. He warded off his wife angrily glowering at him by raising his cards to eye-level.

'No bid,' said Mr Robinson somewhat loudly to ease the tense situation building up.

Sarla Sethi's temper rose to a pitch she herself dreaded. How many times had she repeated the name Robinson at the dinner table! Day-dreaming at bridge ruined the game for everyone. And the utter insensitivity—that was most exasperating. Until she swore at him, he would not realize she was upset. But she was determined not to lose her temper. She took a couple of deep breaths and called out as coolly as she could: 'Two, no trumps.'

'No bid,' said Mr Robinson.

'No bid,' added Mrs Robinson without a pause.

Sethi had not expected his turn to call so soon; he was humming again and had his face hidden behind the cards. The blood rose in Mrs Sethi's face.

'Will you pay attention to the game!' said Mrs Sethi pounding the table with each word.

'Oh, so sorry,' replied Sethi, looking very confused and guilty. 'What did you call Mrs ... Mrs ... ?'

'For the hundredth time; Robinson,' shrieked Sarla Sethi. 'And she said no bid.' She could control herself no more. She jumped up from her chair and flung her cards in her husband's face. With a sweep of her hand she swept the tumblers of whisky-soda off the table and sent them crashing on the floor. She stamped her feet in impotent rage and ran into her bedroom crying hysterically.

The flood of tears drained the temper out of her system. She lay on her bed. She heard her husband apologize to the Robinsons as they left and the servants clean up the mess and switch off the lights. Her husband had stretched himself on a sofa for the night. The situation was familiar to her. He would not apologize for his behaviour. He would not even realize that he had done anything wrong. On the contrary, he would sulk as if it was he who had been wronged. How she loathed the man! Adenoidal, dense, flabby, impervious to change. And this was taken by others as good-natured, absent-minded! How little they knew! She wished she could divorce him and finish with the business once for all. It wasn't right to corrode her entire life wedded to this moron. But divorce wasn't easy. There was the problem of money. There were the children. And their so-called friends and relations who would love to gossip about why the Sethi's marriage had gone bust. Most of all, Sethi's sister—that sanctimonious little bitch for ever talking of family traditions and breeding. She had opposed their marriage. If it came to a break, she would feel vindicated: 'I told you so, didn't I? It would never work,' she would be telling everyone. It had taken Sarla many years to free her husband from the influence of his sister. She had put the woman in her place and put a stop to the comings-and-goings between the families. They met perhaps twice in the year. And now Sarla was able to take her in her stride because she no longer cared about what the woman said or did. Why couldn't she do the same to her husband? Why should she let him upset her so much? All she had to do was become indifferent towards him and lead a life of her own.

Sarla Sethi did not have much sleep that night but she rose from her bed unusually calm. She joined her husband at the breakfast table. They read their morning papers in silence. Neither of them referred to the incident of the evening before. But the dead-pan neutrality of his wife's countenance, which exhibited neither recrimination nor regret, gave Sethi an uneasy feeling that his wife had gained the upper hand.

After her husband left for his office Mrs Sethi took the accounts of yesterday's shopping from her cook, and gave him money to buy vegetables for lunch and dinner. She told the ayah to take the children to the park. She took a cane chair out into the garden. She put her head back, shut her eyes and tried to empty her mind of all thoughts. The Buddha had rightly exhorted that we should make our minds as silent as a wooden gong. Then neither lust, nor anger, neither love nor hate could disturb one's tranquillity.

Peace of mind after a period of mental agony is very much like taking a tranquilizer which deadens pain; it produces an unbelievable numbness akin to sleep. Sarla Sethi was in this twilight world when she heard a voice ask: 'May I enter?' She did not believe her ears and kept her eyes shut. 'May I come in?' asked the voice again very gently.

Mrs Sethi awoke with a start.

'I am sorry to disturb you,' said a grey-haired old white lady. Then unbidden she opened the wicket gate and came across the lawn. 'I am Miss Moore,' she said extending her hand. 'You must be Mrs Sethi. Can I talk to you for a few minutes, my dear?'

Sarla Sethi got up from her chair, shook hands with the visitor and shouted to her bearer to bring another chair. The grey-haired woman covered her face with both her hands. Sarla Sethi glanced nervously at her visitor. If it had been an Indian, she would have demanded her business and dismissed her in five minutes. And though the days of the British Raj were over and though this woman was obviously a missionary type, one had to be more courteous to a white woman. Mrs Sethi waited patiently. After a while the visitor uncovered her face. 'You must be wondering why I have to see you,' she said with a smile.

Sarla Sethi did not answer.

'I've come to tell you about our Group, the Love Group,' the old woman continued. Sarla Sethi mentally switched off her hearing aid. A missionary no doubt. She would let her run out of gas, give her five rupees and send her away. The woman talked on. A nice soothing voice, thought Sarla. But all that clap-trap about truth and purity and integrity! The voice stopped suddenly. Sarla looked up into the old woman's smiling eyes. Had she asked her some question?

'Whats troubling you, my child?'

Nobody had used this maternal tone with Sarla: and her mother had been dead more than ten years. 'Nothing,' replied Sarla jumping up from the chair. 'Nothing at all,' she repeated as she hurried indoors. She took out a five-rupee note from her wallet and came back to the garden. 'Here,' she said holding out the money. 'I am afraid this is all I can afford.'

Mrs Moore looked up. 'I don't want your money my dear; I want you.' Her eyes twinkled.

Sarla Sethi felt very foolish holding the note in her hand. Mrs Moore sensed her embarrassment. She rose from her chair and took Sarla's hand in hers. 'My dear, put that money back in your wallet. I've come for something much more precious than money; I've come for you. Sit down and talk to me.'

Sarla Sethi sat down, utterly deflated. She did not do any talking: Mrs Moore did not give her a chance to do that. But this time she listened to what her visitor had to say. And although there was nothing new about what Mrs Moore said, it had a special meaning for Sarla Sethi. People poison their lives with hate; when they hate others long enough they begin to hate themselves. It is not necessary to hate people or yourselves. On the contrary, it is much easier to live than to hate. And once you learn to love people, they respond by loving you—and you in your turn learn to respect yourself. How do you get about loving people you detest? Easy. Examine your motives for detesting them. The venom is in your own heart. Go to the person you hate and make a clean breast of it, then see the result. It'll draw the venom out of your system. It will disarm your adversary and he (or she) will embrace you in forgiveness and gratitude. Life will become sweeter, nobler, worthwhile.

Sarla Sethi drank in the words like nectar specially brewed for her. 'Ponder over these words, my dear,' and if you have time browse over some of these,' she said, rising from her chair and handing over a sheaf of pamphlets. 'I'll drop in again, and if you then feel so inclined we will welcome you in our Love Group.'

Sarla Sethi resumed her reverie. The words of the Buddha were not occupying her mind now, but those of Mrs Moore. The Buddha had also said 'hate kills the man who hates', but he had not prescribed any specific solution except withdrawal from the world. How could a married woman with children withdraw from the world? Mrs Moore had suggested a practical way—make a clean breast of it. Could she admit that every time she quarrelled with anyone or hated them, she herself was to blame? Who were the people she really hated? Her husband came first to mind. She tried to drive away the thought. What a horrible creature she must be to hate her own husband! No, no she didn't hate him. He irritated her and made her angry. Her sister-in-law? Yes. She had to admit she hated her. Even as she thought of her she became conscious of the swell of angry emotions inside her against the bitch, as she had always called her. Who else? Lots of little hates but none really serious. The English? She had hated the English and, for that matter, all white people. But that was a long time ago when the English were ruling the country and belittling Indians. Since Independence it was different. She actually preferred to mix with the English rather than her own countrymen. How could she hate people like the Robinsons? Muslims? Perhaps. But not as much as she had in the 1940's when there were Hindu-Muslim riots. Since then Indian Muslims had become friendly to the Hindus. The only Muslims she now hated were Pakistanis. But that was patriotic. She hated Pakistan because she loved her own country. Was it necessary to hate Pakistan in order to love her India? And so on.

That afternoon Sarla Sethi did not have her siesta. While the children slept, she read the pamphlets of the Love Group. By evening she was in a daze—like one who has had a heavy dose of antibiotics. And what she had heard and read that day was very much like a shot of antibiotic in a body diseased with hate. The internal battle was on.

The family sensed the change that had come over Sarla Sethi. She was calm, determined and distant. After dinner Mr Sethi buried himself in his files; the children were less boisterous and went to bed earlier than usual. Mr Sethi came to the bedroom after midnight. Even in the dark he could sense that his wife was not asleep. He lay on the further edge of his bed till sleep overtook him.

Next morning Sarla Sethi rang up the Love Group and asked for Mrs Moore. A car came to fetch her. She was introduced to a few members. She was suprised to hear their names—some of them of the leading families of the city. Another surprise was the apparent lack of eagerness to enroll her as a member. As a matter of fact, when she mumbled her wish to join, Mrs Moore asked her to take a little more time to think it over. 'There's no hurry, my dear, read some more of our literature. If you have any doubts, tell me about them. When you are quite sure, we will be delighted to have you join us.'

Sarla Sethi took some books home. Mrs Moore came to see her and the two discussed the tenets of the Love Group. The books and the talk were largely an elaboration of the theory that hate destroys, while love creates. Three days later Sarla Sethi put her signature on the form of membership.

Life became a challenge. Sarla Sethi accepted the challenge with a zeal of a new convert, with Mrs Moore as her spiritual mentor. She set about exorcizing hate from her system. 'Draw up a list of the people you hate. Go to them and make a clean breast of it. As hate goes out love will come in.' It was Mrs Moore's formula. It was Sarla Sethi's turn to take Mrs Moore's hand. 'Let me start with you, Mrs Moore. For many years I hated the English. And look at me now, holding your hand.' Mrs Moore embraced Sarla. 'It works, doesn't it!' she exclaimed. They both laughed. Sarla Sethi could not recall when she had last had a hearty laugh.

Sarla Sethi returned home and drew up a list of the people she had to talk to. She picked up her kitchen account book and found a blank page. She hesitated a while before writing down her husband's name: it was hard for her to admit even to herself that she might hate him. She also realized that if she could not tackle her own husband, she would not be able to tackle anyone else. With a firm hand she put down his initials, G.S. The second name didn't cause her any anguish: it was of her sister-in-law. And oddly enough, she didn't feel that talking to someone against whom her animus had been outspoken would be too difficult. So she put down the name of Kamla Berry. Who next? Sarla considered the many men and women she had had misunderstandings with in the past. None of them deserved to be befriended. She couldn't be such a bad sort after all: only two out of the world's millions. Ah yes, the Pakistanis. Hating a nation wasn't the same as hating a person: one could live with that kind of hate without it corroding one's being. Anyhow, to whom could she confess that hatred and be cleansed of it? And suddenly the face of the Pakistani Consul-General flashed across her mind. She had been introduced to him at a cocktail party. He was an arrogant little man flaunting his Karakul lambskin Jinnah cap (so named after the founder of Pakistan). She recalled having snubbed him. When he extended his hand, she joined the palms of hers and, instead of saying 'Namaste', greeted him with 'Jai Hind'— victory to India. The third name on her list was 'Consul-General, Pakistan'.

Sarla Sethi was amazed by how light-hearted she felt at the simple act of admitting guilt to herself. Making a clean breast of it to the person concerned would surely be immeasurably more rewarding!

The first hurdle was the most difficult to cross. This was her husband. Ten years of marriage had set a pattern of reconciliation after quarrels. Neither had ever learnt to apologize to the other. They both sulked and used servants or the children as bouncing boards to communicate with each other. More often than not the 'making up' was after a cocktail or a dinner party in someone's home where her husband got 'lit up' and the sex urge overcame his sense of injury. Copulation lanced the poison. After that relations became cordial once again. Sarla Sethi was determined to give reconciliation a firmer and more lasting base than that provided by the drink-n-sex formula. She took the bull by the horns, as the cliché goes. She bearded her husband in his own den—his study. It was all very simple. 'I am very sorry. I shouldn't have lost my temper. It was all my fault. Do forgive me.' The pipe almost fell out of Mr Sethi's mouth. Before he could react to this confessional assault Sarla Sethi had run out of the study in confusion and tears. Mr Sethi followed her to the bedroom, as if he was a dog on a leash. He sat on her bed comforting her and apologizing for his behaviour. And although he was already late for office he bolted the door and made love to his wife.

The encounter with the sister-in-law did not present as much difficulty, considering the fact that they had not spoken to each other for almost two years. It was remarkable how smoothly it went off and what dividends it yielded. Sarla Sethi just rang up to say she was coming over. And the sister-in-law was so overwhelmed with the admission of error by Sarla that she broke down and insisted on taking most of the blame for herself. They celebrated the re-union with the two families getting together—a luncheon party at the sister-in-law's, followed a couple of days later by dinner at the Sethi's. Thereafter, the children of the two families were constantly in each other's homes—the two ladies consulted each other on menus and recipes. Sarla Sethi told her sister-in-law about the Love Group and Mrs Moore.

In the honeymoon of reconciliation Sarla Sethi forgot that she had ever hated anyone. It was by sheer accident—when she was checking her kitchen accounts—that she noticed three names scribbled on one of the pages. With a feeling of triumph she scored out the first two—her husband's and her husband's sister. She passed over the third, 'Consul-General, Pakistan'. She was surprised to find that it aroused no feeling of any kind in her. She felt that she had really purged all hate out of her system. Was it necessary now to make a confession to the Pakistanis? After pondering over the matter for some minutes, she rang the Pakistani Consulate. She told the secretary her name and her husband's official position. She said that she had met the Consul-General and he might recognize her name. About her business, she refused to say any more than 'strictly personal'. The secretary took down her telephone number and promised to let her know.

The Pakistani Consulate checked up on Mrs Sethi's credentials. The Consul-General agreed to receive her even though no business was stated.

Sarla Sethi arrived at the Consulate and was shown in to the Consul's room. It was the same little man she had snubbed at the party. The Karakul cap hung on a rack behind his chair. On his table were two large silver-framed photographs of the two Pakistanis Sarla Sethi had hated with a passion—Mr Jinnah, the founder of Pakistan, and President Ayub Khan. There was also a miniature green-and-white flag with the crescent-moon emblem. Sarla refused to let these put her off. She put out her hand. But this time the Pakistani joined his palms to greet her in the Hindu manner. As she withdraw her hand to respond likewise, the Pakistani put out his hand. The comic charade embarrased both of them. He asked Mrs Sethi to sit down and went back to his chair. After a while he asked: 'What can I do for you, Mrs Sethi? Would you like some tea or coffee or a Coke while we talk?' he asked, ringing the bell.

'No, no thank you,' replied Sarla Sethi and waived away the secretary who had come in. 'This is a very difficult moment for me. Mr Ali, please give me a few seconds to compose myself.'

Sarla Sethi covered her face with both her hands and composed herself. H.E. Mr Ali, Consul-General, Pakistan watched her with some apprehension.

Sarla Sethi uncovered her face and looked Mr Ali boldly in the eye; a beatific smile lit her face. And, as suddenly, she lost nerve and became embarrassed. 'Please, Mr Ali, a little more time to compose myself; this is very crucial for me.' And once again Sarla Sethi covered her face with both her hands. And Mr Ali's hand twitched nervously towards the bell.

At last Sarla Sethi was ready. She uncovered her face, slapped her knees and with a loud *hah* said, 'Now I am ready.' It almost sounded as though she was announcing readiness for a wrestling bout. Mr Ali had a wan smile on his face. He played with the flex wire of the call bell.

'Your Excellency, it is like this,' began Sarla Sethi. She unfolded her past life: her childhood in Lahore, the memories of the Hindu-Muslim riots of the summer of 1947, how their home was burnt down by a Muslim mob, their days in a refugee camp in India. And how all that had created a deep-seated hatred in her heart for everything Muslim, particularly Pakistani Muslim. 'You know Mr Ali, hate kills the one who hates,' she said quoting Mrs Moore's words. 'Hate can only be overcome by making a clean breast of it, cleansing your heart by a candid confession. Then you make room for love to enter; isn't that so Mr Ali?' Sarla Sethi's large eyes devoured Mr Ali. Mr Ali's nervousness grew. Was she going to declare her love for him? His thumb was on the knob of the bell.

Mr Ali's fears were assuaged. 'You see Mr Ali, it is not possible to go to every Muslim and Pakistani and ask for forgiveness; so I thought I would come to you because you represent the whole of Pakistan.'

'Yes, yes, yes, yes,' stuttered Mr Ali. 'That, that's very kind of you. We, we all have shown ill will. It is nice to conquer it. Our Holy Prophet Mohammed said love is stronger than hate. We should all love each other.' He put down the bell on the table and relaxed in his armchair.

Sarla Sethi had not come for a social chat. She stood up. To avoid repetition of the handshake or join-palms issue, she joined the palms of her hands: 'I know you are a busy man; I must't waste your time. Namaskar.'

'Namaskar,' replied Mr Ali. And showed her out of the room.

He came back to his desk smiling and chuckling. What a wonderful little incident! He could dine off it for many days. He could liven up many a diplomatic cocktail party narrating this encounter with Mrs Sethi.

He did. For the next fifteen days Mr Ali spoke of his meeting with Mrs Sethi at every party he was invited to. He enjoyed telling the story for the roars of laughter it aroused. People who heard it from Mr Ali told others—and soon all the people who mattered in the city heard of Sarla Sethi's encounter with the Pakistani diplomat. Mr Sethi heard from one of his colleagues: 'I believe your wife called on the Pakistani Consul-General.' From the grin on the man's face he knew that he did not insinuate disloyalty but eccentricity. And since most people had not heard of the reconciliation with the sister-in-law, a number of ladies gave Sarla's sister-in-law the story spiced with details out of their own mental scullery. Frequently the incident was prefaced with remarks like 'that Sethi woman must be going round the bend. Did you hear...' and so on. The hapless sister-in-law confirmed the worst fears of gossip-mongers by adding her own experience to that of Mr Ali's.

Sarla Sethi was prepared for a reaction to her conversion. Hostility she was prepared for. Cynicism and sneering too she would have countenanced. But smiles, sniggers and elbow nudging when her face was turned was not the reaction she had visualized. It angered her. She suppressed her anger. She avoided parties and instead went to the office of the Love Group. She argued that as long as her husband and children and her husband's sister's family felt the change in her, she could ignore the rest of the world. However, she was eager to know what people were saying. Then her patience ran out and she went to call on Mrs Soni—the city's most celebrated gossip-monger.

She did not have to probe the woman. She brought up the subject herself. 'Sarla, I believe you called on the Pakistani Consul. What did you see him for?'

'Who told you?' asked Sarla Sethi.

'Who told me! Why the whole world is talking about it. I must have heard it from dozens of people.' Sarla Sethi's temper began to rise. 'I asked you, who told you?'

Mrs Soni fidgeted uneasily. She had not heard of the reconciliation with the sister-in-law. 'I don't recall exactly who—might have been—your sister-in-law, or...or...somebody else. But just everyone is talking about it.'

'What did she say?'

'I don't know the exact details. Something about loving everyone,' she replied with a snigger...'I hope you didn't make a fool of yourself!'

Sarla Sethi leapt out of her chair and without a word of farewell drove off to her sister-in-law's. She did not even try to control her temper. She pulled up in the porch and stepped into the verandah. The screech of breaks brought her sister-in-law out—beaming and with arms wide open. 'Why Sarla, how nice...!'

Sarla Sethi gave her a stinging slap on the face...'you bitch...you bloody bitch.... You've been making fun of me behind my back.'